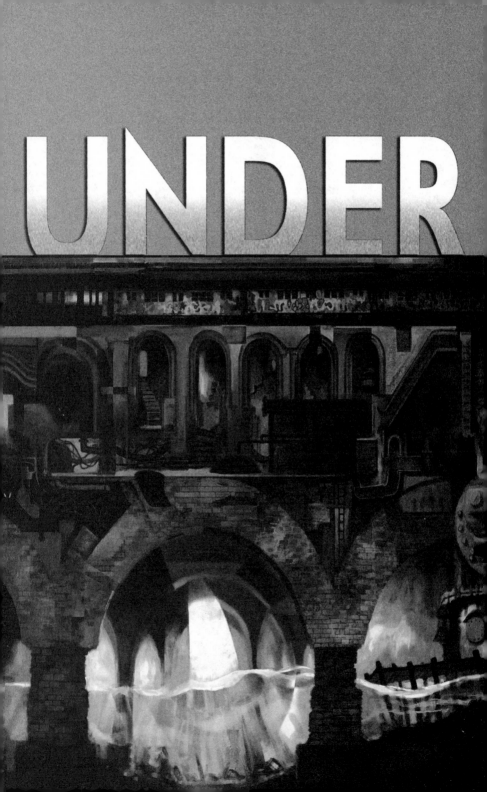

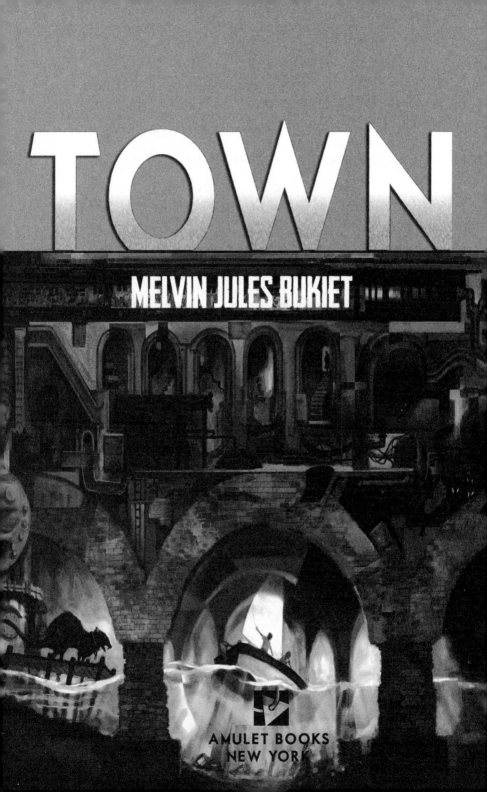

# TOWN

## MELVIN JULES BUKIET

AMULET BOOKS
NEW YORK

Library of Congress Cataloging-in-Publication Data

Bukiet, Melvin Jules.
Undertown / Melvin Jules Bukiet.
p. cm.
Summary: Middle schoolers Timothy Murphy and Jessamyn Hazard career downhill on a sailboat being towed through Manhattan and fall into the sewers, where they meet interesting characters before being caught by the evil "queen" of this underground society.
ISBN 978-1-4197-0589-2
[1. Adventure and adventurers—Fiction. 2. Sailing—Fiction. 3. Sewerage—Fiction. 4. Homeless persons—Fiction. 5. New York (N.Y.)—Fiction.] I. Title.
PZ7.B911147Und 2013
[Fic]—dc23
2012039246

ABRAMS
THE ART OF BOOKS SINCE 1949
115 West 18th Street
New York, NY 10011
www.abramsbooks.com

# CHAPTER

# 1

**L**YING ON THE WARM TEAK DECK, GLANCING UP PAST the gleaming brass struts and rails and fittings adroop with bright-orange life preservers and the tall, tapering mahogany mast from which the jib and mainsail flapped gently in the breeze, Timothy Murphy thought that the balmy summer sky might as well be counted as one more blessing in his nearly perfect life. Timothy spent a lot of time counting blessings.

Then he reached out for the book he'd set on the deck beside him and inadvertently touched flesh—female flesh—and jerked his hand back to rest safely on his stomach. The sky above was perfect; the boat below was perfect. Only one thing was wrong.

*Better return to the blessings*, he thought. To start with, there was his loving father. Make that his loving but likely to be absent father, Tom, who tried to compensate for lack of face time with a sequence of expensive presents. Timothy was the first on his block to get every technological gizmo from an Xbox to an iPhone, though sometimes he had to wrestle them from his dad's grip. Tom liked to think of himself as a kid at heart, in touch with the

3

needs and desires of young people. To some extent that was correct since Tom's Tees, the business that kept him working late five or six or seven nights a week—allegedly so that he could afford to purchase whatever Timothy wanted—relied upon a mystical connection with his ten- to twenty-year-old customers.

Expensive leisure wear provided a comfortable lifestyle for the duo that Tom liked to refer to as the Murphy Men, as if he and Timothy had chosen to embark on a grand adventure after Timothy's mother died. That hadn't been much of a blessing.

Yet there were other things in life besides death. Timothy reminded himself of this as a cloud in the shape of a cauliflower drifted across the spar from which the sail hung.

To start with, there was school. Timothy was a good student, perhaps too good for his own benefit. He wasn't smart enough to frighten anyone, but he was smart enough to irritate. Thus the atmosphere at Montclair Junior High was for him a toxic mix of social and physical torture. Often, Timothy spent class silently debating whom he'd most enjoy throwing into a pit full of starving hyenas: moronic, dictatorial history teacher Mr. Tasman or handsome, loathsome, popular Brian Pfeiffer, who'd mastered the art of twisting his gym towel into a lethal locker room weapon frequently aimed at Timothy's butt. Only one thing Timothy had to admit about school: It wasn't as bad as cancer.

Lots of things were better than cancer. Sunshine was, and so was rain. Actually, Timothy rather preferred damp, soggy days—at least until the *X-tra Large* arrived. During precipitation he wasn't expected to join a neighborhood version of whatever professional sport was in season at the moment. Nor was he expected to bike aimlessly, seeking adventures on the dull suburban streets of northern New Jersey. Whenever it was raining, he could lie back on the wicker couch on the sunporch with a black-and-white milk-

4

shake—another thing that was better than cancer—and lose himself in a book, which was not only better than cancer but better than a milkshake. Reading on a sunporch in the rain might very well have been Timothy Murphy's favorite activity in the world.

At least until the *X-tra Large* arrived. Since then, reading on the deck as the boat rolled over the currents by the Jersey Shore was his absolutely favorite activity. Still gazing at the clouds that had shifted from vegetable to animal, now resembling a whale, a weasel, a camel with one—no, two—humps, or Brian Pfeiffer in a guillotine, he groped blindly on the deck for the novel he'd been immersed in over the last few days. It was Philip K. Dick's *Do Androids Dream of Electric Sheep?*, infinitely superior to the Hollywood movie.

Sometimes Timothy would lose himself so completely in a book that he'd miss the dinner prepared by Loreen, the Murphy Men's housekeeper, and wake up on the couch the next morning unsure whether he was in Montclair or Orbis Tertius. Fortunately, his favorite author was Isaac Asimov, who had written over five hundred books, so he wasn't afraid of running out of titles. Even if he read every one of the millions of words Asimov had written, he suspected that he could start over again without it spoiling any of the plots.

Another blessing was money. Well, not money itself—Timothy considered himself a socialist, or maybe an anarchist, if someone could explain the difference—but the goods and services that it brought into his life. Timothy knew that he was fortunate to have enough money to purchase however many books Asimov or the other science fiction gods he worshipped wrote. Vaguely, he remembered a time before the family had real money, enough to purchase all the nifty stuff a half-orphan could want, except for a mother or time with his dad.

After his mom noticed a strange mole on her shoulder, the night-mare, as ferocious as it was rapid, began. Doctors diagnosed the mole as a symptom of stage 3 breast cancer and "gave" her three months to live, and, sure enough, she sickened and died sixty-two days later. That was two years ago, and Timothy hated that verb ever since; life was more than what doctors "gave" their patients. He couldn't help but think that if his mother had never gone to the doctor, she never would have gotten sick.

"No," his dad insisted. "It's not anyone's fault." Which helped exactly nothing. Having someone to blame might have been a blessing, but all Timothy could do was retreat.

Gradually the Murphy Men grew further apart, until late one Wednesday night when Timothy, having fallen asleep on the sunporch couch, a hardcover tome splayed out on his chest, was shaken awake.

"What are you reading?" It was a question his dad had never asked before.

Timothy held up the volume he'd borrowed from the school library. The book wasn't his usual science fiction fare. The title was *Two Years Before the Mast*.

"Hey," the shirtmaker said, struck by inspiration, "you want to go to the shore?"

"When?"

"How about now? The roads'll be empty, so there won't be any traffic. We'll find a motel, get some sleep, and then have a whole day together tomorrow."

"But it's a school day."

"I dunno. Looks like a shore day to me."

"Play hooky?"

Tom shook his head. "Not play. This is serious." He grinned.

"You mean it?"

"Last one packed is a broken egg."

What the heck did that mean? How could a person be a broken egg? Another one of the worst things about being Timothy Murphy was that there was so much to ponder. But he hustled to avoid broken-eggness—or was it eggitude?—and fell asleep in the car before they reached the shore. All he remembered of their arrival at the oddly named Snowcrest Motel was his father practically carrying him to their room.

The next day, however, after a leisurely breakfast of waffles with enough syrup to drown Britney Spears, he had blessing after blessing. Father and son started on the boardwalk, but all they could see out in the ocean beyond the roller coasters and skee-ball booths and candy apple stands were two paunchy cabin cruisers and a few distant container ships bound for Port Elizabeth. Not much quaint sailing on the Atlantic that day. Refusing to give up, they gravitated to the bay side of the spit of land that separated a score of resort communities from the Jersey mainland. There, in the protected enclosure, half a dozen small sailboats glided across the surface of the water.

"Look." Timothy pointed to a tall two-master.

"Nice." Tom nodded, then said, "But, hey, what about that one, by the bridge."

"Yikes. And, hey, is that a boat or an iceberg . . ."

"What about her?"

"Too big. Ostentatious."

"A little broad in the beam, I think."

"Yeah, but . . . Oh."

"Oh."

Eventually, they found the marina that housed these boats when they weren't out on the bay. They walked onto the gently bobbing docks, getting right up close to the boats. Each one was an object of beauty in its own way. The day was close to heaven.

Not every weekend, but any weekend that his dad could slip away from his business, they drove out to explore another marina in the region. They checked out Stamford in Connecticut and City Island in the Bronx and Amagansett on Long Island and half a dozen spots on the Jersey Shore, gradually becoming more expert in their appreciation during the only pleasant hours they'd had since the evil diagnosis. While other fathers and sons bonded over the Yankees' infield or the Rolling Stones, the Murphy Men compared the merits of a fiberglass Pearson ketch to an all-wood Catalina sloop.

They agreed that size was not the measure of value. It was hard to define, but certain boats simply had good lines.

"Like women," Tom said.

"Mom?"

"The best."

In general, it was best to forget what you could, the good more so than the bad, because it hurt more to dwell on what was missing than to deal with life sucking. That went for a mother who would never return, as well as a father who was suddenly invisible. As swiftly as Tom had gotten interested in sailboats, he abandoned ship. For several weeks, he seemed to disappear into his computer, doing some sort of obscure research, too busy to pay attention. "What? Hmm. Let me get back to you."

Yet when Tom suggested another trip, this time to Newport, Rhode Island, for a boat show, Timothy hopped. Maybe, probably, he'd get hurt again, but he couldn't resist.

In the car, he squirmed and enthused, "I've heard that Newport is the best harbor in the country."

"Yep, and this show is supposed to be the best for sailboats."

"Better than the New York convention center?"

"Too many motors there."

"Yep."

They spent the first day getting the lay of the land. A gigantic hangar on the edge of the harbor contained dozens of boats displayed by Chris-Craft and the other big manufacturers, while hundreds of boats on sale by individual owners were moored in the harbor a mile from the convention center. Tom and Timothy wandered appreciatively, licking at ice cream cones, until they arrived at the farthest, most remote dock in the marina, and there sat the most beautiful boat that Timothy had ever seen.

It wasn't the biggest; in fact, it may have been smaller than anything besides the most functional dinghy, but it was small like a diamond bobbing on the lapping waves in the shadow of several crude behemoths.

Tom explained, "It's a Herreshoff 12½. Built in 1926, it's one of only three hundred and sixty-four of this dimension from the original manufacturer. Rebuilt in 1953—that's when they added the brass trim and an engine to make it easy to get in and out of the harbor. Overhauled again in the 1980s, with the latest radio and radar communications. As far as I can tell, it's the finest sailboat ever made. I mean, on an inch-by-inch basis."

He was right. It was perfect. Well, almost. Strangely, the boat had no name. A wash of fresh white paint covered a rectangular plate mounted on the stern.

"So?" asked Tom.

Timothy didn't understand what his father was asking. "So what?"

"So, what do you think?"

"I . . . I think it's great. A real jewel."

"You want to try her out? C'mon." Without asking permission, Timothy's dad stepped off the pier and onto the deck of the unnamed sailboat. He reached out a hand, and Timothy, fearful but giddy with excitement, took it. The boat wobbled a bit initially but regained its balance after a second. That proved that it not only looked beautiful but was excellently built. They paced back and forth, then stepped up on top of the raised platform that contained the instruments, where Tom encouraged his son to pretend to man the wheel.

Timothy was sure they were going to get arrested, especially when his father suggested they explore the cabin via a three-rung ladder bolted into a hatchway behind the wheel. Flanking the ladder was a tiny bathroom and tinier kitchenette with a below-counter refrigerator and a grandfather clock–shaped pantry. Beyond the facilities were two slim teak-sided berths on either side of a narrow aisle. "Try it out," Tom insisted.

Stiffly, Timothy lay on the snug bedding.

"Nice, huh?" Tom asked.

"Sure, Dad."

Then, even more brazenly, Tom rummaged inside the pantry and said, "Look at what we have here."

It was a paper bag containing a white sailor's cap with the words *Captain Timothy* stitched across the brow.

"I don't get it," said the boy, half humored and entirely baffled.

"Actually, you've already got it. Happy birthday."

"But my birthday isn't until the winter."

"So it's a surprise."

For a second, Timothy kept trying to find some logic to the situation, but then a light flashed, like the aurora borealis from over the horizon. "What? You didn't . . . You did? Are you kidding? Really? You mean it? We got it. *We got it!*"

A Herreshoff 12½ was miles better than cancer. All week after bringing their prize back from Rhode Island, Timothy and his father discussed what to name it. *Dana* was a good possibility, and so was *Queenie*. Over a dinner of take-out Indian food, they'd nearly settled on the *H.M.S. Vindaloo*, but that seemed too cute come morning.

While they were discussing other names, an emergency call arrived from Tom's factory. He lifted a "Wait a second" finger to Timothy, and was soon yelling into the receiver. "No, no, no! Take that load and get rid of it. Store it somewhere. Burn it, for all I care. If our shipping agent wants x-tra large, we're going to make x-tra large if we have to run shifts around the clock."

By the time he returned to the table, his son was grinning.

"What's so funny?" Tom asked.

"Not funny, exactly, but if it's x-tra large T-shirts that allowed us to get this teeny-tiny boat, then maybe the teeny-tiny boat should be called . . ."

Tom jumped in: "The *X-tra Large*."

Timothy laid his palms flat on the deck on either side of his legs and felt the wood, so warm that it seemed to be emitting heat rather than absorbing it from the sun. He couldn't do more than squint upward because of the sun, but he refused to glance sideward because someone else lay next to him, intruding, invading, intolerable.

The *X-tra Large* was the single best thing in his life now, better than any video game. She was more than a boat, more like a creature that he'd learned to ride—not to tame—over the course of the previous summer. Tom helped and so did a few marina bums, who affectionately referred to her as a minnow and welcomed the father-son team with the theme song from *Gilligan's Island*.

Mostly, however, it was the boat that let Timothy know what she wanted, be it an extra coat of oil for the mast, an hour's worth of polishing brass, a run-through of emergency procedures on the radio should a squall arise when they were out to sea (though in fact they never left sight of land), or, of course, the actual sailing.

Generally, the *X-tra Large* lived in Matalon, New Jersey, in the Albanese Brothers Marina, but along with the boat Tom had purchased a kind of elongated metal cradle on wheels. This contraption allowed the Murphy Men to tow their vessel to any other harbor they pleased.

Still, Matalon was home. It was in the calm bay that Timothy took lessons to master the rudiments of sailing. Circling or figure-eighting around three concrete pillars that supported a drawbridge, he learned how to manipulate the *X-tra Large* in the tightest situation. Races never particularly appealed to him, sheer speed being a crude measure of nautical skill, but tests of instinct and dexterity brought out his inner sportsman.

And then, finally, the ultimate test: He steered the *X-tra Large* between two curving jetties that extended into the Atlantic like a pair of crab claws. It was in the ocean that other sailors feared that he discovered the beauty of the tack, a maneuver that allowed him to move the boat into the teeth of the salt wind.

Above all, sailing was a way for Timothy and his father to escape their workaday, school-a-day, day-to-day worlds, together. Part of the vessel's appeal was that no one would have suspected either of the Murphy Men to be a natural born sailing man.

As for Timothy, well, he had been happiest alone on the sunporch, until the *X-tra Large* brought the Murphy Men out of their shells. The vessel was like a private club with a membership of two, until Tom apparently peeked out of his shell and ruined everything.

How could his father have done such a thing? Bringing strangers on board shattered the privacy they'd shared on the waves. It was a violation of the very essence of the boat. Again, he gazed up the mast to avoid the awful reality beside him on the deck.

Timothy had been dreading this day of infamy from the moment his father had approached him three days earlier.

As usual, before introducing a delicate subject to Timothy, his dad ventured slowly. "I've met a woman."

Silence was Timothy's usual reaction when faced with an unusual condition.

"I think you'd like her."

Maybe, if he concentrated hard enough, Timothy thought, the buzzing in his ears would obliterate all other sounds.

"I think that your mom would have liked her."

The buzzing ceased. Timothy couldn't ignore his father anymore. "You mean, like, they would have been friends, saying, 'Your turn.'"

"Don't be crude. I mean that your mom would have wanted me to meet someone new, eventually."

Timothy was furious. "And that sounds exactly like the kind of self-justifying junk that people say when they do what they want."

"Easy there, pal."

"What? You want me to just forget my mom, like a penny that slips out of my pocket to fall between the cracks? Oops, she's gone! Sorry, but moms don't disappear just like that. Not so easy . . . *pal*."

"Whoa, Timmy, I—"

"You know that I hate being called Timmy."

"Sorry, but it's not simple for me, either. Remember, I've been going to the bereaved spouses group every Tuesday for two years."

"Oh, so you go to this club and eventually they tell you that it's, like, totally OK to do whatever you want. Besides, where'd you meet . . . Ohhh, I get it."

Yes, he did.

Tom hung his head, not that there was anything to be ashamed of. As if it would make any difference, he felt obligated to explain. "Her husband died in a car accident."

A bell was ringing somewhere, but Timothy didn't heed it. Instead, he continued to pour salt in his own and his father's wounds. "I hear that the Tuesday bereaved spouses group is the best place to find a date this side of the bowling alley."

"That's unfair."

"Life is unfair. Suck it up."

"No, Timothy, this time I won't. I like Miranda a lot."

It was the first time Timothy had heard the woman's name. He didn't like the sound of it.

"I'm not saying there's a big future, but this is the first time I've thought there might be something. And that's good. I've invited her to come sailing with us."

*"What?"*

"And . . ."

"And what?" What could be worse than sailing with someone named Miranda?

"And best of all . . ."

Worst of all was what his dad thought was best of all: Miranda had a daughter. "Maybe you know her," Tom said, and that's when he mentioned the second horrible name of the day—Jessamyn.

There was only one Jessamyn that Timothy knew of at Montclair Junior High School. Only one Jessamyn whose father had died in a car accident. As far as he knew, there was only one Jessamyn in the whole world, but he prayed that he was wrong.

Tom put an end to his prayer. "Jessamyn Hazard."

The last name was appropriate. She was as dangerous as blind sailing in a hurricane, and nine feet tall. Well, almost. Seven or six, or at least a head taller than any boy in their grade. She certainly made Timothy feel like a runt. Then, she was smart, really smart. Not a focusing-to-get-an-A student like Timothy but some sort of creepy genius. She was the last human being on the continent that he'd want to be seen with.

"They're coming over this weekend."

*Three days.* Timothy had three days to commit hari-kari, but he didn't. Nor did Jessamyn, whom he surreptitiously observed in their school cafeteria the next day. She was so cagey that he couldn't tell if she, too, was aware of their repugnant double date.

D-day arrived. About ten in the morning, Sunday, the mom and daughter drove up to the Murphy house in a cheerful, silver convertible. Ugh. How, Timothy wondered, could either of them step foot in a car after Mr. Hazard's gruesome end? It was a sign of their heedlessness.

Timothy considered hiding under the couch. Or imitating one of those street performers who strike a pose and remain so immobile that no one can detect them breathing. Or he could actually stop breathing. That would take care of things.

"This must be Timmy," gushed the attractive middle-aged woman. She was wearing flip-flops, a silky blue skirt, and an inappropriately tight Tom's Tee.

Under his breath, "Timmy" muttered, "Timothy."

"What?"

"I prefer Timothy," he said.

"Oh. I feel like we already know each other because your dad has told me so much about you. I'm Miranda."

Timothy smiled weakly.

"And," Tom said, welcoming the girl beside the woman, a red-headed giraffe wearing a regular T-shirt under a Hawaiian shirt tied at the waist of a pair of orange shorts, "you must be Jessamyn."

Her lip curled.

"And," the two grown-ups chimed together as if they had rehearsed their lines, "you two must know each other?"

To which both Timothy and Jessamyn did credible imitations of deaf-mutes.

"Hey," Miranda chirped, "where's this fantastic boat I've heard about?"

"C'mon," Tom said, "around back."

Timothy noticed that Miranda Hazard knew her way through his house, as if she'd been there before. Must have been when he had visited his grandfather in a retirement community in the Poconos. Gross!

Nevertheless, he was proud of the *X-tra Large*, parked at the side of the house in its wheeled cradle, hitched to the back of a Chevy pickup that Tom had bought for just that purpose. He noticed Jessamyn's eyebrows rise a quarter of an inch—more reaction than she'd shown when Michael Standring sliced off the tip of his finger in art class and it landed on the table in front of her like a tiny pink eraser. While everyone else stared, she picked it up and said to Michael, "Is this yours?"

But now she was impressed. Timothy could tell. How could anyone fail to be impressed? The *X-tra Large* was a beauty when at home in the water, but sitting up on the metal cradle, her mast rising high enough to pierce the clouds, her keel and rudder striking down from the curved hull like fins, her exposed flank like a frozen wave, she was stunning.

"Let's pack and get started," Tom declared.

"I've brought food," Miranda Hazard said. Indeed she had, enough for a lunch for twelve: two chickens cut into pieces, containers of coleslaw and potato salad, bags of chips, several bottles of soda, and a blueberry pie for dessert. Timothy and Jessamyn climbed up the short ladder attached to the boat and hauled her mother's food over the side like fishermen bringing in the catch.

"Remember, Tim," Tom said. "Everything . . ."

Timothy finished the sentence: "in its place." It was one of Tom's sea mantras. Fifteen minutes later, with everything stowed inside the *X-tra Large*'s pantry or in an ice-filled cooler, they were off. Tom and Miranda shared the truck's cab while Timothy and Jessamyn remained on the deck of the boat itself, which faced backward for easy release into some distant body of water.

"Ready astern?" Tom shouted cheerfully from the driver's window.

Timothy sighed. "Ready as we'll ever be."

At first, the two teenagers stood at the rail at the rear—and the scene from *Titanic* occurred to Timothy—but neither said a word. He always liked riding in the boat to the shore, playing it cool when people in other cars stared at the small beauty cruising down the Jersey Turnpike at a steady fifty miles per hour.

Getting to City Island, however, meant that they'd have to cross the George Washington Bridge and, Timothy feared, take a side trip down memory lane. Whenever Tom was anywhere near New York, he couldn't resist showing off the tough neighborhood where he'd grown up. He felt it proved how far he'd gotten in life.

Resolved to enduring the worst—well, *one* of the worst—days of his life, Timothy lay down and, without saying a word, Jessamyn lay down, too, separated from him by the shadow of the boom that bisected the narrow deck. They were silent for a good

17

twenty minutes as the truck wound down from the ridge where the Murphys lived, entered onto Route 46, and started in toward the city. That was when Timothy reached out for his book and inadvertently touched his unwanted companion. "Sorry," he blurted, and withdrew his hand as swiftly as if he'd inserted it into an electric socket.

She answered unexpectedly. "You think they really like each other?"

Timothy turned to make sure that the giraffe beside him had actually spoken. She was lying on her side, staring at him, her T-shirt gaping slightly at the neck. He replied, "Um, I guess so. I mean, why not?"

She shrugged. "They could be pretending, you know, just to drive us crazy."

"Hmm." He considered the proposition. "Yes, that's a common parental motivation."

"Deflects attention from their own inadequacies."

"Which are many and varied."

An eighteen-wheeler as long as the pickup's cab and cradle combined blew past them in a rush of hot air that made Jessamyn's reply hard to discern. "Abundant beyond eeee-lief."

"What did you say?" he asked.

"Abundant."

"After that?"

"Beyond belief."

"Oh."

"What?"

"Nothing."

Well, nothing creates curiosity like nothing, so she insisted, "You've got something on your mind."

"No . . . it's just that I thought you said something else."

"What did you think I said?"

He knew, absolutely, in the pit of his belly that his bad hearing was going to get him into trouble, but he couldn't think of anything but the truth. "I thought you said 'abundant beyond bereaf.'"

Snickering, Jessamyn, who obviously knew as well as Timothy about their parents' shabby history, replied, "I bereave I did."

So Timothy confessed. "The way the two of them met. It's so yucky. I need something to bereave in."

Quoting, or deliberately misquoting, a book they'd both been assigned to read in school, Jessamyn got a sly look and said, with ostensible sincerity dripping with sarcasm, "In spite of everything, I still bereave that people are truly good at heart."

He nodded, serious. "You must bereave in miracles."

One bad pun led to another. They pushed each other further into outrageousness as they moved from plain language to literature and then, finally, to song.

Cruising along Route 46, passing mall after Jersey mall, she crooned, "I beee . . . reeeeave in yesterday."

Besides the Beatles, they did Cher and the Angoras and Potluck Explosion.

He sang, "I'm a bereaver. I couldn't leave her if I tried."

She, and then they, sang, "Daydream bereaver . . . homecoming que-e-e-een."

By then they were running low on the belief/bereave motif, but one tiny moment of inspiration led them to "Good Mourning Starshine" and "I Heard It Through the Graveyard."

It was the fastest trip Timothy Murphy had ever made from Montclair into Manhattan, on or off the Herreshoff 12½.

Bent over in hysterics and pounding on the deck—partially to keep rhythm with the song, partially to let loose the pain that had been stoppered inside themselves for as long as they could remember—the teenagers hardly noticed when the vessel and the vehicle that towed it came to a halt. Then Timothy and Jessamyn glanced over the side, where, instead of a gentle or strong sloshing tide, they saw the tops of hundreds of automobiles. Ahead loomed the interlacing steel towers of the George Washington Bridge.

On the bridge, Timothy and Jessamyn sat with their knees up and hands flat behind them, the best position to anchor oneself on a bumpy passage over either water or tar. They paused to behold the great city stretched out as far as could see. There were the bulky structures of Columbia University's New York–Presbyterian Hospital just south of the bridge and then the ranks of apartment buildings marching down Riverside Drive to a gothic church, and midtown office buildings, and a few downtown towers visible from ten miles away.

Minutes later they were in Upper Manhattan, where the streets were not nearly as smooth as those in the suburbs and where it was harder to pretend that the jolts and bumps were waves and swells.

"Why did we get off the highway?" Jessamyn asked.

"Egg creams."

"Anyone ever tell you that you don't know how to give a straight answer, Timothy Murphy?"

"That's how my mom and dad met. She was this girl from the suburbs who got lost in the city and asked for directions at Katznelson's Luncheonette. He was there sipping an egg cream. It's sort of the founding myth of the family. So whenever we're within fifty miles—OK, fifty blocks—of Katznelson's, we pay homage."

"Um?" Jessamyn raised one finger.

"Yes?"

"What's an egg cream?"

"Well, to start with, it has no egg and no cream. It's a drink made of seltzer and chocolate syrup, preferably Fox's U-bet, and a little milk. Never mind. Just give thanks that you're not in the front seat or my dad would start bending your ear about the day the Polo Grounds closed. Mrs. Katznelson must be at least ninety-five. She's the only non-Dominican left in the Heights. But I will tell you one thing . . ."

"Yeah?"

"The egg creams are the best."

As soon as they drove a block east of Broadway the atmosphere changed entirely. Spanish names appeared on storefronts. Groceries became bodegas sporting orange and yellow awnings. There were hair-braiding salons, and discount furniture shops advertising their installment plans, and salsa music blasting out of windows and from rusty iron fire escapes.

Jessamyn took in the exotic landscape and said, "It looks like a set from *West Side Story.*"

And just as they gazed at the city from their fine vessel, so were Timothy and Jessamyn gawked at by people along the street. It wasn't every day that a sailboat cruised the Heights.

"Ahoy there," shouted a pedestrian waiting for the bizarre apparition to sail across Saint Nicholas Avenue.

Jessamyn saluted and the man grinned and saluted back.

Traffic clogged where an enormous pit had been dug to facilitate a construction site—electrical repairs, a new subway entrance, it was hard to tell what was going on—at 184th Street. Scores of cables and hoses snaked in and out of the pit, which was surrounded by orange traffic cones and concrete pylons. Several trucks filled with rubble blocked traffic.

At last, the pickup towing the *X-tra Large* passed the construction site and pulled up beside a fire hydrant halfway down the block from Katznelson's.

On a stoop, three teens looked at the boat as if it was a UFO.

Timothy and Jessamyn leaned over the railing. In one direction was the busy excavation, and in the other was the dusty, once and surely never again to be illuminated neon sign for Katznelson's.

Tom Murphy and Miranda Hazard exited from opposite sides of the cab and circled around to the cradle. Timothy could tell that his father's eyes were scanning the street for signs of his T-shirts, which were rare in these environs. Tom suggested, "How about you guys stay here while we bring back some refreshments?"

Timothy nodded. Actually, Jessamyn wasn't bad company. That didn't mean that he liked her or anything, just that he could tolerate her presence on the deck overlooking the urban sea.

"Hon?" Miranda asked her daughter.

Jessamyn grunted affirmation.

The two teenagers watched the adults saunter down the street, uncertain whether their hips were touching. That would have been too gross.

"They'll be a while," Timothy said.

"How do you know?"

"The second he gets inside he's gonna start telling stories. Take my word for it. Been there."

"So what do you wanna do?"

Interesting question. He wasn't sure. Usually he accompanied his father inside while the truck was illegally double-parked outside the luncheonette. "What's the worst thing they can do," Tom would say, "give me a ticket?"

This was the first time Timothy had been left alone, though he wasn't really alone. In any case, he was tempted to explore, but the neighborhood looked sort of dangerous. And if he left the *X-tra Large*, someone might steal its brass railings or the radio or even the steering wheel. No doubt, a boat was safer in the water.

"I've got it," Jessamyn declared. "Let's play Pick the Scariest Person on the Block. I'll go first." She peered left and right and then said, "OK, guess who I chose."

"Easy," Timothy said, "the guy with the machine gun."

"Very funny."

"That lady there. Her ankles are like tree stumps."

"Guess again."

*"Moi?"*

"Sorry, dear, but you are the least-scary person between here and Afghanistan. Last chance."

*Dear?*

"Um . . ." He watched Jessamyn's eyes, which glanced briefly to the west side of the street. He immediately saw a man wearing shorts, and a vest over a bare, hairy chest. The man was clutching a large book that you knew, just knew, had to be a Bible. "King James?"

Jessamyn nodded. "Two points. Your turn."

They played a couple of rounds, and then discussed the difference between Washington Heights and Montclair.

"I mean," Timothy said, "who would I be if I was born here? If my dad never moved to the burbs."

"You wouldn't be," Jessamyn answered.

"I know that. But what if? What if everything else was the same except for the place I grew up."

"You'd probably be the same jerk you are now."

Timothy twitched.

Jessamyn noticed. "I'm sorry. What I meant was—"

"Never mind."

23

"—that I think that character is something inside you that comes before circumstances."

"Never mind."

"You want to be a sullen baby, have it your way. Besides, I'm tired."

"If you want to take a rest, there's a cabin down below."

"Not that kind of tired. I'm tired of talking. Let's play a trick on the rents."

He could tell that she was trying to make up for her insult. "What?"

"How about we unattach the boat from the truck. That way they'll leave us behind."

"You mean the *X-tra Large*?"

"I don't see any other boat around here."

Timothy knew that he'd asked a stupid question, but he was still reluctant. "That doesn't sound like a great idea to me."

"C'mon. How far will they get before they notice? Twenty feet. A block at most."

Deep down, this felt like a mistake. He was about to heed his intuition when Jessamyn made the one argument he couldn't refute. "C'mon. It'll be funny. Bereave me."

He melted and bereaved, and thought for a quarter of a second of his mother, so distant and so beautiful, on this deck, preparing to embark on a mysterious voyage.

A nod from Timothy was all it took for Jessamyn to jump from behind the wheel to the stern of the boat, beyond the tip of the boom. She leaned over to examine the gizmo that yoked the cab and the cradle together. It was simple, like a hook and eye that might lock an old-fashioned bathroom door, except sturdy enough to withstand highway driving.

She leaned over and reached down, pressing a thick steel button while tugging at the single round peg set into the single round hole until it finally jolted free with an odd uncorking sound, and what happened at first was . . . nothing.

Just as planned. Tom and Miranda wouldn't notice; they'd drive off; there'd be a moment of parental panic; they'd return, reattach the peg. Everyone would laugh. Then they would go sailing.

The cab stood still. The boat stood still. The apartment buildings and the great gray bridge spanning the Hudson River stood still. The only things that seemed to move were people, some coming, some going, some jaywalking across the middle of the block. Both Timothy and Jessamyn paid special attention to the two people coming out of a storefront about a hundred feet away, beneath a defunct neon sign. The man was gesturing broadly, the woman smiling and gazing up at him. Timothy was stunned to realize that they were happy.

If that wasn't strange enough, as Tom Murphy and Miranda Hazard continued walking forward, they appeared to Timothy to be receding. And so did Katznelson's and Guayabera Bodega, and the teenagers on the stoop, who had been parallel to the *X-tra Large*, were now sliding backward, laughing and pointing at the boat.

Timothy and Jessamyn did not have to wait long for their parents to notice that something was amiss. At first, a quizzical expression crossed Tom Murphy's face, as if he was confronted with a "What is wrong with this picture?" puzzle. Then enlightenment came. It took less than a second for him to thrust the bag with egg creams into Miranda's hands and break into a run.

One by one, the rest of the people on the block noticed. Like the teens on the stoop, some gaped and gestured. Others just stared, while, at first, Tom gained on the gradually moving *X-tra Large*.

But the pitch of the street, which neither Timothy nor Jessamyn had taken into account, was inexorable and the runaway cradle holding the vessel began to pick up speed, heading eastward on 184th Street.

"Stop!" screamed Tom, arms pumping, racing after them.

"Stop!" shrieked Miranda, also running now, tossing the brown paper bag of egg creams to the curb.

"How?" shouted Timothy.

The boat clipped the edge of a cart selling flavored ices, which spilled several gallons of crushed ice and thin streams of cherry, chocolate, and coconut syrups into the street. *"Ayyy,"* screamed the man who owned the cart.

Faster and faster the boat went, as if driven over the surface of the sea by a gale. Maybe if the sails had been taut, Timothy could have tacked, brought the boat about, executed some nautical maneuver he'd learned the previous summer. Unfortunately, he hadn't trained for steering a boat on a wheeled flatbed tearing downhill.

Nor did any of the pedestrians who crossed its path expect a speeding boat in Washington Heights. A drug dealer's black SUV cornering over a post box at midnight ahead of a screaming police car, sure. Motorcycles with howling hooligans, yes. A thirty-year-old station wagon kept together with duct tape and a bent-wire antenna, look on any block. But a vessel that was inch for inch the finest in its class with teak decking and brass trim, no way.

At the excavation at the end of the block the construction workers saw the danger and leapt out of the path of the speeding sailboat, which snapped a chain surrounding the area and crushed the traffic cones until the cradle slammed into one of the concrete pylons protecting the site. The steel folded in upon itself like an accordion.

For maybe a quarter of a second, both Timothy at the helm and his father in rough pursuit thought that the runaway vessel had been halted. For that moment, each could begin to imagine the repercussions of the accident: Screaming. Yelling. Insurance.

What a luxury.

In the next quarter second—or less, or an eternity, since time was both shrunken and expanded from Timothy's and Jessamyn's perspectives—the boat illustrated the first law of physics. Bodies in motion tend to remain in motion. Thus the vessel intended solely for water use slid off its base, over the top of the stubby concrete, en route to an inclined ramp into the excavation. Most of the floor area of the ramp was covered with eight-foot steel squares, like gigantic rusted tiles, set in place by a backhoe to facilitate the workers' entry and exit from the site.

For the next stunning quarter of a second, it seemed as if the *X-tra Large* might skate on the edge of its keel across the crude steel rink to land safely on the far shore, but one brutally realistic moment later, both the keel and most of the rudder broke off the boat's curved bottom as cleanly as chicken bones. Yet before separating from the rest of the boat they had absorbed the brunt of the impact, so the hull remained intact even as it ground down the steeply inclined plane, where an underground workforce was busy in the city's basement.

For the last quarter of a second, Timothy imagined the maiden voyage of some grand, new ocean liner or aircraft carrier, more like an edifice than a vehicle in dry dock until a ritual bottle of champagne is smacked across its prow by a queen or politician or giggling starlet and the stately vessel gradually drifts into the sea, where it will live for the rest of its life.

Only, the *X-tra Large* wasn't drifting. More like a Jet Ski than an ocean liner, it scraped down the incline with fantastic velocity as workers leapt out of the way and their tools bounced off the walls, and electric sparks jumped from severed wires.

And instead of a great placid ocean looming beyond an enclosed dry dock, the open air of West 184th Street gave way to a dank tunnel, which if Timothy wasn't mistaken was considerably shorter than the height of . . .

The mast.

Fourteen feet of lathed hardwood hit the underside of the street and snapped in the middle, the bottom portion of a now jagged spike remaining upright and the rest collapsing to the deck like a tree cut down by a lumberjack, landing directly between Timothy and Jessamyn. A foot in either direction and one of them would have surely been crushed.

The *X-tra Large* was near the end of its journey, or so thought its two stunned passengers and their parents huffing and puffing along the street. A horn blared. At them?

A police whistle.

Jessamyn had the leisure to find that amusing. Like the Herreshoff 12½ would pull over to the side of the pit and Timothy, abashed, would confess that maybe he was going a little over the speed limit, without a license to cruise. What would the policeman do, give him a ticket?

But she couldn't follow any train of thought amid the cacophony nor distinguish its specific notes what with the rasp of the hull and the slam of the mast still echoing in her ears as the boat plowed relentlessly toward the wall at the end of the tunnel.

Timothy and Jessamyn braced themselves for impact, but the wall had been shaved to the width of a single brick by the city workers and the *X-tra Large* rammed straight on through. Chunks of mortar hit the deck about the broken mast, battering the prow, denting the brass railings, and scratching and tearing at nearly every inch of the boat's surface.

Already ten feet below street level due to the incline, Timothy thought they ought to be on sheer bedrock, but at that moment came a final surprise greater than their initial release, greater than their race to the pit, greater than their entry into the pit. For what had to be the ultimate millisecond of their adventure, the *X-tra Large* was . . .

*Flying?*

Airborne. The whole world was upside down. Planes don't float; boats don't fly.

Just before everything went dark, Timothy caught a glimpse of Jessamyn's face: eyes wide, mouth open. Was she crying? A screaming filled his ears. It was his own.

They weren't flying underground. They were falling.

Dropping deeper, having pierced the thin roof of some cavern that may have existed as a geological formation for millions of years.

But God didn't make barrel ceilings. He didn't build His caves with rusty steel beams and columns, one of which grabbed at the jib, ripping it down the middle, the tearing sound taking the place of the scraping and screaming until they all came to a splash landing.

The fall seemed endless, but it probably wasn't more than another ten feet, yet Timothy and Jessamyn collapsed into the wreckage until gouts of water from somewhere below rose up and rained back down upon their heads. Now everything was still, and they were bobbing upright on what appeared to be a body of water.

Lying on the boat's deck, as they had at the beginning of the outing, but surrounded by the toppled mast, the shards and remnants of a brick wall, the torn sail, soaked to their skins, Timothy and Jessamyn listened to the sound of themselves breathing.

Far above, where there had once been an endless sky, a pinhole of light from the opening in the earth was shrinking by the second. After the speed and roar of the accident it was difficult to perceive that they were still moving, floating with a current on a black river.

"You OK?" Timothy asked.

Jessamyn breathed deeply. "Yeah. Only . . ."

"Only what?"

"I don't think we're in Manhattan anymore."

"No, we're *under* Manhattan."

# CHAPTER

## 2

**T**HE RIVER, OR CHANNEL, OR CANAL, OR WHATEVER IT was, wasn't black but dark, faintly illuminated by several rectangles of light hovering above the boat. Already the hole the kids had plunged through was distant, and the face of a single workman staring at them over the edge disappeared. Just as Timothy Murphy and Jessamyn Hazard had watched one cloud recede and another advance during their progress through suburban New Jersey, just as they had watched the western tower of the George Washington Bridge recede and the eastern tower advance while they crossed the Hudson River, so now they charted this new journey from one glowing rectangle to another.

"Where are we?" Jessamyn whispered.

Of course there was no need to whisper, but the strangeness of the environment made her cautious.

Timothy lay back on the deck where the top half of the broken mast lay like a felled tree. He listened to his and Jessamyn's breathing gradually settle. How curious, he thought, to be able to distinguish individual breaths after the clamor of the city and the insanity of their accident. He couldn't remember hearing his or his father's breaths during previous trips on the *X-tra Large*, but the ocean was a noisy beast.

"If I had to guess, I'd say 183rd Street, between Broadway and Saint Nicholas."

"I meant—"

"I believe that we're in the sewer."

"The sewer!" she yelped.

"Not the sanitary sewer with house waste, but the storm sewer. Although it probably has its share of dog poop." He pointed to the nearest rectangle, forgetting that there was no way that Jessamyn could see his arm in the dark. "That's probably the catch basin on the corner of 182nd."

"Catch what?"

"Basin. The drains at street corners that collect runoff."

At that moment, the *X-tra Large* brushed against something. A harsh, rasping sound filled the space and the teenagers immediately hushed. But a second later, they were moving smoothly again, carried by a faint breeze or a pitch in the system.

Jessamyn said, "I hope that wasn't an iceberg."

Timothy smiled in the dark. Something about their horrible accident wasn't very horrible at all.

Jessamyn observed, "It doesn't smell bad."

"No reason it should. I mean, aside from the dirt that washes off the street, it's all rainwater."

"But there hasn't been any rain lately. So why is it full?"

"That's because . . . um . . . That's a very good question."

Frequently, Jessamyn stumped their teachers by asking an obvious question to which there was no obvious answer. Timothy therefore ought not to have been embarrassed because he couldn't explain their situation, yet he felt that he should be in charge while they were on his boat. He aimed to concentrate on their surroundings.

To begin with, the sewer was hardly silent. Besides the current lapping against the sides of the channel, street sounds drifted down from the catch basins. Once, there was a prolonged beep—an angry driver warning another vehicle, maybe. But the sewer—or at least the underground—had its own sounds, too. A distant rumbling emanated from elsewhere beneath the surface. Timothy wondered if it was a pump that kept the water flowing.

The light from the catch basins was so thin and diffuse that it might have been a tease. He made out as much as he could of the tunnel as they glided under each fixture but still sensed rather than saw that they were in a tight space. The air was thick. Once, extrapolating from a breeze or the way his voice carried, he believed they had entered into a more generous space, a cavern perhaps, but then, when the familiar constriction returned after a minute, he realized that they must have crossed an intersection. Of course, the sewers followed the pattern of the streets above.

Jessamyn said, "It's peaceful here."

"Hmm."

"A bit like a burial. Or the way that I imagine a burial. Only conscious."

"That's morbid."

"Look who's talking, Mr. Bereaver. Besides, aren't there certain cultures that imagine dead people setting sail on an ocean voyage?"

"Or the River Styx that runs through Hades."

"Right."

He felt pleased that he was able to match mythological references with the most intimidating girl in Montclair Junior High, and repeated her initial comment, "It is peaceful here. I could stay for . . . well, not forever, but for a while."

"How long do you think we have?"

Again, a very good question. Moreover, a complicated one that implied more than its ostensible meaning. Upon crashing through a concrete barrier and plunging into a sewer beneath a city street, most people would wonder how swiftly they might be rescued. Yet neither Timothy nor Jessamyn had been hurt in their fall. Nor was either of them dramatically upset about floating along on a subterranean stream with no particular source or destination.

Just the opposite. In fact, the sewer was oddly beautiful. It was as if they'd been given a special, secret opportunity and the time underground was to be treasured. How much time did they have? How much time do any of us have?

"I don't know," he replied. "But my guess is there's going to be all sorts of folks after us pretty quickly."

"Ya think?"

He laughed. "Of course, we might not be so easy to find if we encouraged this motion, put ourselves out of range."

"How would we do that?"

"The *X-tra Large* is a sailboat. I'd sail."

"Can it still do that?"

Again their conversation was replete with double meanings. By asking how they'd escape their parents and presumed rescuers, Jessamyn was not explicitly suggesting that escape was desirable. Likewise, by explaining how they'd enact such a flight, Timothy wasn't implying the wisdom of flight. Neither knew the other well enough to be so daring, so reckless. His answer had to be as hypothetical as her question. Was the *X-tra Large* up to the task? Was the boat literally shipshape?

He groped around the dark deck, feeling the scratches and dents, and crawled over the toppled mast, under the intact boom. Significantly, there was no damage to the great wheel used for steering nor, as far as he could tell by touch, to a stub of the rudder that hadn't snapped off in the initial fall.

"Been better, but she seems to have taken the abuse. But let me check a bit further." He stood carefully, for without the bottom of its keel and the top of its mast, without its metal cradle, the *X-tra Large* was extra tippy. He held a hand out in either direction like a tightrope walker and reached as far up the broken mast as he could. He couldn't feel the top, which meant that they still had at least seven feet.

Otherwise, the boat felt solid beneath him, a testimonial to old-fashioned construction. A modern fiberglass hull would have shattered into a thousand pieces. You could always count on a Herreshoff. "Yep," he declared. "We have enough to work with."

"Which is?"

"Let's take inventory. It's important to determine what our assets are. Then we can tell what our potential is."

"But how can we see?"

"Because asset number one is a lantern."

"You've got a lantern?" Jessamyn practically squealed with excitement.

"Standard operating equipment. You never know when you're going to lose electricity. It might be exactly what you need for the Coast Guard to save you if your boat is struck by lightning or disabled by a crazed tiger shark."

"Just for example."

"Yeah."

He'd heard all of this from the old salts at the marina who'd given him and his father lessons, but he hadn't believed a word of it. Now, however, he was speaking as if he was on intimate terms with nautical emergencies that sent lesser men to Davy Jones's locker. "Just wait a few minutes and I'll find it."

He kept to the center of the vessel and tiptoed forward. Once he found the narrow ladder bolted to the inside of the hatch, however, things were easier because there wasn't anyplace for something to go wrong. He climbed down the ladder and turned to orient himself in the absolute pitch.

Right away there was good news. For a few heartbeats as he descended, he realized that, despite his bravado and despite the surprisingly good condition of the rest of the vessel, he was fearful that he'd step into a pool of water. But the floor was dry; indeed, the hull had taken the brunt of the shock and held strong.

There was barely enough room to squeeze between the beds built into the side walls of the cabin. He paced three steps to the end of the sleeping area and opened a cabinet tucked under the stern.

Everything that had been neatly stowed had tumbled during the boat's fall, but it was easy to feel around for the heavy cardboard box in which the lantern was packed. Aside from one night out on Barnegat Bay, he and his father had never used it. They were day-trippers.

Holding on to the top rung of the ladder with his left hand, he balanced the box on his right palm like a waiter carrying a tray from Poseidon's realm. "Here."

Jessamyn's hands reached out, touched his.

Instinctively, he let go of the rung and fell backward, but the hatchway was so small that his spine smacked against the opposite side and he remained upright. "Oh, um, sorry, I was surprised."

"My bad. I was waiting for you."

"OK. But we'd better take this stuff to the stern because of the mast and boom."

The two intrepid travelers crawled toward the rear of the boat, where they sat cross-legged with the box containing the lantern open between them. There were only a few pieces, but fitting them together in the dark was not so simple; the contraption had a round metal base and a glass tube that screwed neatly into it, and a few smaller but presumably vital parts. There was also a jug of some sort of liquid that they set aside.

Jessamyn said, "Hold on to everything."

Timothy replied, "Especially the instructions."

"Yeah, because then after we get this thing lit we can see if we did it the right way."

For a moment, a shaft of light from the next catch basin, set too low into or sunk too wide from the aboveground curb, did indeed pierce the darkness, illuminating Jessamyn's red hair as if the lantern had already been lit. Reflexively, Timothy glanced away.

She reached out and helped him attach the base to another piece of metal that she had fished out of the box. Then she observed, "There's a hole in the side."

"That's where you insert the wick."

"Yes, here in the envelope, a long stretchy thing like a shoelace."

"There should also be a key to adjust the flame."

"Got it."

Working together was a maritime necessity. Timothy's father had always insisted on it when the Murphy Men set sail. It was, perhaps, a little like surgery, this operation. How long it took, neither teenager could say, but every action was crucial. At last, most of the pieces fit snugly, but there was one remaining object that didn't seem to belong anywhere. It was a narrow oval about six inches long. Most of the oval was made of smooth metal, but it ended in a tiny surface that measured about a quarter of an inch by three quarters of an inch and was rough to the skin.

"What is it?" Jessamyn asked.

"I don't know, but it feels like, um, a nutcracker," he answered. "It's flexible. I can squeeze it."

"Then you know what you should do, Timothy?"

"Squeeze it?"

"Yeah, the worst that can happen will be that the planet explodes."

He did squeeze, and—it wasn't exactly an exploding planet, but both of them jerked back when the thing sparked.

He laughed. "It's a lighter."

"This bottle . . ." Jessamyn lifted up the jug, about the size of a carton of orange juice, stored in the box with the lantern. Timothy could sense her exertion as she twisted off the top. There was a sloshing sound, and a biting alcoholic odor wafted into the air. "Fuel," she announced. "But I don't know where to fill it."

He felt around the base of the lantern where the wick poked through the hole. A miniature sliding door opened. The design was ingenious because it allowed the wick to absorb as much fuel as it required to stay wet while keeping the rest of the flammable liquid in an independent compartment safe against spillage. If the lantern toppled over on a wave-pitched boat, the light would shutter, but the fire would not spread. "Here."

She poured several ounces into the cavity while he held the mechanical flint to the tip of the wick. "This better work."

"It's gonna work or . . ."

"Explode the planet."

And then there was light.

🦫

Timothy's sense of enclosure had been accurate. The sewer was barely wider than the boat. The walls consisted of great rough-hewn gray stones that gradually curved upward to meet in a barrel ceiling. Because of this, it was vital to balance the *X-tra Large* extra carefully. Tilt too far left or right and the boat could lose the rest of its mast.

At the next intersection, a pair of catch basins on opposite sides of the tunnel showed the perpendicular barrels meeting in a groin vault from which a stream of water trickled in and splashed the deck. Perhaps a hydrant above was spraying a street full of happy children in wet shorts and T-shirts. Or maybe there was a fire and the water came from a leaky hose.

"Say," Jessamyn said, no longer whispering.

"What?"

"I was just wondering . . ."

"Yes?"

"What do you do for light when you're not being attacked by sharks or hit by lightning?"

"What do you mean?"

"Well, you said the lantern is for a nighttime emergency. So what about when it isn't an emergency?"

"There's a battery. It's charged at the marina and . . ."

"How do you turn it on?"

"With a key . . . that I, um, have right . . . here." He fished a ring of keys out of his pocket.

"And . . ."

He saw the logic. With the key, he could have turned on the engine. With the engine, he could have turned on the regular lighting system. Their labor spent putting the lantern together was unnecessary. "It didn't occur to me."

In the dark, it didn't occur to him to flip a switch to turn on the light? He changed the subject to something that could be seen by the emergency lantern, a narrow ledge that ran above the water line beside the channel for a block or more. "Look at that."

"What's it for?"

Timothy hazarded a guess. "Um . . . promenading. You know, for people who are allergic to the sun."

39

"Very funny. What do you really think?"

"I'm not sure, but I'd guess repairs." The lantern cast a flickering light, and Timothy reached out to let his fingers stroke the wall as they passed a tight spot in the channel. "It's wet," he said.

Jessamyn nodded and then looked down at the water and repeated the question she had asked earlier in the dark. "Where's it coming from? I mean, there's no rain today."

Timothy shrugged. "I don't know. Maybe there's always some seepage. Or maybe they keep a certain amount in the system to keep it—"

"Moist?"

He ignored the wit and tried to focus on his surroundings. The wall seemed mossy and cold even though the temperature had to be 85 degrees. The channel smelled fresh despite stray cigarette butts and Styrofoam cups and other urban detritus washed down from the streets. Again he listened to the rumble in the tunnel. Part of the hum definitely came from the surface, yet some vibrated through the walls on a regular but discontinuous basis, every few minutes. Perhaps a dentist was working in a basement office on the far side of the wall. No, there would have to be a team of dentists busily drilling their patients' teeth for block after block.

And then there was one other small sound that Timothy or Jessamyn might have called a rustling if they'd been in the forest, because it wasn't mechanical or industrial; it was biological. Neither mentioned it.

"We've got work to do," Timothy announced.

"Aye, aye, sir." Jessamyn saluted.

He couldn't tell if she was being sarcastic, but he didn't mind. For Jessamyn Hazard, sarcasm was a form of salutation.

He explained that it would be a good idea to use their light to take inventory of the rest of the community's assets. To begin with, there was rope. Sailboats are basically made out of rope loosely held together by planks of wood and stretches of cloth. Some of the rope lay in neat coils at the bottom of the utility cabinet in which Timothy found the lantern, but more was strewn across the battered deck, hopelessly tangled when the mast broke.

"What are we supposed to do with rope?" Jessamyn scoffed. "Lasso some wild horses?"

Patiently, he explained, "We don't know what's going to come in handy. Remember, this is uncharted territory."

"Yippee-i-o-ki-ay."

Ignoring her, he propped the lantern at the top of the ladder so that it illuminated both the deck and the cabin below. Then he descended again into the newly lit interior and opened the door to the pantry next to the bathroom and started calling out the items of the inventory before passing some upward and stowing others. "One pair of bright-orange inflatable life vests."

"Is that a fashion statement?"

"No, it's for an emergency."

"Like the lantern? What are we going to do, drown in two feet of water?"

"You never know. Gas. One medium-size propane tank."

She sat at the top of the hatchway, legs swinging, casting shadows, just watching the underworld go by. "Pro-pain, you say. In my neck of the woods, most folks are anti-pain."

"That is really bad."

"Not as bad as forgetting that you had the key to the boat."

"OK, are we even, then?"

"Even Steven. But about the propane . . . is that for barbecues?"

Perennially the best student in her class, Jessamyn happened to be correct. "How else do you think you cook on a boat? So yeah, here, add one glorified hibachi."

"Speaking of which . . ."

He knew what she had in mind. "Yes, indeed, food is a priority. To start with, there's the stuff we packed today. You and your mom brought most of it, so why don't you tell me what treats we have to look forward to."

"Two chickens, marinated, cut into pieces . . . potato salad . . . coleslaw . . . chips . . . a blueberry pie."

"No partridge in a pear tree?"

"Couldn't fit it on the forklift."

"But wow, good for your mom for cooking all that."

"I didn't say that she cooked any of it. Underpaid ethnic minorities who work at Whole Foods did. My mom hasn't cooked since . . ."

She allowed the pause to linger a second. That was how long it took for Timothy to figure out how long it had been since Jessamyn's mother had cooked anything. Then he filled up the airspace. "We also carry staples in the pantry: ramen noodles, canned vegetables, ketchup, mustard. Maybe some other stuff. We should check. And there's a brand-new five-gallon container of fresh water. All in all, I'd say this could last us a few days if we're careful."

Aside from their first double-meaning-laden conversation, neither had mentioned a word about how long they were likely to go unfound underground. Or, perhaps more pertinently, how long they might hypothetically prefer to go unfound. In either case, food was a limiting factor unless they discovered more. That was highly unlikely. Maybe they could go fishing.

Timothy pulled out two flexible titanium rods that his father had purchased in a moment of enthusiasm but seldom used. Timothy loved the process of the cast: arm extended backward, and then a flick of the wrist that sends the line, with an oblong rubber bob attached, whizzing into the distance. Sometimes it flew so far that he couldn't see the tiny splash. Then he'd hit the autospool, which retracted the line like a zipper through the waves. But the one time they tried to actually fish for blues, the lines got totally tangled and they ended up going out for a lobster dinner.

On the recreational side, the closet contained an extra set of swim trunks, male, and some snorkeling gear. More practical was a toolbox and a first-aid kit that came with the boat. Also various pulleys and tackles and sail attachments. Domestically, there was bedding and several striped towels, and a plastic container with soap, toothpaste, and shampoo.

The goods lay spread out on the deck as the vessel continued to float gently along the tunnel.

"Um . . . ," Jessamyn hemmed, "about that barbecue?"

For one second she looked like an eager little kid rather than the brittle wiseacre she'd been until now. "Fine concept," he enthused. "But we still have work to do."

"Like?"

"First the checklist."

"I thought we just did that."

"That was stuff in storage. This will be of what we really need in order to get moving."

"Gotcha."

"Better say 'ready as they go.' "

"What does that mean?"

"I have no idea. But it's a nautical tradition."

"Is it a nautical tradition to go for a sail in the sewer?"

Timothy was growing impatient. "Look, are you going to cooperate or not?"

Jessamyn rolled her eyes. "Ready as they go."

"Mast?"

"Broken."

"Well, then, half-mast?"

"More like three-quarters."

Exasperated, he conceded, "Three-quarters mast?"

"Present and accounted for, sir."

"'Check' will do fine."

"Check."

"Engine?"

She peered over the stern of the boat, where an outboard motor had been mounted for putting around a harbor. "No."

"No?"

"We must have lost it in the fall."

"Hmm. Spar?"

"Is that the crosspiece that used to be on top of the mast?"

"Yes."

"No."

"OK, we're going to have to work on that. Boom?"

"Ummm . . . Bah?"

"What?"

"You know, sis-boom-bah."

He smiled. "Not exactly. This"—he patted the thick horizontal pole that extended along the spine of the deck, making two sides of a triangle with the mast—"is the boom. It's used to change direction."

Jessamyn paused for half a second, just long enough to convey how silly the exercise was but not long enough to complain. "Check."

"Wheel?"

"Do you have a driver's license?"

"Wheel, mate?"

"And why is the second-in-command a mate? I thought mates were equal rather than—"

"Wheel?"

"Check."

"Sail?"

"Check."

"Controls?"

"Where are they?"

"Here." He tapped the panel.

She tried every available button, dial, and switch, and all that came up was a harsh crackling noise. "Radio's berserkers."

"How about the light?" He folded his arms smugly and waited for the answer.

She nodded. "You got lucky."

"My father always said that a sailor makes his own luck."

"Or *her* own luck."

"Fine. So except for the controls and the engine and the spar, all things necessary are accounted for. Let's rig this baby."

Immediately, Jessamyn stood up. "Just tell me what to do."

"Start with the rope there. Untangle it and coil it up nicely."

Jessamyn paused. If this was make-work or, worse, woman's work, she was ready to quit on the spot. But Timothy himself was tidying the deck, separating torn bits of sail from chunks of broken wood. In a small boat—in any boat—organization was vital. As Timothy said Tom said, "Everything in its place."

Unfortunately, neatness wasn't going to set the *X-tra Large* straight after the damage from the fall, but his dad also said that a real sailor had to be prepared for anything.

"What's this?" Jessamyn had found an object that looked like a thick metal clamp under some of the torn sail and knotted rope.

"That," Timothy said, grinning, "is exactly what we're going to need to hang a new sail. Please give it to me." He threaded a stretch of rope through a device on the side of the object and stood on his tiptoes but couldn't reach the splintered peak of the mast. He climbed onto the boom but was still a few inches shy of his goal. That was good news and bad news. The former because it meant that a large portion of the sail would be available to catch the underground wind, the latter because the sail wouldn't make a difference if he couldn't attach the thing. "Um . . ."

Jessamyn reached up and easily collared the mast. She didn't get any thanks for making her companion feel like a munchkin.

He tightened the rope that rode upward, doubled it for good measure, and let out some slack. Then he attached the other end to a pulley at the base of the mast and handed it to Jessamyn to stretch out along the boom. Eventually, they'd bring that end back to the mast, thus creating a hemp triangle. But due to the new and lesser height of the mast, several feet of sail flapped over the boom.

"We're going to have to reef it. That means adjust the bottom of the sail, like a pant cuff." He handed her a knife from the toolbox.

"Do I look like a seamstress?"

"No, a mathematician. First, you've got to figure out the dimensions."

An hour later, they were ready, maybe. The damaged mast had to hold, and so did the damaged sail.

"Now, on the count of three, we hoist."

The second the surprisingly heavy fabric creaked up the mast to the block, the breeze in the chamber picked up. At least it seemed that way because the sail puffed boldly outward. In reality, they were going only a wee bit faster than before because the exposed canvas was a quarter of its previous square footage. Nevertheless, they were moving, without a care in the world. Sailing.

# CHAPTER

# 3

**I**F IT WAS DARK AND FASCINATING BELOW THE STREETS, there was plenty of light above but little worth seeing. Miranda Hazard and Tom Murphy stood, out of breath from their mad dash after the unstoppable vessel, at the ragged edge of the hole in the earth through which their children had disappeared. For perhaps five seconds, Miranda was like a three-year-old who's fallen and needs to figure out the correct response to her pain. Then she screamed.

The only reason Tom didn't join her was that Murphy Men didn't show that sort of weakness, but he leaned over the gash in the ground and called out his son's name. "Timothy! *Timmmothy!* Can you hear me? Timothy!"

The younger of the Murphy Men may or may not have heard his father, but beat patrolman Johnny "Angel" Bosco did. He'd been collaring a teenage shoplifter at a drugstore around the corner when mayhem broke out in the street. He looked at the young offender, said, "Don't do this again," and was first on the scene.

Bosco scanned the smashed cradle and the Con Ed workers

fleeing their excavation, checked to make sure that no one was injured, and then radioed to the precinct house for backup. By then, however, several 911 calls had preceded him, and a squad car was already sirening down Broadway, followed moments later by an ambulance.

"My daughter!" Miranda wailed.

Bosco looked at Tom Murphy beside her. "Are you with this woman?" he asked.

Quietly, Tom gasped, "My son."

More police arrived every second, yet before any of them could discover more about what was fast developing into the SDJ—situation du jour, in cop lingo—a dinged-up, unmarked Chevy with a portable light and siren attached to the roof roared the wrong way up 184th. From the reckless driving, Bosco knew who was in the car: brass.

A barrel-shaped man wearing a brown suit and a bad toupee, the kind that dares people to notice it, climbed out of the passenger seat. Bosco immediately acknowledged the occupant. "Captain Mullane."

The head of the 34th Precinct didn't bother to return the greeting. He looked at the hole in the ground, at the increasing number of police officers circling it for no ostensible purpose, at the gathering crowd, at the distraught couple, and only then at his subordinates. "Everything under control?"

"Yes, sir."

Mullane spat into the gutter. "What do we have?"

Johnny Angel briefed him as best he could. "From what I can figure, a boat with a couple of kids on it fell into the hole."

For a second Mullane thought Bosco had said "a goat" and wondered what the heck two kids in Washington Heights were doing riding a goat, but once the story had been confirmed, the goat made more sense than the actual truth. He scratched his toupee, which shifted slightly to the left, exposing a line of gray stubble over his right ear. "What are we talkin', the *Queen Mary?*"

"It was apparently attached to that pickup over there." Bosco pointed to the truck with New Jersey plates.

"The driver?"

"One of them." He pointed to Miranda and Tom, who stood frozen like statues amid the rapidly increasing chaos.

"Parents?"

"Yep."

"And . . ." The major question. "Where are the kids?"

Bosco shrugged and gazed into the crevasse like a tourist at the Grand Canyon. "We haven't made our way down there yet, but we don't think there are any fatalities. It seems as if the boat got away."

At that moment another caravan of cars and vans arrived to block traffic, which was just as well since the street had taken on the atmosphere of a carnival. A crowd of locals amassed on the edge of the pit.

The second group of vehicles belonged to the representatives of the utilities whose work had been damaged. Con Ed sent a crew; so did the telephone company. Then the fire department set up a pair of floodlights to illuminate bits of wood floating below. The only agency that did not appear was the New York City Department of Environmental Protection, a.k.a. sewer and water.

And then there was the press. Every daily tabloid and local TV station monitored police reports. Traffic accident? Didn't rate a stringer. Construction accident? Ho-hum. Two children on a boat disappearing into the sewer? The next day's front page had just been written!

Once the captain had absorbed the minor data his officers had gathered, he interrupted. "All right. Done. First, I want several men down there. Stat. Now . . ." More carefully he eyed the two parents. Mothers and fathers of lost or hurt kids were a police officer's worst nightmare. Grotesque if guilty, pathetic if innocent. They wrecked you.

Calmly, he introduced himself. "Excuse me, folks. Seems like we have a little problem."

Tom Murphy turned on him, eyes blazing. "A *little* problem? You call your street swallowing my boy a *little problem* and—"

"Sir! Sir! I apologize if I spoke wrongly. Now, let's start at the beginning. Are you sure that your boat was attached to the truck up the street?"

"Yes," Tom snapped. "How do you think it got here from New Jersey?"

Miranda interrupted. "When we came out of that luncheonette the boat was already rolling downhill. We tried to catch up with them, but we couldn't."

"Yes, ma'am."

"We were going to City Island. We stopped for an ice cream."

"Egg cream," Tom corrected her.

To calm down the parents, Mullane needed to shift them away from the gruesomely compelling wound in the earth. "Why don't we step out of the sun over . . . there." He led them to the trailer parked on the far side of the hole to oversee its excavation. At the door, the captain flashed his badge at several shaken Con Ed workers. "Out," he declared. "This trailer is temporarily impounded by the NYPD. Thank you," he said before anyone could object.

Mullane returned to the business at hand. "We've already determined that there have been no injuries, and we're going to find your daughter. And your son, sir. But we need to find out exactly what occurred."

"No." Tom Murphy was still unhelpful. "What you need is to get down there."

🐀

Patrolman Bosco knocked on the door of the trailer. Glad for the break, Mullane said, "Excuse me, please. I'll be back in a moment," and stepped outside.

Bosco reported that he had done a preliminary forensic examination of the site. He'd also walked uphill to the pickup truck, which was duly registered, though it had a three-month-old unpaid parking ticket from this block. Most important, he noticed that the six-inch solid-steel hook meant to fit snugly into the trestle's eye was hanging loose next to a stiff button that had to be pressed before the hook could be removed. Though simple, it was a fail-safe mechanism that couldn't bump or shake loose. Tension on the connection made it impossible to budge while in motion and difficult at rest. "In other words . . ."

Mullane concluded, "This was no accident."

Yet attributing cause to the SDJ was irrelevant at the moment. They'd have plenty of time to sort out the mess. For now, the father was correct. It was imperative to find those kids. Preferably *rescue* those kids, though it remained a theoretical possibility that their parents had committed about the weirdest crime the captain had ever seen.

He looked at the trailer's smeary window, then up the block to the truck and nearby stoops. They'd have a hundred witnesses to interview. Someone surely noticed. Someone surely would talk. He was just thinking that they'd get a clear picture when a tall man entered the restricted area clutching a tan briefcase as if it contained diamonds.

"Excuse me, excuse me," the man demanded. "Who's in charge here?"

51

Tom and Miranda stepped outside to see what was going on.

"That's me," Mullane said.

"Seth Rothbart, troubleshooter for Time Warner. Now, we have over five thousand customers who are currently without service. So here's what I expect you to do . . ." He pulled a sheaf of official-looking papers out of the briefcase.

For one slight, light moment, the policeman's eyes met those of the father of the lost boy. Then the captain picked up the papers as if to examine them. He strolled over to the edge of the pit, now blocked by yellow tape, and dropped the batch over the edge.

"What are you doing?" yelped Rothbart. "I have customers, Captain, and . . ."

"And I've got two kids down there while you're worried about whether your precious customers can see *Dancing with the Stars*? I'll tell you what, Mr. Cable Man. I'm going to count to ten to give you a sporting chance to get out of here before I throw you into that pit with your forms."

"If you think—"

"One . . . Two . . ."

The man from Time Warner fled the scene as fast as anyone can move without running.

"Thanks," said Tom Murphy.

"It's nothing. I should have fed him to the crocodiles." And then, seeing the sudden alarm on the mother's face, Mullane corrected himself. "Not that there's any crocodiles down there."

In fact, he was glad for the bureaucrat's interruption. It had given him the opportunity to earn the parents' trust. "Tell me more about your kids."

🦫

Suburban kids. Good grades. Each had some friends, but neither was going to be voted Most Popular. Actually, NYPD Captain Walter

**52**

Mullane had been voted Most Likely to Do Time by the senior class of Bensonhurst High School.

Mullane asked both of the parents a lot of questions about their children until he began to feel like he knew Timothy and Jessamyn. Geeks, both. No special trouble that the parents knew about. Or, to be precise, no special trouble the parents were willing to mention. He also learned about the boat: age, origins, dimensions. It was described like the getaway car in a bank robbery. No, it was described like the accomplice in the getaway car. It had a personality, like another child with its own desires.

There was one more element in the equation that had to be taken into account. A force perhaps more similar to the *X-tra Large* than to its passengers. Inanimate, but with a character, a nature that needed to be understood. Hopelessly, Mullane looked at the polic and firefighters milling around the site and asked, "Anyone here know anything about the sewer?"

"I can help you." Another man, tall and thin with ridiculously large black plastic glasses, had slipped underneath the ring of yellow tape that now separated official New York from the excited crowd of gawkers.

"And who are you?" Mullane snapped. If there were any crocodiles, they'd be well fed.

"Cass Wainwright. From the civil engineer's office," the intruder said, identifying himself. "And I have here . . ." Fast as a magician, he whipped an enormous roll of papers that Captain Mullane hadn't noticed from behind his back onto the hood of Mullane's Chevy. "Plans."

"Hope yours are better than Time Warner's."

"Much." He pulled loose a ribbon, and the roll unfurled like an Oriental rug at a bazaar. The top page was a map of Manhat-

53

tan, entirely different from any street map that most police would have any reason to use, a topographical map with contoured hills and meandering streams and a small portion of familiar urban grid down at the bottom. Semi-familiar, because the map's proportions were wrong. Downtown appeared skinnier than it should. There was no Battery Park City, and the Village didn't seem to extend as far west as it ought. Mullane tried to make sense of the top half of the map, where a dozen irregular lines curled across the big page like snakes. He raised his chin to the CE.

Wainwright explained, "This is the Viele Map. 1865. Viele was the chief engineer of Central Park, the last man to chart the city's original topography. If you're going underground, you're going to need to know what's there."

At last, some real help had arrived at the SDJ, and yet Mullane was sure that none of his officers had been bright enough to invite the engineer to the party. "How did you get here?"

"Subway."

"No, I mean who asked you to come here?"

To Wainwright, the answer was apparent. "No one. I heard on the radio. Sorry it took me so long, but the archives are closed on weekends. Getting the guard to let me in was like pulling teeth. Then the uptown train was delayed for . . ." He looked at the pit. "Obvious reasons."

Unlike the jerk from Time Warner, this man had simply come because he had something to offer. Incredible.

"Basically, the island of Manhattan is pitched from north to south," said Wainwright, beginning his tutorial. "There are still some hills and outcroppings like the one we're on, Washington Heights, but also Murray Hill and Morningside Heights, and then there were those that were leveled a century ago to make way for development. Still, if you think of the Staten Island Ferry Terminal downtown, you basically step onto the island about ten feet above the waterline. Up here—well, if not for the buildings—you've got a view."

"Are you saying we put a net at the Battery and we'll catch our fishies?"

"Unfortunately not. Besides, that could take a long time. Who knows where they could get stuck between here and there? After all, the island is nearly seventeen miles long and we're pretty close to the northern tip. Approximately . . . here." The engineer pointed to a large empty space where streets hadn't yet been built. A series of squiggly lines rendered streams.

Mullane made the obvious point. "But they're gone."

"Of course they're not. Just because some guy wants to put up a building doesn't mean the stream that runs across his property is going to disappear."

"Couldn't he just plug it?"

"No. The water's going to come out and it's going to go someplace. However, if you can't stop it, you can divert it, change the path—basically, shove it out of your way. You wouldn't believe how many culverts are under these buildings. Now, take a look at this." He unfolded a slightly more familiar second page over the first. In this map, the hills and streams were gone, and something geometrical—not streets—filled much of the island. "This is a map of the sewer that dates back to about 1910. Unfortunately, it's incomplete and doesn't have the entire system."

"So let's get a newer one."

"That's not possible."

"Why not? The sewer had to be built according to a plan."

"True, but a lot of the charts were drowned in the Municipal Building Fire of 1965."

"Pardon?"

"In many cases, there was only one set, and when a garbage can

**55**

fire got a little rambunctious, the fire department decided to soak us down a tad more than necessary. The result was that several million one-of-a-kind documents became . . ."

"None-of-a-kind."

"But we can reconstruct the most obvious decisions that were made—or should have been made—and draw conclusions."

"Like water flows downhill?"

"Not always," Civil Engineer Wainwright explained. "Sometimes pressure from elsewhere in the system can push it uphill. Think of a trap under a sink. Also, underground topography is not obvious from the surface. In some places the storm sewer is only a few feet beneath street level; in others, where there are hills, it may be more than a hundred feet deep. Also, some grades are so minimal, less than one percent, that the slightest impetus would carry a vessel uphill."

"In other words, a motor?"

"A motor, a sail, it could be a team of oxen. Think of the sewer as a canal. Whatever can impel a vessel through Panama can do the same here."

"So we should look for those kids in the Pacific Ocean?"

The captain was pleased with his wit until he glanced up and saw the stricken expression on Miranda Hazard's face. "Sorry about that, ma'am. We will find your daughter and her friend."

He was sure. That's why he'd allowed himself a moment of inappropriate levity. A hundred people had seen the kids disappear. No bodies had been found. It was therefore clear that they had landed safely. And there were limits to where they could have gone. Thus, they were bound to be found. How the trestle bearing the boat had been released from the cab remained a mystery. That was the next problem he had to solve.

# CHAPTER

# 4

**H**AVING TAKEN INVENTORY AND STRUNG AND hoisted the sail, the teenagers suddenly had nothing to do but float downstream as if they were on a raft in the sunlight. Timothy and Jessamyn sat on the deck of the *X-tra Large*, considering their present situation. Timothy stated the obvious. "They're going to be coming in exactly where we entered."

Jessamyn, however, mulled over another, unmentionable truth. Quite simply, this was a major adventure. To quit would be to forgo the saga of their young lives. They might not have chosen to risk those lives or scare the heck out of their parents, or have chosen each other as partners in this day's wild exploit, but none of those options were left up to them. Well, maybe that item about scaring the rents. She could make her peace with that. Miranda would survive. "So the best thing we can do is put some serious distance between us and them."

"Yes, but we have to do more than that."

"What do you mean?"

"We've got to think the way *they're* going to think. Anticipate their next move and avoid it in advance."

"Like chess."

"Um, sure." Timothy played chess. And he was good. Had come in third in an elementary school tournament. But he was pretty sure that he wouldn't stand a chance against Jessamyn. The extra-large girl probably knew every move from the DeCristoforo Opening to the Curran Gambit.

Indeed, she began to spool out the logic of the situation. "So they'll enter the tunnel, discover the stuff we left behind, like the motor. But the boat will have done what boats do. Traveled on the water."

"Right," Timothy concurred. "After all, they know we couldn't have sunk."

"Why not?"

"To begin with, the water's no more than a few feet deep."

She peered into the dark channel. "How can you tell?"

"The keel broke off, but it also broke our fall. We weren't swamped. So the bottom can't be too far below the hull."

Jessamyn nodded. "OK. So what will they think?"

"They should be able to figure out our maximum cruising speed and then enter the sewer ahead of us. They might put up a blockade. But we have several advantages."

"The first is that you're so smart."

"What?" Absurdly disconcerted, he asked, "Do you really mean that?"

"No, but I figure I've got to flatter you."

Instantly deflated, he sighed. "Really?"

"Whatever I say now wouldn't make a difference because I've already established the principal that I can assert two diametrically opposite propositions. Thus, you couldn't be sure if I was telling the truth, so there's no point in your asking and less point in my answering."

He looked at the enormous girl in her Hawaiian shirt and orange pleated shorts sopped from the splashed-up water of the sewer. Trying to count his blessings, he smiled. "Did anyone ever tell you that you're a sociopath?"

"You mean a psychopath."

Once again, she had him. "What's the difference?"

"Actually, I don't think there is one. Or maybe it just depends on who's making the determination."

"Then why are there two separate words?"

"Because psychologists and sociologists can't agree on anything. They each had to make up their own word."

"Which basically means someone who doesn't play well with others?"

"I thought that was the definition of success. Speaking of which, what are our advantages?"

"Well, the first is that I'm so smart."

She put the tip of her finger to the tip of her tongue and made an imaginary score mark in the air.

"And the second is that this sewer system is pretty labyrinthine." He felt pleased at using the fancy word.

"And the third?"

"Well, they're going to assume that we want to be rescued and that we're going to do everything we can to stay as close to the place we went into the ground as possible. And even if we were hurt or unconscious or something else made it impossible to maneuver the boat, they'd still assume that we'd be carried in the direction of the current. So if we put a little energy into putting some distance between us, and if we go off at an angle, they won't be able to catch us until we're good and ready to be caught."

With the boat moving swiftly now, Timothy and Jessamyn both noticed that what initially seemed like a single, uniformly designed sewer system actually varied enormously from block to block. In some places, like intersections, the space widened. In others it narrowed. The ledge they'd seen came to an abrupt end and then recommenced farther on. Pipes and conduits hung from rusty brackets here but not there, fortunately above the height of the partial mast.

A series of metal rungs set into the stone wall climbed out of sight. An ancient louver door, rusted into rigidity, protected what must have been the tunnel's pumping, mechanical, or storage space. Or, for all they knew, it was an abandoned gift shop that once sold posters and snow globe souvenirs of the sewer.

Nor was this an entirely man-made world. Vegetation grew in the sewer. Moss furred some of the stonework while here and there a twiggy tree sprouted from the cracks.

Jessamyn's thoughts returned to mortality and she wondered again, "You think this is what burial is like?"

Timothy took the question seriously. "The enclosure. The quiet. Could be."

"My mom says that it's unfair that rock stars die."

"My dad says that's how you tell that the world is fair."

"What do they see in each other?"

"What does anyone see in anyone else?"

"Or," she continued, "what do we see in ourselves? I mean, do you think of yourself as having one parent or not having one parent?"

"Like, is the glass half empty or half full?" Timothy asked.

"Sort of."

"Well, I'm not sure it's possible to be a half-orphan."

"And if two half-orphans meet, do they become a whole orphan?" she asked.

As they spoke, the *X-tra Large* sailed into another open space, like a cavern or an aquatic public square. It couldn't have reflected an intersection up top, because they had just passed one. In fact, they were beneath a traffic triangle where two avenues scissored at an angle. Down below, this created the kind of interlacing architectural pattern that Timothy had once seen in a black-and-white poster at a friend's house. More important, it meant that the *X-tra Large* had plenty of room to tack. "How about we turn off here?" Timothy suggested.

"Good as any, I suppose," Jessamyn agreed.

"Ready and about?"

"Yes, sir."

Timothy slackened the sail while Jessamyn pushed the boom a few degrees leeward to take advantage of a slight shift in the wind. Obliging as always, despite its recent shock, the *X-tra Large* responded beautifully, but the moment it rounded the corner onto what they assumed was a street in the 170s, the sailors were met by a wall blazing with color.

The sight practically knocked Timothy off his feet. "Yow!"

Even in the dank and once again cramped tunnel, the wall could have been a massive stained-glass window. It glowed. It shone. Automatically, the pair leaned backward, as if to protect themselves from its splendor and also to better perceive its message. Vivid red at the waterline shaded upward to orange to bright yellow, clearly the image of a flame spelling out a single three-letter word in nine-foot-tall capital letters that began under the surface of the water and extended up to the curve of the vault: DUO.

At a loss for her test-prep vocabulary, Jessamyn said with a sigh, "Awesome."

Timothy remained silent, staring at the huge letters. In a way, he and Jessamyn might have been like European explorers hacking through a tropical jungle to suddenly come across Mayan pyramids or Angkor Wat. Or, thinking of the science fiction he loved, like Captain Xakerax in Briana Morton's intergalactic, epistolary, feminist trilogy, *Sarah Lawrence of Pedagogia*. Behold, the remnants of a civilization that flourished and perished eons ago.

Then again, maybe DUO was just a couple of kids, rather like themselves, who snuck into the sewer. Well, maybe *not* so like themselves.

"How did they get in here?" Jessamyn wondered aloud.

Timothy thought for a moment and then posed another question. "And who is it for?"

Jessamyn shrugged. "Graffiti for graffiti's sake."

"Like art?" he asked.

"Still, how many people do you think get down here?"

"At least four."

She looked at him. "You and me and DUO."

"And . . ."

Ahead of the boat, another wall of graffiti loomed, and then another, each in a different style, each bearing a different name. There was the hard, almost glassy edginess of Lazer and the ornate curlicues of Terf 161.

"Look at that." Timothy pointed to an elaborate cityscape by Mango.

"And here!" Jessamyn reached out to touch the muzzle of a gun that seemed to pop out of the wall as if it was three-dimensional.

And then, in the largest open space they'd yet come to, at what must have been another traffic triangle above, appeared a graffiti gallery, with a dozen or more painted surfaces. Each was more extraordinary than its predecessor, but this latter work still seemed crude in comparison to the grace and precision evident in DUO.

Timothy imagined a party, the graffitists' ball, strictly BYOP: Bring your own paint. At some point in the evening, Terf may have been inspired to start on one wall. Then Lazer and Reef and Themboyz took to the opposite side of the tunnel. At last, DUO set up their studio around the corner and the flames started licking at the walls until the visual arsonists had ignited their three immense letter-shaped candles. Awesome.

Alas, the graffitists must have run at last out of paint or space because one final panel of tunnel spelled out the end of the group show in jade green outlined in cobalt blue: "Adios Amigos," by someone named Latin Sam.

At least Timothy and Jessamyn thought the show was over, until they drifted a few blocks farther. There, stretching from one catch basin to the next—Timothy's best estimate of its extent and location being the entire span from 172nd to 173rd Streets—was the true coda to the exhibit, a final masterpiece by DUO.

It consisted of a subway train of a dozen cars with DUO's tag sprayed across its doors and windows. However, there were other tags, too, some by the contemporary masters they recognized from the gallery and some that they couldn't know referred to graffiti legends of the past, like Zephyr and Dondi. It was a mural that contained the whole history of graffiti, as if some modern artist had re-created *The Last Supper* with Jesus in the style of Picasso and Judas as portrayed by Dali.

More extraordinary yet was the context, for the subway itself was entirely realistic, and so were the southbound passengers partially visible between the letters of the spray-painted graffiti. There was a black-hatted Hasidic man reading a Yiddish newspaper in Zephyr's *e* and an Asian woman with a baby in a backpack on her shoulder in Lazer's *a*, a uniformed transit cop glancing at his watch in the dot over Dondi's *i* and, in the center of DUO's very own *O*, a young black boy peering out at the world.

The train was so authentic that Timothy thought he could hear its rumbling, and then he realized: He did hear a train rumbling. It was the sound that had previously reminded him of a dozen dentists' drills, and it grew louder, then quieter. There must have been a subway track on the other side of the wall, just another part of the active subterranean life. Perhaps the graffitists had gained access to the tunnel by means of a door between the transit and sewer systems.

Timothy and Jessamyn found themselves speculating about that, as well as nearly every subject in the world. "I mean," she suggested, perhaps provocatively, "what's the difference between DUO and Michelangelo? They both decorated great public spaces. Actually, they both worked on arches and had to take into account perspective and the curvature of ceilings like the Vatican."

"Yeah, but DUO doesn't do naked people," Timothy said, more daring than he'd ever imagined himself.

She took his reply seriously. "Maybe. But maybe this is only their uptown gallery. Maybe they got sexier when they went downtown."

"And how do you know that they started here? Maybe they live on the Upper East Side and go to some Catholic boys school."

"Hmm." She considered his point seriously but took one issue. "Why do you assume they're boys? Maybe DUO is a pair of twin girls from Park Avenue."

"Or Montclair?"

"Don't be silly. No one from Montclair could ever find their way into the— What's that?" Jessamyn heard a familiar sound that couldn't have been a . . . cough.

"Nothing."

Together they worked in silent communion as the vessel continued forward as if of its own volition. They didn't question whether to try and steer it to take a turn or avoid a turn and could no longer be quite sure how far they'd traveled. Nor could they be certain what time it was, though the glow from above had weakened. It was afternoon and Jessamyn had forgotten her hunger—until now.

"Hey," she said. "Didn't you promise me a picnic?"

"Excellent idea. Let me show you how to work this thing."

They unfolded the hibachi, screwed the propane tank into a nozzle on the side, and used the squeezy igniter from the lantern to spark the gas into a deep-blue flame.

They grilled one of the marinated chickens and set the fixings on a couple of paper plates. Instead of eating blueberry pie for dessert, however, they broke out a box of Twinkies from the pantry. It was all as delicious as it was supposed to be out on the open waters of the Long Island Sound with their parents.

And yet something was missing from the picture.

Oh: the parents. Also the sky, the ocean, seagulls, maybe a few other boats out on what had promised to be a beautiful day that both Timothy and Jessamyn had originally dreaded.

Instead of anxiety, however, they both felt a sense of profound calm. Indeed, to look around after a frightful accident and be able to count one's limbs and digits might give anyone that "but for the grace" chill, and yet both of them knew—not to speak it, but deep down they *knew*—that they had escaped a far worse fate.

If not for the "accident," they would have arrived at City Island a bit after noon, gotten the *X-tra Large* into the water by one o'clock, puttered around on the Long Island Sound for a few hours, and returned to the same dull life they'd always led. *That was truly humbling.*

"Um . . ." Jessamyn, who seemed willing to make any brash statement at any given moment, hemmed awkwardly.

"What?"

"Does the bathroom work?"

"I didn't check. Let's go down."

Together, they descended into the hatch, and Timothy held up the lantern with its wick turned low to conserve oil. He peered into the tiny room he called a "head" and announced, "Looks good." Then he climbed back on deck and sat on the prow, feet dangling into the water, and thought how funny it would be if he lost a flip-flop. A minute later, Jessamyn returned and glanced around the deck with a quizzical expression.

"Um, Timothy?"

"Yes."

"Did you clean up?"

"No, but I will."

"Were you hungry?"

"No thanks. I just ate."

"I mean it. If you didn't clean up, you must have been really, really hungry."

"Not so much."

"Well, you must have been if you ate every bite of the chicken, including the bones."

Timothy turned. The half-filled plates they'd left were empty. Only the Twinkies remained. He lifted the lantern and a foot-long tail slipped into a hole between the bricks.

"Ewww," Jessamyn said.

"It must have been drawn by the food."

"As long as it's not drawn by the company."

"OK, it means that from now on everything, every single edible bite, goes in the refrigerator, whether it works or not."

She nodded, but once the paper plates were disposed of and the rest of the food was stowed, all they had to do was make tiny adjustments to the sail, lie back, and appreciate the scenery. Indeed, the tunnel began to seem like a grotto with moldy papier-mâché stalagmites growing on the ledge in heaps of sodden garbage bags, and newsmagazines studded with shiny cellophane and glittery foil cigarette wrappings ornamenting ancient headlines.

Timothy said, "Talk about yellow journalism."

The tunnel was its own busy ecosystem, but what else was in it besides rats and graffitists and them? "You think there are reptiles here?"

"How'd you get that idea?"

"Some book."

"No."

"I always heard there were alligators."

"No, but there are bugs the size of rats."

"You know, that isn't what bothers me, but . . ."

"But what?"

"If the bugs are the size of rats, then how big are the rats?"

"Maybe we really should get out of here."

They lay back, less easily than they had earlier, pondering where circumstance might take them before the end of the day.

"How far do you think we've gone?" she asked.

"I don't know. Say that it takes about ten minutes to get from one catch basin to the next, and that's a block. We've been down here maybe an hour, an hour and a half, so we may have gone six or nine blocks. I'd say we're approaching New York–Presbyterian."

"What's that?"

He looked at her as if he'd said they were under the White

**67**

House and she'd failed to recognize the reference. "It's the big hospital you can see when you're crossing the GW Bridge. A real campus with a bunch of buildings connected by skyways and . . . Oh, of course, you'd have no reason to know. It's . . . let me put it this way . . . My mom never cooked dinner after she went to New York–Presbyterian."

🐀

Aboveground was the site of Columbia's Business and Technology Center, formerly the Audubon Ballroom. Originally a film and vaudeville theater, it later became a Jewish synagogue that rented out space to the OAAU, the Organization of Afro-American Unity, for its weekly meetings. There, on February 21, 1965, Malcolm X was lecturing when two men with pistols emerged from the wings and shot him dead. Currently, the old facade is all that remains of the original structure.

# CHAPTER 5

**K**LIEG LIGHTS WERE MOUNTED AROUND THE PERIMeter of the excavation. It wasn't yet dusk, when they would glow and hum with eerie beauty, but someone—not Walter Mullane—had decided to go for the gala Hollywood-premiere look.

The captain surveyed his world: tense parents, insatiable press, and immense crowd. Even though it had become obvious that no bodies were going to be raised from the pit, word had spread through the Heights that 184th Street was hotter than any old street fair. Several couples were salsa dancing to the beats from multiple boom boxes, while every kebab vendor within ten blocks had rolled his cart over to feed the dancers, as well as the police and the utility workers and the media. Vast quantities of useless equipment were being unloaded from a truck that belonged to Lord knew who.

At least he did have some tidbits to feed the ravenous journalists. Rope finally obtained, two police officers were being prepared for their expedition, equipped with lights and walkie-talkies that Cass Wainwright believed would maintain better underground reception than cell phones. If necessary, more officers would follow, but it was most likely that the missing kids were around the corner.

"Men!" Mullane addressed them.

"Yes, sir," they both said.

"When you get down there, I want you to separate. Keep in contact with us and with each other, but separate. Cover as much ground as possible."

One of the officers couldn't help himself. "Ground, sir?"

"Whatever." Mullane sighed and sidled up the block, aiming to get lost in the crowd, grab a bite to eat, and find someone who wasn't present for the show but had been present all along— a witness.

Mullane went over the SDJ. It was difficult to avoid the assumption that this case was like that of some toddler who was holding his mother's hand in FAO Schwarz one second and gone the next . . . taking a nap with the stuffed bears. Most lost children were found in ten minutes, most of the rest within an hour. A few, however . . .

That's why the first principle in a search was speed; the odds of finding a kid to whom something genuinely scary had occurred decreased dramatically with the passage of time. Obviously, kidnapping didn't seem a consideration for Jessamyn and Timothy, but finding their bodies washed up in a cul-de-sac was a possibility mentioned quietly among the searchers. Not to the parents.

He checked Katznelson's, which had sold out of doughnuts but confirmed Tom and Miranda's story, and then looked across the street to La Iglesia de la Casa Sagrada, a bit redundant if you asked the captain. Could some young padre have been gazing out the window while counting his rosary beads? No such luck.

Still, there had to be at least one observer Mullane's predecessors had missed. Every neighborhood had its own unofficial concierge who maintained a 24/7 watch on the streets. Then he heard snickering from the adjacent stoop. Three teenagers in jeans and expensive sneakers sprawled over half a dozen steps each. Two of them sipped beer, theoretically illegal in public, but they didn't care. It tasted better that way, a tiny dare to the man. *You got your rules. I got my street laws. Let's see who wins.*

"Hey," Mullane said.

They didn't respond.

"You guys comfortable? . . . You look comfortable."

One of them scratched his belly, either an itch or body language declaring himself the leader of the pack.

"Some big to-do at the corner." Mullane spoke as if they were buddies, been gabbing all afternoon, and that they didn't know damn well what he was doing there.

The scratcher finished his beer, smacked his lips, stood, and, in a practiced basketball move, pushed the can off his fingers in the direction of an overflowing garbage can next to the nosy stranger whose badly fitting gray suit screamed "cop" as loudly as a blue uniform.

But before the can had a chance to score an imaginary two points, the captain snatched it out of the air and whipped it back so fast it bounced off the kid's chest.

The boy collapsed back onto the steps. "Man, what'd you do that for? I wasn't doing nuthin."

"You weren't saying nuthin, either. Now, I'm going to be polite and you're going to answer politely. Did you see anything happening on that boat before it rolled down the street?"

"Just this white kid and his girl."

"What were they doing?" Mullane glared at the boy's two companions, who were leaning backward out of reach.

"Nuthin, 1 don't know."

"What's your name?"

"Carlos."

"Were they on top of the boat the whole time, Carlos?"

"Er . . . ," said the second wiseacre on the steps, the one next to the leader.

Mullane raised his chin at Carlos, who nodded, permitting the other kid to speak. "Don't you guys remember? For about a minute, the girl jumped off the boat."

"Is that true?" Mullane still addressed Carlos, allowing him to recover his memory and pretend that it was his decision to come forth with the information. Sources had to maintain face on the street.

"Yeah, yeah, she did," he said. "I thought that maybe she dropped an earring, because she was bending over near the ground by the front of the boat."

Mullane asked if any of the boys could tell what Jessamyn was doing, but her back had been to them. Still, that hardly made a difference. He didn't have proof, but he knew what had happened. The girl had unattached the boat. It was some sort of practical joke on the parents, who probably deserved it. There'd be hell to pay once the truth came out. Still, he had to find them first.

By the time he got back to the trailer, one of the spelunkers had already returned. Bosco was helping the shivering officer strip off his sodden uniform.

Mullane snapped, "What's going on?"

The man shook his head. "It's nasty down there, sir."

"What did you see?"

"Nothing."

"What do you mean, nothing?"

"Junk, debris from the boat right below. No trace of the boat itself or the kids."

"How far did you get?"

"We each went as far as we could, sir." He looked frightened.

"Did you hear anything?"

"Like what?"

"Voices. A splash maybe."

"It's a world of water, Captain. I couldn't hear anything but splashes and . . ."

"And what?"

The officer thought of the odd scratching sounds in the tunnel. And squeaking sounds, too. Not the squeaking of a boat's timbers, but something organic, something enormous. "Nothing. Nothing helpful, sir."

"OK." Mullane addressed the men in the trailer while the parents stared out the window, as if in a trance. "If it was uncertain until now, it isn't any longer. Those kids have a boat. And if they have one, I want two. Someone call the Coast Guard."

In fact, the NYPD was in possession of a number of vessels, which were mostly used to chase boats like the *X-tra Large* away from fireworks barges in the Hudson on the Fourth of July, though they occasionally came in handy when dredging a floater out of the river. Hopefully it wouldn't come down to that in the underground river, but still.

"Wait." Mullane addressed no one in particular. "Maybe we can cut off the kids before they get too far." He looked at the civil engineer, who'd remained on-site, poring over his maps. "Right?"

"No," Wainwright replied. "Our boats can't get in anyplace else. We could open a manhole or rip out a catch basin. There are even a couple of staircases for individual workers to enter, but the only place large enough for a boat to enter is at the start or end of the system. Queens, the Bronx, the river, or here. But I don't believe we're going to find them this way."

"Why not?"

"I'm not sure. What do you call it, a hinch?"

Mullane looked at the engineer in his cartoon glasses. "A hunch." Sadly, he had the same hunch, but he still had to try every option. "C'mon, give us some expectations. How far could they get?"

Wainwright shook his head. "There's more than sixty-six hundred miles in the system. I think that they may have gotten out of range. Maybe they got turned around."

"But how fast could they go?"

Wainwright shrugged. "Not my field."

Mullane looked at the group of police officers. "Anyone know the speed of a sailboat?"

At last, one of the cops in the background, an occasional Sunday sailor himself, said, "A good vessel might ride the current, catch the breeze, go maybe ten, maximum twelve knots."

Captain Mullane was frustrated. "We're not on the briny main, man. We're in the sewer main. Speak English."

"Five miles an hour."

The speed was insignificant, yet it made the predicament worse. Mullane did the math. The kids had several hours' head start. Three times five was fifteen. Manhattan was seventeen miles long. "You're saying they could be anywhere on the island."

Wainwright answered, "Theoretically. It depends on the circumstances."

The captain was confused. "What circumstances could there be?"

"To start with, rain."

"So, they're waterproof." It was one of Mullane's favorite lines.

Whenever his detectives complained about the weather, he'd say, "Don't worry, you're waterproof." They hated it.

Wainwright, however, explained, "Every drop that lands up here finds its way into the system. As the volume and level rise, the water moves faster because it's confined to traveling through a limited circumference. It can reach seventy-five miles per hour in some tunnels."

The captain looked at the sky. It was clear, but to be on the safe side he turned to Patrolman Bosco and said, "Get me a forecast for the next few days."

"Days?" Miranda yelped.

Every police officer in the room turned as one. They'd forgotten the parents.

Mullane hastened to calm her. "Worst-case scenario, ma'am. We'll have them out in hours. Now get me that forecast, Bosco. So what else could affect speed or direction?"

Wainwright gestured to the gigantic hole outside the trailer. "Stuff like that. It's possible that some stones or mortar were loosened elsewhere in the system before the collapse. But the biggest variable is the people themselves. They can facilitate the natural speed and direction of the boat. They can also work against it."

"Er . . ." Tom Murphy made a sound.

"Yes, sir?"

"Timothy is a good sailor. Unless he was incapacitated, he'd halt the *X-tra Large* on a dime."

Unfortunately, the captain already knew why the boy didn't stop the boat. Why Timothy Murphy and Jessamyn Hazard were using their head start to sail as far from Washington Heights as possible. Because it was fun. Because it was there. Because they were stupid, privileged suburban brats just like their parents.

Because they were the architects of their own catastrophe and were afraid of being caught and punished.

Nonetheless, it was the NYPD's job to find them, and pronto. "Well then," he asked the engineer, "once we get our own boats down there, where should we go?"

"Basically south." Wainwright flipped through his plans until he came to a page the captain could recognize. It was of contemporary Manhattan. Wainright took a pencil from his breast pocket and chewed on it for a while. Then he licked the tip and drew an arc on the regular map. He drew the line to about 125th Street and said, "It's hard for me to imagine them drifting any farther south than this. Also, we've got to hope they don't, because the system gets really hinky under Central Park what with the ponds and the reservoir. Also, you should keep an eye out here." He tapped the pencil near the edge of the map, at 145th Street.

"Why?"

"North River sewage plant. It's the destination for all of the waste in the sanitary sewer of Upper Manhattan, but it's a major outlet for the storm sewer, too. If these kids are going really fast and the natural flow is carrying them, that's where they'll leave the system."

"Meaning?"

"Just pop right into the Hudson. Except there's a cast-iron grate over the opening to keep kids from trespassing. It would also lock kids in. Can you remove it?"

Mullane was already on the phone, ordering a police cutter to the Hudson River at 145th Street. He turned back to the engineer. "And then?"

"Well, it depends."

"On what?"

"See, none of these maps tell me exactly how wide the tunnels are. If the boat gets stuck, but they continue without it, they'll be exposed."

"And."

"Whether they do well or not also depends."

"On what?"

"If they can swim."

Another police officer was sent out for Chinese food.

Everyone settled in for a long haul.

# CHAPTER

## 6

"COULD BE A WHILE TILL WE'RE FOUND," TIMOTHY said as they finally cruised out from under the crushing weight of the hospital.

Oddly, Jessamyn replied, "Do you read the *New Yorker?*"

"Huh?" He knew about the magazine from his ophthalmologist's office: the pastel covers, endless articles, incomprehensible reviews of avant-garde performers, stark black-and-white photographs; it was the epitome of sophistication for a suburbanite. He didn't understand why she was asking but replied, "Sure."

"My favorite cartoon ever is from there."

Yes, the magazine had cartoons, too. He didn't admit that they were all he looked at while waiting for Dr. Koestler to adjust the prescription on his ever-worsening eyes.

"You wanna know what it is?"

"Sure."

"There's three fish in a row. A little fish is about to be eaten by a medium fish about to be eaten by a big fish. Three thought bubbles are over their heads." She peered into the murky sewer waters as if to discern any bubbles. "The little fish is thinking, *There is no justice.* The medium fish is thinking, *There is some justice.* And the big fish is thinking, *The world is just.*"

"What does that mean?"

"What does anything mean? That's what I mean. In fact—"

A slim, gray figure glided along the narrow ledge of the channel beside the *X-tra-Large*. At first Timothy thought it was a shadow of the mast cast by the lantern, but why hadn't he noticed it until now? For a moment he considered cranking up the engine, but then he remembered that he no longer had an engine. In order to better confront their observer—and also because he was curious—the captain turned the lantern key to expose more wick to the flickering flame.

Caught in the light, an old man with a beard immediately cried, "Don't hurt!" and turned away, as if attempting to hide in a crevice in the wall.

Timothy shifted the boom and slacked the sail so that the boat halted next to the man. He was difficult to make out, huddled against the stone wall, but he wore a tattered overcoat with holes in both elbows. A belt around his waist was so long, or the waist itself so slim, that the tongue dangled halfway down his thigh. Glancing over his shoulder, he blinked continuously and held his hand against his forehead to protect his eyes from the lantern and repeated, "Don't hurt!" and pulled a shapeless felt hat tight to his scalp.

"We won't hurt you," Jessamyn said softly.

"Really?" He allowed his eyes to linger for a second on the girl. "Why should we?"

"People hurt."

"Not us."

For a second Timothy thought the creature was not a man

at all but a mouse, because his face, except for a tiny upturned nose, seemed to be covered in a thin coating of gray fur. In fact, the skin between his beard and hairline was of an ashen pallor. It was obvious that he lived here. The teenagers were the intruders.

Jessamyn repeated slowly, "We're not going to hurt you."

"Hunting?"

"No, we're just . . . visiting," she said, and immediately wondered why anyone might believe that someone was hunting in this subterranean environment. "What's your name?" she asked.

"Name?" He looked nervous, confused.

"What are you called?"

He puzzled over this question as if asked for the square root of pi. Names were for the sun-blessed who lived up top. How long had it been since a mother, a friend, anyone had spoken his name? He replied, "You."

For a second, Jessamyn thought he didn't understand the question, but then she recalled that her two-year-old nephew called himself "You" until he went to preschool. Everyone thought it was incredibly cute, but it was actually quite obvious. After all, people were always asking him, "Are you tired?" or "Are you hungry?"

Could this graybeard be thinking like a two-year-old? She tried an experiment, "Hello, You."

He peered out from under his brow, clearly a major risk, though his eyes also darted left and right, and he started sidling along the stone wall toward a corner about fifteen feet away.

Timothy rummaged through the leftovers saved from the rats and found the Twinkies. Just the thing. Snack of universal friendship.

The man cringed at the angry sound of crinkling plastic but immediately took notice of the aroma that entered the sewer.

Timothy proffered a Twinkie over the damaged rail of the *X-tra Large*.

The man's eyes lit up, but he was clearly afraid of a trap.

"Go on." Timothy nodded. "It's OK. It's for You."

Tentatively, the man reached out. Careful to avoid touching his benefactor, he grabbed the offering of bright yellow cake and white cream and stuffed it into his mouth, devouring it in one gulp. His eyes brightened, and he moaned with pleasure. "You like."

"I like, too," Jessamyn said, and then, maybe a mistake, she brought up her worry of moments earlier. "Who's hunting?"

He shrank into his collar, only a dab of white cream showing where the Twinkie was smeared on his nose.

"Please, tell me who's hunting . . . You."

"Everyone in Undertown."

"What?"

"Undertown, here. The cremblers and the crawlers and the civvies and DUO. And, and, and now there's . . ." He jabbed a finger at the sailors on the *X-tra Large*. The gesture seemed accusatory, but Jessamyn instantly realized that it took the place of language since he couldn't logically call them "you."

"I'm Jessamyn and this is Timothy," she said, hoping to sound friendly.

"J-J-Jessathy," he said, conflating the two. And, strangely, once he had a name for them, he seemed to lose his fear. "Th-th-thanks for the cookie," he blurted, and dashed around the corner. By the time Timothy was able to angle the ship away from the wall and raise the sail enough to catch the faint breeze in the tunnel, You was gone.

"Cremblers and crawlers and civvies," Jessamyn said. "Who could they be?"

Timothy speculated. "Civvies could be municipal workers. And crawlers . . ." He didn't want to mention the rats that infested the tunnel.

"How about cremblers?"

"I don't know."

"And DUO. Maybe they'll paint us."

"You was really afraid," Timothy said.

"No I wasn't."

"I didn't mean you. I meant . . ."

"You?" Jessamyn laughed. "I think it's possible that You is afraid most of the time. That doesn't mean that we should be. We've got the biggest ship in the sea. It even has a name."

"Everyone does." Such a simple thing. "Except for You."

"Yeah." Jessamyn sighed, oddly thoughtful. "But I don't like mine."

"Really?"

"Truly."

"Why?"

"It sounds like the name of an English spinster. It should be served with scones and marmalade. I feel that I should be wearing a dirndl or something."

"How do you spell that?"

"D-i-r-n . . ." She had won a spelling bee the year before with that word, which she automatically recited until she realized that her companion had just asked the question to make her feel better. "Useless talent still doesn't make up for J-e-s-s-a-m-y-n."

"What would you prefer?"

Without missing a beat, she said, "Kat . . . with a *K*," and swiped at him as if she had claws.

Timothy jumped back, and then confessed, "You know, I'm not so crazy about my name, either."

**82**

"Yeah?"

"Yeah, it sounds like 'timid,' and even worse is . . ." He didn't dare utter the diminutive.

"Timmy."

He cringed.

"Sorry. So how'd you get the name?"

"I don't know. It's some sort of grain. My mom was a bit of a hippie, and my dad thought it had a *foine Oyrish rrring*. Like I have anything to do with the *auld sod*!"

"What would you rather be called?"

Unlike Jessamyn, he'd never imagined a different name for himself. "I don't know."

"Well, I do," she declared. "You seem like more of a Jake to me."

*Jake.* What a radical concept.

Jakes were the kind of guys who were, well, they were guys, not boys. Jakes wore hats instead of baseball caps. They drank amber liquids and probably smoked, even if it was bad for their health. They had a fatalistic attitude toward life, because they knew the dangers. Tobacco was too slow to get them when there were guns, or gats, in the world. Other men looked up to Jakes. And as for women, Jakes knew women who had sultry, enticing names like . . . Kat.

Just for example.

"Yeah," he said. "I'd like that."

Upward—they couldn't say "upstairs" because there weren't any stairs—may have been a balmy summer evening, the kind in which they might once have gone out for ice cream or taken a late swim at a friend's pool, but down below was a whole other world as the light from the catch basins continued to dim. The walls seemed to emit drafts of cold air captured during the previous winter, and their clothes were wet.

**83**

Jessamyn gazed longingly at the ceiling.

Timothy followed her gaze and quietly suggested, "I think it's better if we let the current take us a bit farther along by morning." Still, he detached the sail so the *X-tra Large* couldn't travel too fast. If there was an obstruction, he didn't want a collision. For the same reason, they decided to remain on deck rather than rest down below. Each sat, back against the rail, alone with their own thoughts.

In Jessamyn's case the thoughts led, natch, to food. "Hey, how about dessert?"

"Good idea." Timothy brought up the blueberry pie, which they ate directly from the tin.

Then Jessamyn heard a scratching, and she saw what looked like a good-size dog dip its snout into the water farther down the ledge and grab something and run away.

Unfortunately, it wasn't a dog.

Jessamyn shivered. Without thinking, she reached out to hug Timothy. He reciprocated, but their seated embrace felt awkward. Maybe five sleepless minutes later, arms holding each other stiffly, Timothy couldn't help but say, "Um, Jessamyn?"

"Yes."

"You know . . ."

"I know," she said. "When I was a scout we learned that if we were ever lost in the woods—"

"Lost together with someone else."

"Of course. Then the most important thing to do was to keep warm . . ."

"If it's cold outside."

"Right, because . . ."

"Because," he continued, "there's a danger of hypothermia. That's what they told me and my dad when we took boating lessons."

"Well, since you know so much, just huddle and go to sleep."

"I'm just saying that it's good to be warm."

"Warm," she repeated sleepily.

They turned down the lantern's light and let the current take them wherever it would.

# CHAPTER 7

**U**P **TOP FOR REAL, CAPTAIN WALTER MULLANE** looked at the children's parents, sitting like statues amid the ad hoc rescue operation. They had refused to leave the trailer. He didn't blame them. If his kids were lost, he wouldn't leave, either.

Yet he wondered what Tom and Miranda thought of the party in progress outside the trailer. As far as the community was concerned, the lights around the pit were an open invitation to a new disco. Word spread block by block and people strolled over to check out the show. The coconut ices of the afternoon gave way to adult refreshments. Some people were dancing to boom boxes in the street, while a few couples pressed fervently against each other in the shadows of the fire trucks.

Bosco delivered a progress report. New police fanning out from 184th Street ought to have covered most of Washington Heights by now—though "covered" sounded wrong since they were beneath the streets. Nor did "undercovered" work. "Right?" he asked the civil engineer, who'd diligently penciled in the tunnels that had already been investigated on his master map of the system.

Mullane considered the other information he'd received regarding different aspects of the SDJ. He took the parents' descriptions of their children's saintliness with plenty of salt, but a pair of detectives dispatched to New Jersey confirmed this. No contraband was found under the kids' beds, no map to the sewer system.

"Only thing is . . . ," one of the detectives started to say.

"Tell me, Cosgrove."

"I don't think they knew each other. We hacked into their computers; there's no e-mail. Phone records show plenty of calls between the houses, but of course that could have been the parents. Still, the kids are two of a kind. Each has a sort of shrine in their room."

"A shrine?"

"Photos. Objects of personal significance: Invitation to a party. Tickets to an amusement park. The boy's shrine is to his dead mother, the girl's to her dead father. Tell the truth, they made me feel creepy. I don't mean that there was anything creepy about them, but I felt like an intruder. Nothing wrong, Cap."

Yet something had to be wrong for a lost suburban boy who wasn't a druggie or a political zombie to run away, or sail away, from the police. Mullane had been over the contents of the boat a dozen times with Tom Murphy—tools for operation and toys for leisure—none of it of any significance. The only unusual items on the *X-tra Large* that day were her passengers.

Mullane was on the verge of an idea when Jerry Dodds, an eager rookie who'd been monitoring communications with the men below, dashed into the trailer. "Captain. Captain, sir. I think we might have something."

"What?"

**87**

Dodds handed him the walkie-talkie.

"Who's this?"

"Warshowsky."

*Better yet.* He was one of the officers who had traveled farthest, seen the most. "Come in."

"It's up ahead."

"Are you sure?"

"I know a boat when I see one, sir. Doesn't seem to have a mast, but that may have broken off in the fall."

"Any trace of the kids?"

"Not yet, sir."

"Where are you, Warshowsky?"

Like the teenagers he was searching for, the policeman couldn't do more than estimate his location. He gave his best guess, and two teams were dispatched with a municipal backhoe and union crew to tear out catch basins in the vicinity so that more officers could help Warshowsky in case the kids had proceeded farther on foot.

Mullane turned to Cass Wainwright. "C'mon, Mr. Sewer Man."

The engineer looked up in a daze. He'd been so focused on his plans that he hadn't heard a word. "Are we going someplace?"

"Yeah, and if you're good, I'll let you play with the siren."

Tom Murphy stood up.

Mullane met the father's eyes. "I know. I know. But this is police business. We'll call the moment we find anything. I promise."

Of course, reporters weren't so accommodating. Three vans tailed Mullane's Chevy and four patrol cars as the procession screamed about thirty-five blocks south, past Columbia's New York–Presbyterian Hospital toward Audubon Terrace.

America's Acropolis, the terrace was established on the homestead of the famous bird-watcher along 155th and 156th Streets from Broadway to Riverside Drive. Eight Beaux-Arts structures (designed by, among others, Stanford White) originally housed the American Academy of Arts and Letters, the American Geographical Society, the American Numismatic Society, the Hispanic Society of America, and the National Museum of the American Indian. Several of these subsequently moved in order to escape the deterioration of the neighborhood. The others remained as cultural beacons.

Throughout the half hour it took to break open the street, Civil Engineer Wainwright stood quietly, leaning against a bus shelter.

"Cat got your tongue?" Mullane asked.

"No."

"What are you thinking about?"

"I don't know. I just don't like this."

"Why!" Mullane had to shout to be heard over the jackhammers.

Wainwright shrugged. "Not sure, but I've seen more weird stuff down there than you can imagine. Animal, vegetable, mineral. Rats and roaches—common city vermin—but also raccoons. Once found an otter." He continued talking as several workers threaded a heavy chain between the bars of the drain and a backhoe tore it from its setting in the curb like a dentist removing a rotten tooth.

Immediately, they dropped a ladder and several officers, led by Johnny Angel clad in hip boots, descended.

"Then there was a whole flock of chickens nesting under a manhole near a slaughterhouse in Chinatown."

Mullane spoke into the walkie-talkie. "We're coming in, Warshowsky. Can you see us?"

"Not yet."

"Salt that's etched what looks like hieroglyphics in granite. Yep, I guess you'd have to call that a real natural wonder."

"OK, listen up." Mullane signaled to Johnny Angel at the base of the ladder.

With his free hand pressed against his left ear, Bosco pulled the trigger on an air horn.

"Remember the CowParade a few years ago? One of them statues was placed on the Upper West Side. Right in front of a vegetarian restaurant. Couldn't be sure if it was a protest or coincidence." The engineer chuckled in fond remembrance.

"Can you hear me now?" Mullane asked Warshowsky.

"Loud and clear. You must be around the corner, sir."

"Which way?"

Warshowsky gave directions, and a minute later he saw the lights of the team wading toward him. Another minute and they united beside the vessel he'd found.

"What do you have?" Mullane called, so excited that he was about to go down into the sewer himself.

Bosco said, "It's a boat, all right. Only I don't think it's the right boat."

"Why not? How many boats can there be in the sewer?"

"Well, it's old, sir, and it's not that the mast broke off. From what I can tell, this boat never had a mast."

"Motor?"

"Actually, it's more of a rowboat, sir. Also, we can make out the name on the rear."

"What is it?"

Bosco took a breath. "The SS *Red Herring*."

# CHAPTER

# 8

**T**HERE WAS EVENING AND THEN THERE WAS MORNING. Timothy stretched and realized that he was not bobbing gently, attached to a solidly anchored line in the Long Island Sound, his dad above with a plate full of bacon and eggs and a loaf of his favorite cheddar bread and a jug of fresh-squeezed juice. And yet, he must be on the water. At home, onshore, in bed, his feet dangled free.

Nor would he be lying next to a girl at home, in bed. He scooted away as if she was a six-foot-tall, red-haired iguana.

"Pretty scary, huh?" Jessamyn laughed.

"Nooo," he drawled with as much cool as he could muster. "It's just that, well . . . it's a lot warmer now than it was last night."

"Quite warm." She grinned.

"True."

"You know what else is true?"

"What?"

"I could eat a horse."

"Only one you're likely to find is a sea horse."

"Very funny," she said. "How'd you sleep?"

"Not bad. Not bad at all." He blinked toward the glow from above and saw the dented and discolored railing that it had been his job to polish with Brasso. Next to him were sections of the broken mast that he used to polyurethane twice a season, once before Memorial Day to prepare for the annual launching of the *X-tra Large*, and once after Labor Day to set the vessel straight for a recuperative winter in dry dock.

Stuff was certainly different here. The very coordinates of existence—up, down—were different from the normal east, west, north, and south categories above.

Where they were, however, he couldn't say, since they had allowed the current to carry them farther into the system, away from their entry point. Unfortunately, that wasn't sufficient, because they both heard a faint voice calling, "Timothy . . . Jessamyn . . ."

"Police," Timothy said.

A prick of light flashed in the distance. "It's true," Jessamyn said.

"What?"

"There is a light at the end of the tunnel."

It waved and circled, searching for them. Rescue was imminent, and both of them were hungry. That dream of eggs could come true with a single shout.

They looked at each other.

"What do you say?" Timothy asked. He was surely the captain, but he'd abide by the wishes of his sole passenger. After all, the law of the sea was ladies and children first. He may have been the latter, but she was both.

"Heck," she replied, "let's get out of here."

Hoisting the sail was easier than it had been the previous day.

Since Jessamyn's alterations, it was cut to the right size and considerably more maneuverable than the original. Of course, their maximum velocity was less than half of what it would have been with a full sail, but there was nothing to do about that. Or was there? As the vessel began to float southward, Timothy considered the spears of mast that had splintered off during the initial accident. He lifted one and it wasn't too heavy. Then he wedged it into a crack in the wall of the tunnel and shoved as hard as he could.

Without a word of instruction, Jessamyn took the other pole and planted herself by the starboard rail. Before Timothy, she understood the benefits of synchronization and started counting, "One. Two. Three. Push." Then she hummed four beats and began counting again. "One. Two. Three. Push."

He sang in as low a register as he could reach, "Volga booooatmen . . ."

She added nonsense lyrics. "Are big and oooorange."

He sang, "They eat their poooorridge."

She finished, "And beg for more."

The walls ripped by as the wind puffed out the sail, and the poles provided additional impetus. Basin after basin came into sight above. They passed the familiar corner where they'd met You. At that intersection, they paused to consider which direction to take.

"That one." Timothy chose a narrow lane to the left of the *X-tra Large* precisely because the wind was blowing outward. It would be a tricky turn, and therefore seemed an unlikely path for the police.

"Good idea," Jessamyn said. "But how are we going to get there?"

"We're going to tack," Timothy declared.

As far as Jessamyn knew, tacking meant inserting a flat-headed pin into a bulletin board. But she'd read *Moby-Dick*, or enough of it, to write a bogus essay on the nature of cosmic evil, and she recognized nautical vocabulary.

Timothy saw her uncertainty. "It means we're going to change direction, but watch out because the boom will swing wide in the opposite direction to our turn. Stay low. We don't want you knocked out." He loosened the sail to cut its power, sort of like braking a car at a corner; this allowed the timber that bisected the boat to swivel. The boom was just about to hit the right-hand wall when he tightened the ropes and let the sail catch the breeze again. Sure enough, the *X-tra Large* angled left with only the tiniest scrape of the hull against the base of the walkway. Immediately, he straightened the boom so the flat of the sail was perpendicular to the axis of the boat.

*Choreographed*, Jessamyn thought. His sequence of motions was like a dancer's.

The light behind them blinked out. That meant that they were temporarily invisible to their benevolent pursuers and able to ignite their lantern.

And yet, the second they left the police behind, both of the underground sailors had the feeling that something else had changed in the tunnel. There was still the drip and gurgle of water, but the rest of the background noises, including the frightening scratching sounds, disappeared. It was as if the sewer had been vacated by its natural inhabitants.

For a while it was possible to imagine that nothing else existed in the entire world. No school. No dead parents. No living parents, either, beloved but irrationally demanding. As long as the sailors tightened the canvas when it loosened, and loosened it when it strained, the boat pretty much took care of herself.

"It's weird," Jessamyn said. "You think you're on an island that's surrounded by water . . ."

"Like a block of buildings is surrounded by the street."

"Right, but actually the water is beneath you. And we're the reverse."

"On the water, surrounded by rock."

They spoke about geology and also geometry, which Timothy claimed that he never fully grasped.

"Ridiculous. Look at the way you automatically balanced the angles of the prow, the mast, the sail, the boom. If that isn't geometry, I don't know what is. Now, English, that's another matter." It was Jessamyn's turn to confess that literature was not her best subject. "Of course I get A's," she said in that way he found so irritating, "but I don't really feel that I'm earning them."

"How so?"

"With math there's a right answer. You have to find the correct formula and you have to use it properly, but the numbers will never betray you. As for what the meaning of *The Scarlet Letter* is, it seems like a game. A game that I win because I know the rules."

"Go on."

"Like, I know that if the answer to an essay question is longer, it will seem more thoughtful, but if it's too long, then the teacher may get pissed off that she has to read it. So you hit the right length with the right number of five-dollar words and you end with some fake profundity like, 'That is why the obvious is more mysterious than you think.' And the teacher will roll over like a puppy dog."

"Arf. Arf."

"C'mon!"

"Well, you're right about tests. But writing doesn't really have a message. Not good stuff, anyway. It's not *about* something; it *is* something. So what you were doing with those essays was what the writers were doing when they wrote their books. Which means that you did fine." He looked around the dim cavern, thinking how strange it was that he was explaining anything to Montclair's resident genius. In a way, she was as dumb as he was.

"I'm hungry," Jessamyn said.

"Oh, yeah. Good idea." He handed the tiller to Jessamyn while he foraged in the cabin. There wasn't much, since they'd finished the pie the night before, but he found a chunk of only slightly moldy cheese in the ship's refrigerator, crackers from the pantry, and various condiments: mustard, ketchup, soy sauce, mayonnaise, and a crusting of strawberry preserves. "Voilà."

Her face dropped at the meager pickings. "It's not much."

"It's OK," he said. "I'm not really hungry."

But Jessamyn wouldn't have any of this game. "If you're not hungry, then I'm not hungry."

"If we're both not hungry . . ."

"Then we'll both starve."

"After you."

"Don't be so damn gallant."

"Did anyone ever tell you that you're a pain in the—"

"Yes."

"Then let's eat."

Jessamyn nodded, and Timothy set to slicing the cheese and distributing an equal number of crackers slathered with each of the condiments. It wasn't the most elegant meal in the world, but it was filling.

If the first stage of their voyage had been fraught, both of them felt more at ease now that they knew their ship was sound and they'd both gotten a decent night's sleep and put a little nourishment in their bellies.

Above the tunnel, above the hot tar of 160th Street, one of the highest points of land on Manhattan Island prior to the invention of the elevator was the Morris-Jumel Mansion, the oldest remaining Colonial residence in the city, now a museum. Once upon a time, General George Washington stood on the porch and watched the smoke from the British army encampment a dozen miles downtown.

The lady of the house, Eliza Jumel, started her auspicious career as a woman of low morals and high finances but spurned her paying customers to host the men who governed the new nation, among them John Adams, Thomas Jefferson, and both Alexander Hamilton and his killer, Aaron Burr, whom Madame Jumel married. Allegedly, her ghost haunts the premises.

Under the Colonial veranda, the atmosphere wasn't exactly dreamy but simply other. When it came time to shift the sails or replenish the lantern's fuel, Timothy and Jessamyn rolled up their damp sleeves and set to the task.

One thing still bothered Jessamyn. "Where do you think the rats went?"

"I don't know. It's curious. But I'm glad. Maybe they're afraid of us."

She shook her head. "Or maybe they're afraid of something else."

Timothy didn't reply. He was enjoying a new breeze and daydreaming about a boy named Jake.

Then Jessamyn glanced over the edge of the vessel and noticed that the water was running perpendicular to the hull of the *X-tra Large*. "That's strange," she said.

Still distracted, Timothy murmured, "Yes, strange."

"But I guess the sail is stronger." Approvingly, she noted the taut canvas.

"Hmm."

But where, she wondered, could the water be heading if not directly ahead in the ten-foot-wide tunnel? Then she realized that she couldn't see the left wall of the tunnel anymore. Also, the water itself seemed to disappear about a foot past the side of the boat. The side that was drifting in the same direction as the water.

"Um, Timothy?"

"Yeah?"

"Can you pass me something?"

"Sure. What?"

"Oh, anything will do." Taking her eyes off what was surely an optical illusion, she peered across the deck of the *X-tra Large*. "How about the cooler?"

He was still mulling over the thought of a Jake at the helm of the boat and passed her the empty plastic box without paying much attention.

Watching the rivulets disappear wasn't too disconcerting in and of itself, but there was something about the way the sound also vanished—as if it was sucked into another dimension—that unnerved Jessamyn. Just to reassure herself, she tossed the cooler a few feet overboard, expecting a nearly instantaneous splash.

No sound.

"Timothy?" she repeated.

It took a moment to rouse him from his pleasant reverie. "Yes?"

"I'm not sure, but I think—"

*Splash*. A tiny sound came from a great distance.

"*Help!*" she screamed as the rear of the vessel swung wide over the edge of a waterfall.

Number 555 Edgecombe Avenue housed the crème de la crème of the Harlem community for decades in the mid-twentieth century.

Among the musical residents were Count Basie and Paul Robeson. Joe Louis represented sports, and Supreme Court Justice Thurgood Marshall was a frequent visitor. The lobby was all marble and mahogany elegance, the apartments spacious. But the main thing that gave the Three Fives its cachet was the view over Highbridge Park at Coogan's Bluff, site of the former Polo Grounds. The view spanned half of the Bronx and at least five bridges, and beyond the bluff was a hundred-foot sheer drop.

Jessamyn was unaware that the basement of Sugar Hill's finest abode was on the other side of the tunnel wall. All she knew was that if the boat continued five more feet in the direction it was heading, the balance would shift and gravity would surpass momentum. They'd plunge down to whatever rocks the cooler had smashed upon. This was far worse than their initial ten-foot drop into the sewer.

Timothy stood, befuddled, while the tallest girl at Montclair Junior High School—maybe the world—loomed over him and worked frantically to untie the ropes that kept the patched-up sail on its course to catastrophe. He shouted, "What are you doing?"

"We've . . ."

"What?"

"There's a cliff."

"Where?"

"There. We have to go straight. Straight!"

He couldn't help but think that she sounded like one of the antidrug spokespersons who lectured at school assemblies. Yet her warning was more dire. "When?"

"Now!"

Without asking the captain's permission, she grasped the boom with both hands and pulled it as hard as she could, as if chinning, and ducked as it flew over her head, and the ship angled away from the falls.

The change in the prow's direction meant that the stern swung in the opposite direction, toward the falls, and Timothy could now perceive the danger. "Yikes!"

In a quarter-second he, too, was doing his best to drag the sail into position to catch the wind rising out of the depths to drive the ship to safety. The sail flapped like a puppet on a string, but if they took one more of those pleasant easterly gusts, the *X-tra Large* would surely fly right over the edge of the waterfall to perdition.

Maybe, thought the boy who'd dared to consider himself a sailor, Columbus was wrong. Him and Magellan and Da Gama and all of the other explorers they'd learned about in the first month of a world history course. And the scientists, too—Galileo and Copernicus—and the Vikings. The earth really was flat, and the proof was a breath away. The sound of the wind turned to a roar.

At that moment the *X-tra Large* hit a bump in the floor of the tunnel. Fortunately, this meant that there was a slight lip at the edge of the Edgecombe drop into Highbridge Park. Unfortunately, the jolt tipped the lantern. The glass broke and the light blinked out. Timothy heard the broken fixture rolling across the deck. He reached out blindly to save it but managed to grab only the device used to light it as the lantern slid under the rail.

It was nearly impossible to communicate in the dark, and yet the two acted in concert as if they'd crewed together on Jason's *Argo* or Odysseus's *Penelope*. Instinctively, both Jessamyn and Timothy threw their weight onto the deck away from the pit.

And then, instantaneously, the roar ceased, as if they'd passed through a wide and horrific opening to another world. The enclosure of the New York sewer system tunnel returned. The opening was designed to allow overflow from the system to cascade dramatically into the park. It must have been a great sight from below, even if no one bothered to consider that it might be tricky to navigate.

Then, as the masters of the *X-tra Large* took charge of their destiny, rather than merely going with the flow that could have destroyed them, the downward grade of the channel increased. Edgecombe was the steepest hill in Harlem. Even without the massive quantity of water diverted over the falls, the sewer again grew noisy. Timothy caught a glimpse of white foam like boiling milk.

It wasn't a sheer drop, but that was small comfort as the front of the boat tilted down and pitched forward.

"Hold on!"

Jessamyn yanked the ropes like the reins of a bucking bronco, hoping to impede their sudden velocity. Overhead, one then two then three corner drains flew by like strobe lights. The peak of the tunnel receded as the base of it dove. *Rapids.*

The last of the food and supplies rolled off the deck.

A branch growing out from between great granite stones on the wall of the tunnel whipped against the top of the mast and a shower of leaves came down, incongruous in the roaring channel. But that might have been the worst of it: a vicious crashing above, with a din alongside and who knew what beneath. In less than a minute, the grade began to level off and the pace of the *X-tra Large* to slow. They hit one last vertical drop that took away their breath, but both teenagers could tell that they were near the end of what had been the ultimate amusement park flume ride.

At the bottom, they came to a blissful halt in an enormous pool that stretched from one catch basin to the next.

Behind them the stream poured endless water into the pool.

Timothy collapsed onto the deck. "Wow."

Jessamyn sat on the boom that she'd wielded as eloquently as any nautical maestro. "Double wow."

He looked at her and couldn't say much more. "Nice job. Really nice. You saved us."

"Oh, c'mon. Anyone with an ounce of brains would have done the same thing."

"You know, it's not really the brains. It's the instinct." And then he gave her the nicest compliment he knew. "You're a natural sailor."

On the other hand, he wouldn't have blamed the natural sailor if she'd had enough adventure for two days—or fourteen years. He was thinking of how comfortable his bed was and how nice the sun always felt on his skin. Surrounded by water, drenched again by the splashing and spray, he was utterly filthy. There was crud from the initial collapse in his hair, grime and sweat from their labors in his pores. Tentatively, he said, "You think that we should . . . maybe . . ."

"No." She cut him off, fully aware of what he was thinking because she was thinking the exact same thing. Then, whether it was false bravado or sheer brazenness, she declared, "And the good thing is that we've left anyone who's chasing us far behind."

"What about us?"

"We're just getting started."

# CHAPTER

# 9

L OST!" CRIED THE *NEW YORK POST.*

"The Sewer That Eats Children," yelled the *Daily News*, whose headline was next to a photograph of the 184th Street crater.

🐀

As far as NYPD Captain Walter Mullane was concerned, Monday mornings always sucked.

Then again, so did Tuesdays through Fridays, as well as the one weekend a month he remained in the precinct house, holding the hands of the rookies while beefing up his pension.

Mullane grumbled about his bad luck, but if he hadn't been on duty he still would have had to clean up whatever mess was made of the SDJ. Fortunately, Civil Engineer Cass Wainwright stayed with him through the long night after the discovery of the unfortunate ghost ship. First off, there were pained explanations to the media. How could the NYPD lose a sailboat in the sewer, reporters wanted to know. Pointing out that it was a small sailboat didn't help. "Oh," replied one snide columnist for the *Times*, "you mean it's like losing a small whale in a bathtub."

The SDJ grew minimally more tolerable around dawn when a crane finally arrived and they lowered the temporarily designated PB-1 and PB-2, motorboats borrowed from a cop who used them for weekend outings in Sheepshead Bay, into the sewer. Both boats were now cruising, presumably making more progress than the teams wandering on foot under Washington Heights. Also, the Coast Guard was working to launch more boats into the system via the exit pipe onto the Hudson at 145th Street.

Better yet, the crowd had finally dissipated, though a few early-morning dog walkers sniffed at the scene of civic disruption. On the other hand, they were bound to return when they saw the morning's newspapers. "We currently have several dozen teams exploring the sanitary water removal system," the mayor declared at his press conference, making the rescue effort sound like D-day on 184th Street. Greatest show in town.

"Ouch," whispered Cass Wainwright, partially because of the exaggeration and partially because the storm sewer should never be confused with the sanitary.

"As of now," the mayor, partial to sports metaphors, reportedly went on, "I am giving orders to my team to flood the zone."

Mullane slammed the paper down in disgust and stepped out of the trailer to piece together his own ideas about what might have happened. The two children had been alone for nearly twenty-four hours in circumstances that would try anyone's sanity. Who knew what they were going through? But when he stepped back into the trailer, the civil engineer was repeating the mayor's idiotic words as if they had some meaning. "Flood the zone," he said.

As if in a parallel universe, Mullane replied, "I was just thinking that the boy may have lost or—"

"Flood the zone."

"Or may have left behind—"

"Flood . . . Flood . . . Something the mayor said, it got me to thinking about another problem we may have."

"Great. You wanna tell me what it is?"

"No, I shouldn't be the one to tell you."

"Who, then?"

"A meteorologist."

"We got a forecast yesterday."

"That was yesterday. I don't like the look of those clouds today."

# CHAPTER

# 10

**T**IMOTHY AND JESSAMYN EACH MULLED OVER THEIR adventure in a different way until Timothy finally broke the silence. "You think this is how Indiana Jones feels?"

"No."

"Really?"

"Really," Jessamyn asserted.

"How do you think he feels after something like this?"

"Hungry."

"We just ate."

"Well, I guess that almost going over a waterfall at a hundred miles an hour naturally builds up a girl's appetite."

"Except that we don't have any food left. It all washed away."

"Then . . ."

Both knew that their adventure, already extraordinary, couldn't last forever, but having no chance of returning up the Edgecombe rapids, neither knew when they might be rescued.

"Where do you think we are?"

"Can't be sure anymore. I'd guess the 140s."

They weren't giddy but dreamy after an episode of such high adrenal intensity. Besides, the cavern was a fine place to rest compared to the dank, enclosed sewer line. The ceiling was high above them and the endlessly churning water at the entry invigorated the atmosphere.

Each vaguely remembered a time when their families were intact; when they had helped a now-missing parent set the table, tend a barbecue, run an errand; when they had shown an elementary school report card to two parents. They also thought about the current state of affairs in their respective households.

Neither Tom nor Miranda was a bad parent. In fact, Jessamyn said, "I just wish she wouldn't try so hard to be a supermom."

Timothy understood. "Right," he said. "Although there are occasional benefits, like—"

A light went on—not a flashlight glinting from afar but a direct beam—shining from above as if they had suddenly been teleported to a stage. Both sailors froze, and the boat came to a halt under a rusted cable. The light held them as fast to a single spot as a thumbtack would a photograph to a bulletin board above a desk. A photo of a bunch of friends with their arms around each other's shoulders, celebrating a birthday or a football victory or a day at the beach.

A voice came from somewhere behind the light. "Nice maneuver."

Trying to be cool, Jessamyn replied, "Thanks."

"You don't see that sort of skill down here too often." It was a youthful, confident voice.

"Thank you," Jessamyn repeated.

The voice continued. "Now, don't you think it would be polite to introduce yourselves?"

Squinting toward the light, the captain said, "Um, sure. I'm Timothy Murphy."

"And I'm Jessamyn Hazard. And you are . . . ?"

There was silence.

"OK, then," Timothy hemmed. "We'll be heading off now. Bye." His hands tensed on one of the spears of wood, ready to fight if necessary.

Still no response. No objection. Some other resident of the underground world was just making his presence known.

"Why don't you come out?" Jessamyn said, thinking that perhaps he was hiding, afraid, like You.

"Why don't *you* come in?"

Timothy and Jessamyn looked around. They'd drifted to one side of the cavern, where an inlet lapped against a natural harbor.

"Or should I say, why don't you come *up*? That's what folks outside Undertown say all the time."

It was the second time Timothy and Jessamyn had heard that word: Undertown. Was this place real enough to have a name? Timothy looked at the ceiling, lower in this corner of the cavern than elsewhere. Sure enough, there was an open hatch in the barreled vault about equidistant from two catch basins, and a hand extended down from the opening.

Timothy made an instant calculation: Accept the hand and he might be drawn to doom; reject the hand and he'd surely insult this person who'd been able to track them from Washington Heights down the Edgecombe rapids to Central Harlem, a person who knew the subterranean world far better than the police. Also, Timothy was curious. He looked at Jessamyn and whispered, "I'll go first."

He stepped up from the deck onto the boom and reached toward the hand. It was a small, black hand. The hand clasped his wrist and helped him shimmy up the mast until he could bend the upper portion of his body into the opening.

It took a moment to pull his legs over the rim of the vault and more time to stand upright—or semi-upright—since the convex surface of the floor above reflected the concave ceiling of the tunnel below. Also, the space's own ceiling was so low that Timothy had to stoop to keep from hitting his head. Jessamyn would have to kneel.

And yet, as vertically challenged as it was, the space was horizontally abundant, stretching farther than Timothy could see in the light cast by a single bulb attached to the ceiling. Most important, it appeared as if nobody else was there besides the boy—small enough to stand. He had an anachronistic seventies Afro and wore a shiny pleather jacket. Timothy had the weird feeling that he'd seen him someplace before.

"Your friend coming?" the boy asked.

Timothy took further measure of his host and the place itself. The walls were covered with paintings that had to come from the graffitists DUO, though the team's work here was in an uncharacteristically domestic mode. The team had painted an old-fashioned, Victorian living room, complete with brocade sofa, dark wood chairs, end tables, fringed standing lamps, and bookcases. Each object had the glossy veneer of subway work and yet each also exhibited a magical specificity. Some of the threads on the painted couch were loose and one section of marquetry on the back of the rocking chair was missing. Every painted book on a painted shelf had a title. Timothy recognized one: *McElligot's Pool,* by Dr. Seuss.

It was that book that led him to make a quick decision. "Yes, but . . ."

"But what?"

"The boat. It might float away."

"Feel free to tie up to Pier 145."

So Timothy had been more or less correct about their location. He was pleased that he was able to determine where they were with relative accuracy. Such judgment might come in handy later.

Also, if he was right about one thing, he might be right about another, like the harmlessness of this kid in this place. He leaned over the edge of the opening and said, "Come on up."

Five minutes later, Timothy Murphy and Jessamyn Hazard were leaning against the inside slope of the roof—rather how the two of them had rested on the deck of the *X-tra Large* on the New Jersey Turnpike what seemed like a hundred years earlier, before they learned that an entire world existed beneath the world they knew.

Jessamyn tried again to get their host to identify himself. "Um, you said you were . . ."

"My birth name is Calvin, but you can call me DUO."

*Of course.* Timothy knew where he'd seen the boy before. He'd placed a self-portrait in the center of the *O* on the side of the painted subway car uptown. He didn't happen onto this space with the wall drawings; he created it.

"Really, we've seen some of your . . ."

"Work. You can call it work. 'Art' sounds pretentious."

"It's beautiful."

"Well . . ." The kid crossed his hands behind his neck and considered this. "Yeah."

Jessamyn noted that he didn't thank them for the compliment. He merely acknowledged it.

He must have overheard them back at the gallery. That's why he invited them into his atelier.

Jessamyn realized that this attic crawl space ran the length of the tunnel. That was how he'd spied on them, knew what they'd said. He could keep an eye on anyone.

"Snack?" he asked.

He'd also overheard Jessamyn complain about her perpetual hunger.

She said, "If you don't mind."

"Great. I'll get something from the kitchen." He walked past the wall of painted couches and chairs until he came to a six-paneled door painted on the rough sewer wall. Beyond the door was a mural of a kitchen, complete with a cozy oak table with claw feet and a bulging 1930s-style Frigidaire. And yet a real shelf protruded from the wall under a painted shelf, and the bottom half of the painted refrigerator was actually a real, mini refrigerator painted to look like it was . . . painted. The boy knelt and opened the refrigerator and held forth two Mason jars. "Lemonade?"

"Sure." Timothy accepted the offer even though it seemed weird. Then again, everything seemed as inverted here as the floor that was actually a ceiling, or a wall painted like a paneled door, or a refrigerator painted on a stone wall. But he'd experienced stranger things over the last day than he had in all his years. He took a sip and smacked his lips. "Good."

"Made it myself," the half of DUO said. "Hey, have a seat."

Jessamyn looked around, saw that half of the chair and table legs were cut so that the furniture sat level on the curved floor. In fact, it was comfortable. The room on top of the tunnel felt like a luxury hotel overlooking Times Square.

Make that a very strange hotel with limited amenities. No TV, no telephone, no room service, and one narrow mattress on the other side of another "door" painted on the opposite side of the "living room" from the "kitchen" of the . . . What was the right word to describe DUO's place? Timothy wondered. Habitation? Studio? Or simply premises, which were about five feet tall, ten feet wide, and seventeen miles long.

"I don't get many visitors," the kid declared as he set his lemonade on the coffee table and passed a bowl of guacamole and a plate of tiny stuffed empanadas to Jessamyn. "This is a real party. How long you folks thinking of staying?"

"Um, we haven't quite made up our minds."

"Take your time. Everybody's welcome in the sewer." He chugged half the jar of lemonade.

"Apparently," Timothy ventured.

"Some days it's nearly as busy as up top. Specially now with Dora the Explorer here." He smiled at Jessamyn.

She suddenly wondered where the electricity for the lamps and the refrigerator came from. "You're pretty comfortable down here."

"Yep," he said. "It's a pad. You just got to know how to tap into the lines that supply the streetlights. But I've got to say that the cable reception leaves a bit to be desired."

Then she thought about what You had told her about how DUO had been hunting him. Trying to put this delicately, she said, "But not everyone feels welcome."

"If you're talking about that old skell, he's nuts."

"He seems afraid of you."

"Well, he shouldn't be. I painted a bunch of him around one day, for fun, and it sort of drove him nuts. Damn geezer should have been flattered. I mean, I don't do portraits too often, but every time he saw a picture of himself, he started screaming."

"We didn't see any of them."

"I blacked them all out after he freaked, but he still skedaddles whenever I show up. Whenever anyone shows. Except of course . . ." He paused and then changed the subject. "Him talking to you guys was a first. And you were kind to him. That's why I figured that I'd say welcome."

"Who else is here?"

"Bunch of homeless guys, make their home around 110th, near the park. Some explorers—they call themselves urban archaeologists—like to poke around the place. Show up with silly hats with lights and cameras and notebooks. Once in a blue moon, civvies come by to plug leaks and cement loose drains. And then there's the cremblers."

Both Timothy and Jessamyn noticed his use of You's words, first "civvies," then "cremblers." So the terrified homeless man wasn't making them up.

"Who are they?"

"Bad guys. Keep away. Mostly they're interested in money. If they smell it on you, they can be dangerous. You see, you run."

"But how can we tell if someone's a crembler?"

"Until you know any better, assume that anyone down here is a crembler . . . except me."

"About you," Jessamyn asked, "where's your partner?"

"Huh?"

"DUO."

"So?"

"So it's not UNO." Timothy felt clever for using a single word of junior high school Spanish, but he still had the logic all wrong.

Calvin explained. "You know, I heard you earlier. That stuff about not assuming DUO's a male. Not assuming DUO's color. All true. But how about not assuming that DUO is a they. Maybe it's a he. Just a one-man game. Can't trust no one else. God bless the child that's got his own." He broke into song. "That's got his o-w-w-own."

Timothy wondered how old this kid was who knew the sewer like Timothy knew Brookdale Park in Montclair, and produced "work" as easily as Jessamyn wrote papers for school. All Timothy did was read and daydream. The captain of the *X-tra Large* suddenly felt like a little kid in this company.

Then DUO let out a yawn and said, "I got to go back to school."

"Where's that?"

"Up top."

"Really?"

"Well, yeah. For some of us, Monday's a school day. I just like to come home for lunch now and then." He grinned.

Like Timothy and Jessamyn, DUO had people who cared about him: two parents, it turned out, and two siblings—one more of the former and two more of the latter than either of the voyagers. It wasn't that the suburban teens had forgotten life aboveground. They simply hadn't thought that some people were capable of moving between realms, that the streets and the sewer were part of the same urban system rather than parallel universes.

"But you guys make yourselves comfortable," DUO said. "What you did was pretty impressive. Take a rest and feel free to raid the fridge. *Mi casa es su casa.*"

Timothy and Jessamyn watched him lope away down the long attic with a touch of envy.

# CHAPTER
# 11

**S**HH!" JESSAMYN INTERRUPTED TIMOTHY, WHO WAS rattling on, speculating about their strange host. "Someone's down below."

The kids tiptoed over to peek through the slats of the closed louver that separated their aerie from the temporary mooring of the *X-tra Large*. From above, the deck looked even smaller than its twelve (and a half) foot length and five foot width, because those dimensions had been adequate for its purposes—either cramped or cozy, depending on one's tolerance for other people.

Two shabby, ill-dressed old men were on board, holding flaming torches that flickered in the damp. A third man, younger and muscular with a tattoo of a snake winding up his arm, emerged from the cabin and turned toward the narrow ledge, out of sight beneath the louver. "They must have abandoned ship."

A high-pitched, female voice from the ledge wondered, "Why?"

"Bored?" suggested the man.

"Noooo, I don't think so," mused the disembodied voice. "But . . ."

Timothy thought back to his mother; he couldn't help it. Every new woman in his life compelled comparison to the one departed.

But even though his mind was occupied, he instinctively drew his head back from the louver, and so did Jessamyn, as both of them sensed eyes roving over the entry to their hiding place.

"I think . . . ," the voice said, just as another voice entered the picture.

"Timmmothy . . . Jessssamyn . . ."

Timothy peeked through the louver. The men on the deck froze.

"Timmmothy . . . Jessssamyn . . ." It could have been the voice calling again or an echo.

"Who's that?" whispered one of the elderly men, his torch shaking with fear.

"Timmmothy . . . Jessssamyn . . ." The voice gave way to a puttering sound.

"Police?" worried the second old man.

"Yes," declared the female on the ledge. "They got here faster than I expected. Take the boat. It's valuable."

"But I don't know how to sail, Malomi."

Timothy nudged Jessamyn, who was peeking out the louver now, too. A name. They had a name. An unusual name. Too bad that DUO wasn't nearby to provide further information.

"Don't sail it, you idiot," Malomi declared. "Pull up the anchor and tie this scow to my babies."

*Babies?*

From directly above the action, Timothy and Jessamyn saw a shadowy figure dash across the deck and then jump into the channel in front of the boat. A moment later, there was the rattling of a metallic object and a horrible squealing. The muscular man shouted, "Tie 'em. Tie 'em tight."

117

"I can't."

"You better."

"Ow. Don't . . ."

"Tie 'em, now."

"Please don't . . ."

"Tie 'em, you damn skells."

Jessamyn nudged Timothy. DUO had used the word *skells*. It was one of the categories of sewer inhabitants. Another was cremblers. She mouthed the word.

Timothy sat back and nodded.

Again, squeals came from whatever creatures were out in front of the *X-tra Large*, though neither of the suburbanites could imagine what could make such a racket. It was as if a herd of pigs were attached to the boat's prow.

"Tie 'em. Rein 'em." The tattooed man kicked out at a figure on the edge of the kids' vision.

"Timmmothy . . . Jessssamyn . . ."

"Rein 'em now, or I swear I'll feed you to them!" The counterpoint of shouts and curses between the distant police calling for the missing teenagers and the cremblers and the skells and whatever was being tied and reined built and built.

"Ready?"

One word from the female on the ledge, and the racket stopped. The skells, beaten by the cremblers, and the cremblers, who'd beaten the skells, awaited further instructions. Even the dumb creatures tied and reined and beaten by the skells breathed heavily but dared not squeal. Maybe they nodded.

"Go home. Now. Take the circular route. If anyone lets himself be followed by the police . . ." She left the implicit threat hanging, and said, "Take me, Lobo."

"Yes, ma'am," replied the tattooed man.

Out of sight of the louver, another engine came to life and immediately putted away.

Jessamyn whispered, "How many boats are down here?"

"Timmmothy . . . Jesssamyn . . ."

Malomi was correct. The police were getting closer.

A moment later and the *X-tra Large* started drifting out of sight of its hidden observers.

"They're stealing my boat," Timothy whispered frantically.

Clear-eyed now, Jessamyn said, "Then let's get it back."

"How?"

"Even if the police can't follow them around whatever circle they're talking about, we can." She drew back the louver and popped her head below the ceiling for a peek.

Already the boat was half a block away and hard to make out in the dim light from the catch basins, but it was surely traveling south. The sail was down and four men walked alongside, two on the ledge that ran next to the channel and two wading in the water that came up to their shoulders. Each held a rope, but it was impossible to discern what horses or sea horses or seals or walruses were pulling the boat.

Far off in the other direction, the engine of another boat reverberated. Obviously, the police had made it this far south, if not by way of the Edgecombe rapids. There were myriad pathways to the same location in the sewer.

"C'mon," Jessamyn said as she started trotting away from DUO's domicile.

Unfortunately, the attic was as difficult for hiking as it was excellent for spying. The low ceiling meant that they had to hunch over. In some spots, they squeezed through heaps of rubble. Finally, no more than a few blocks from where the boat had been stolen, the passage was entirely filled. They groped around until they found another hatchway to the tunnel. It was locked.

Timothy said, "Allow me." Summoning two years of after-school karate classes at the Montclair Y, in which he'd barely broken a pencil, he aimed his heel several inches beyond the louver. That's what his sensei taught about smashing everything from wood planks to cinder blocks. If you aimed at the surface of the object, you'd break your hand. Aim through it. Focus on the result, not the process. The hand is only the tool of the mind. OK, Timothy thought, if he was going to break his foot, so be it; he smashed the louver open.

Jessamyn nodded. "Nice."

How to get down was another matter, a task for a James Bond . . . or a Jake. Timothy held on to the lip of the vault and swung back and forth, hoping to build up enough momentum to land on the ledge. But the jump seemed too precarious and he decided that safety was the wisest course in the midst of insanely dangerous activities. He dropped into the water.

His feet banged the bottom of the channel, but not badly. His head went under the surface for a second.

Jessamyn hung by one hand and pulled the louver over her fingers so as to protect their secret—or DUO's. Then she dropped, too.

It was strange. Even though they'd gotten soaked when the *X-tra Large* plunged into the water back on 184th Street and drenched again while riding the rapids, this was their first deliberate immersion in New York's storm sewer.

Timothy said, "How's your swimming?"

Jessamyn turned to him and grinned. "Last one to the park's a rotten egg." And she took off.

Stroke by stroke they advanced up the channel, keeping pace

with an empty pack of Newport Lights riding the current along with a faded yellow duck that may have come from a child's wading pool. Block after block they followed the *X-tra Large*, at a distance. This meant that they had to stop every once in a while to peer forward in case the boat had turned off the avenue. They also had to check behind them in case the police motorboat had advanced. Once or twice, Timothy put his ear to the side of the tunnel to make out the vibrations.

At several intersections where Saint Nicholas Avenue angled across another thoroughfare, it was difficult to decide which way to turn. No wonder the police—though surely temporarily—had disappeared.

Yet the power of the creatures towing the stolen boat was too great. Mere teenage muscles couldn't keep pace. Eventually, Timothy paused and admitted, "I can't see it anymore."

"Maybe it took a turn."

"Maybe it took a turn five miles back and we've been following a mirage."

"Don't exaggerate."

"Right. Five miles is infinitesimally too short. Fifty miles."

"Like Albany."

"Canada."

"Maybe *that's* where they went."

Timothy and Jessamyn stood in the chest-high canal, breathing heavily and sweating despite their immersion.

Jessamyn gasped. "The pantry has the rest of our crackers."

"Do you ever think about anything besides food?"

"Alternate Thursdays."

"Why then?"

"I have volleyball."

Timothy looked at the water flowing beneath the concrete outcropping. He could see thirty, forty feet ahead to a fork where the current split into two separate streams, one traveling west, the other east.

Jessamyn followed his gaze and declared, "The continental divide."

"Huh?"

"It's the line in the Rockies that separates America in geological terms. All rivers on one side flow to the Atlantic; all rivers on the other side flow to the Pacific. In fact, that reminds me . . ."

"What?"

"Close your eyes."

"I don't under—"

"It has to do with the flow of water."

"Oh." He blushed and shut his eyes and tried not to listen as Jessamyn waded a few feet away to do her business. It took some getting used to the idea that his temporary companion in adventure was a female, but the fact that she knew about things like the continental divide was even harder to wrap his mind around. When she returned, he asked, "What about the Mississippi?"

"What about it?"

"It flows to the Gulf of Mexico."

"Don't be a smart-ass, Murphy."

He tried to hide his grin, but he—or rather, they—still had to make a decision. She beat him to it by pointing to the right.

"OK," he agreed. "Why not, but . . . why?"

"Two reasons. First, if all of this eventually has to empty someplace, it's more likely to go to the Hudson than the East River because it's bigger. You know, path of least resistance. Second, if we're near Fifth Avenue, then Central Park is to the west. It's more interesting territory, so it's more likely to be where someone would hide. It could also include the circle that woman told the cremblers to take."

That made sense. He nodded, and they moved on. Then another idea occurred to Timothy: The flow toward the west that Jessamyn described would only be a path of least resistance if one was traveling in that direction. Coming the other way, it would be the path of greatest resistance. If the cremblers who had stolen the *X-tra Large* were now cruising downhill on their return to port, they would have had to have climbed uphill on their outward voyage. Everything is relative. One man's dinghy is another man's yacht.

That meant that the cremblers could have gone anywhere. It didn't make much difference which underground river Timothy and Jessamyn followed. He explained the quandary.

She shrugged, and tossed her sopping hair over her shoulder.

He reached out and removed a distracting square of tin— perhaps from a stick of gum—from her hair. "Do we have a choice?" He tried to push his vision farther into the tunnel, to the left and right—port and starboard, if they'd been on the ship.

*Odd*, he thought. Up top, on the grid, in the light, under the sun, Manhattan was the most regular city in the world. Except for Greenwich Village and the Financial District, it was so simple to find your way around that Timothy's father occasionally allowed him to take the M81 bus in from Montclair on weekends. He prided himself on his sophistication, especially when, once, he'd been mistaken for a resident and asked directions by a tourist.

What a joke. For example, 55th Street was likely to be some-where between 54th and 56th Streets. Same with Third Avenue between Second Avenue and Fourth Avenue. No, that was Park. Or was it Lexington? Still, if you could count, you could find your way around. But down here, the negative image of the city's grid provided no guidance. And there wasn't a genuine resident to ask for help. He and Jessamyn were on their own, somewhere near Central Park.

The tunnels here had fewer basins than the ones under Washington Heights. They seemed darker, the curved ceilings lower, claustrophobic, although they occasionally rose to great heights. Everything was more dramatic. The tiny skittering sounds they'd heard earlier in their journey seemed louder, closer, fiercer, and the smells, perhaps from the park's soil, were riper, ranker. The water seemed as dense as mercury.

More disconcerting, social customs were abrogated below the surface of the metropolis. What sort of place was this, where the first person they encountered was a demented, homeless man named You and the second a street artist named DUO who wasn't part of a duo and didn't work on the street? They hadn't actually met the next few people they'd seen and didn't want to, while doing their best to track the cremblers deeper into the damp and smelly labyrinth.

Even their relationship with each other was abnormal belowground. Just as an example, Timothy had never been in the presence of a peeing girl. And despite her nonchalance, Jessamyn had never gone to sleep next to a boy.

Thinking large, Timothy realized that the structures of organized life that he'd believed to be potent and eternal were actually fragile and ephemeral. Strangely, this perception did not frighten him. Instead, it gave him strength, because it meant that he was no longer subject to the arbitrary rules of the mundane, suburban world. Here, he could make his own rules. But he had to work first, because the current felt like it had changed to molasses.

"What's that?" Jessamyn halted.

The water slapped up against their thighs, so it took a moment for Timothy to ask the obvious. "What's what?"

"I thought I heard something."

Both remained silent for a few moments, but neither heard anything until they resumed travel. "There it is again."

It was the hum of a motor and it was getting closer. In fact, it was coming from behind them.

"Police?" Timothy asked. "Or is that Malomi's boat?"

"Neither," Jessamyn answered carefully. "The sound is different."

Timothy listened carefully and then agreed. "Yes, it's pitched higher. Each engine purrs at its own rate."

"Like cats."

"Maybe, but it also means this one is moving faster. C'mon."

Why they immediately sought to hide, neither one could have said, yet neither hesitated.

They waded along the edge of the tunnel until they found an indentation midway between catch basins. Then they ducked so that the sewer waters came up to their chins as a kind of barge, with an outboard motor hooked to the rear, cruised by. Several passengers sat on a bench, and a man on the stern was holding a small box to his mouth, presumably a walkie-talkie, but neither Timothy nor Jessamyn could make out anything he said except for a vague negative accompanied by a shake of the head.

When the boat disappeared, Timothy said, "What was that about?"

"It seemed like a . . ."

"A what?"

Jessamyn didn't want to sound silly, but still she replied, "A ferry. Or more private."

"A taxi?"

"Maybe."

"It was coming from the same direction we came from."

"Are you implying something?" she asked. "And if so, would you like me to infer what that may be?"

Timothy never could distinguish between implication and inference. *For heaven's sake,* he thought, *even here, even now Jessamyn is using test-prep words.* "No, thank you."

"Well, then I'll do it for you. They were coming from the same direction we came from because they were looking for us."

It was a sobering thought. What could the cremblers want with Timothy and Jessamyn now that they already had the *X-tra Large*? The duo—not DUO—started a slow march forward, presumably following the boat that was presumably following them, until Timothy once more felt the temptation to give up and call the adventure to a close.

After all, what would happen if they actually found the men who had stolen the *X-tra Large*?

"Oh," the thieves would bluster, "we didn't know this belonged to you." Of course, they'd be lying, but the righteous teenagers would allow them to save face. Just as long as they promised to never, ever steal anyone else's boat.

Ridiculous. Absurd. There were police in the tunnel. All they had to do was holler.

Timothy sighed. "I think that I might be ready to . . ." He was about to succumb, admit that this adventure—perhaps any adventure—was too much for him.

Jessamyn, it seemed, could almost read his mind. "If you're thinking of abandoning ship, forget it. You can't."

"Why not?"

"Because you don't have a ship to abandon."

He spun around, stung. "You!"

"Me, what? You weasel."

Waist-high in the flowing underground waters, Timothy trembled with rage. "And if I'm a weasel, you're a . . . a . . . giraffe."

He could tell he'd hit the target from the way the enormous girl flinched.

Nonetheless, she was tough. "Oh yeah? What are you going to do, hit me?" She jutted out her chin. "Because you don't have the guts to go after what's yours when it's stolen from you? Well, if you won't, I'll do it myself." She started walking.

"Good," he said, too loudly. "Go if you want." How dare she simply leave him there? Or threaten to leave him there? He was as angry as he'd ever been in his whole life except . . .

Except for one afternoon in a hospital waiting room not too far from this underground maze, which, now that he thought about it, was awfully like a tomb. "Hey," he called.

She kept walking.

"Hey!"

She was fifty feet away.

"C'mon, wait up, Jessamyn." He splashed toward her and then just walked by her side for nearly ten minutes that seemed like hours. At last, he said, "I'm sorry."

She replied, "For what?"

"For calling you a . . . well, you know."

"A giraffe?"

He bowed his head in shame.

She stopped and he stopped and the current swirled around them as if they were boulders in a country stream. "You idiot."

"I said I was sorry."

"And you think that makes a difference?"

"I don't know what else to say. I genuinely regret that I hurt you."

"You still don't get it, do you? I don't give a flying . . . pumpkin what you say. It bothered me that I misjudged you, because I thought you had the guts to go after what belonged to you. Instead, you turned out to be just another suburban coward." And then, like a rock finally dislodged after millions of years of pressure exerted by the current, she set off again.

"Hey . . ." He hastened to catch up, huffing a little with the effort. "I didn't— No, I did mean you were a giraffe."

"No!" Jessamyn declared.

He looked up, surprised by her vehemence.

She explained, "That doesn't make a difference. But the *X-tra Large* is not theirs. It's yours. And it's just . . . wrong for them to take it. We've got to retrieve that boat."

"Not bereave it?" he said.

"No, I . . ." She stopped when she got the joke, which meant that he got the point. They were in it together.

Stifling any expression of satisfaction, she nodded curtly, but something in the way she had been able to manipulate Timothy reminded Jessamyn of another male figure in her life. He, too, had been eager to please her. That usually meant ice cream cones and playing catch in their yard under the sycamores. She remembered her father's pride when she started bringing home report cards with ranks of A's lined up like soldiers, and she remembered their last conversation. When he said that he was going on an errand to the local hardware store.

The two teenagers walked along in silent reverie. In places, the ledge by the side of the sewer reappeared, but it was easier to keep walking in the sewer than to constantly climb up and down from the capricious walkway. Besides, the current carried them a few additional feet with each step. Here, under Central Park, the channel no longer had any grid to follow and so it grew twistier, and with fewer and less-regular catch basins above there was less light and it was more difficult to estimate location.

Also, the channel pouched off into coves and caverns with virtually no illumination, though many were graffitied like a medieval grotto. DUO and his peers must have brought flashlights.

In some spots the water level rose to Timothy's and Jessamyn's shoulders, and in others it sank to their thighs, probably because the ground had settled irregularly. Water oozed from the walls, seeping and discoloring the granite stones.

They began to feel that they were wading along a natural stream in a densely canopied forest rather than a man-made water removal system underneath the greatest concentration of people and macadam and money anywhere on earth.

There were so many corners and overhanging catwalks and stone arches supporting other stone arches, creating stone domes, in this part of the park that it was difficult to track the sounds of the strange, underground ferry. Timothy and Jessamyn were in what appeared to be a vast civic dungeon.

Or perhaps it was a catacomb winding eerily beneath a bare, ruined medieval church from an ancient civilization that no one knew had existed on the island that became Manhattan. The tunnel wound and intersected. Wherever they were going, it would be impossible to remember where they had been.

"There!" Jessamyn pointed.

Ahead of them, the motorized barge had paused at an intersection, as if waiting for a light to turn green. Then it puttered to the left.

Timothy and Jessamyn hurried onward, made the same turn, and confronted a blank stone wall.

"I don't get it," he said.

"Listen," she urged.

A woeful cry seeped through the atmosphere like mist. And then faint voices emerged from directly behind the dead end of the tunnel. The teenagers stood there for a moment as the waters continued to flow. Both could feel the current lapping at them, and see it lapping the wall yet continuing, beyond it, and both had the same idea.

Jessamyn felt along the wall until she came to a seam. "It's a door, but I can't find any knob or latch or anything."

Also, it might not have been a great idea to simply open the door and announce, "We're here!"

They could, however, slide underneath it. The door—or, more accurately, gate—came down to the water line, but the channel flowed underneath. Timothy, forgetting his previous reluctance, or remembering it and determined to show courage, said, "Hold your breath."

Simultaneously, they pinched their noses, submerged, and then reemerged a second later into . . .

Light!

# CHAPTER
# 12

**L**IGHT AND SPACE.

After twenty-four or more hours in the dim sewer lit only by their now lost lantern and distant catch basins, the teenagers felt like they were staring into the sun. Both of them blinked furiously to keep the rays from jabbing straight into their skulls until their pupils shrank to accommodate the illumination created by hundreds of strands of tiny white Christmas lights, a night's worth of stars.

And then they saw the panorama beyond the gate. Easily the length of a city block, it was like an underground cathedral carved out of pure rock instead of built out of rock. It wasn't a structure but a void surrounded by earth.

Inside the breathtaking vastness, the sewer's trunk line unraveled into a delta that spread its fingers to every corner and then rejoined to exit in a single channel. Each of the smaller lines flowed past raised apses of solid stone and concrete. In each of these lesser spaces, there seemed to be some sort of cargo, some of which was already laden on what must have been a fleet of motorized barges, like the one Timothy and Jessamyn had followed. The place was a station, a transit hub, and dozens of men scurried busily from one platform to another.

A kind of stationmaster waved colored flags to signal waiting boats to pull in to this slip or that. The flags reminded Timothy of the flags that used to fly from the mast of the *X-tra Large*. In fact, the whole scene reminded him of the Albanese Brothers Marina, where he and his father kept the boat when it wasn't cruising the Long Island Sound or the New York City sewer system. Vehicles bumped up against each other in maritime traffic, though special treatment was apparently given to one boat, which jumped the queue and pulled up at a cement pier.

Jessamyn nudged Timothy and whispered, "There."

"Where?"

Several hundred feet away, the stern of a wooden sailboat peeked out from behind a heap of boxes. Above the top of the boxes pointed the tip of a mast. They'd found the *X-tra Large*. They climbed up out of the water onto one of the platforms and hid behind a pile of rough stones.

Unfortunately, nearly fifty human obstacles occupied the space between the teenagers and their boat. Two men in unseasonal trench coats stood at the edge of one of the platforms, counting out bills while stevedores stacked a row of computers beside them. Elsewhere, a thick manila envelope was exchanged for a shopping bag from which a single translucent baggie protruded. A man on the deck of a third boat tossed a rope to a man on the shore, who wrapped it around a pipe anchored in the concrete.

Closest, however, and more distracting, was the source of the moans they'd heard in the tunnel: half a dozen sad creatures loading boxes onto a barge, and next to them a stout man in a motorcycle vest shouting, "Faster, you slugs. Faster or there's no food. Faster, or I swear . . ."

He was aided by another overseer, snapping a belt in a whip-like motion.

"Ow!" cried a man in a shapeless overcoat and hat, clutching his neck.

"Next time I'll give you the buckle," the overseer growled.

"No, please, no." The laborer groveled.

"It's You," Jessamyn whispered.

Timothy nodded. Once You was identified, however, it became obvious that the underground workers were homeless. They must have sought refuge or warmth or a tiny nook of their own below the city streets but were found and captured by the cremblers, who turned them into slaves.

"And take off that damn coat," demanded the overseer. "It's getting in the way."

"Please, sir, I'd rather not."

"Take OFF the coat!"

You hastened to comply. Underneath, he was better built than one might expect—life, if that's what to call it here, was as vigorous as it was miserable—but he cringed in fear as he offered up his single possession.

"I don't want that disgusting flea-bitten thing," said the overseer, laughing. "Put it over there with the rest of them." He lifted his chin toward a heap of coats in a corner and snapped his belt to send You back to work.

You turned red and rejoined the shuffling laborers. The overseer lashed out against random workers with renewed fury.

Off to the left of the chamber, a dozen homeless men chipped away at the foundation stones of the sewer, while others filled large black garbage bags with the rubble. A third group carried those bags to a different platform, and a fourth loaded the bags onto a barge. It seemed strange that they barely used tools when they obviously had access to sophisticated machinery. Perhaps the meaninglessness of the labor served to emphasize the madness here.

Timothy was reminded of Peter Pan and his lost boys—except these pitiable boys were grown men. What were the odds of coming upon them at this moment, undetected? Or was it always like this below the earth? Was this cave a bizarre haven, safe for the dangerous because it was dangerous for the safe?

"We'll be with you in a minute," one of the overseers called to a man on a waiting boat. Then Timothy understood. To ease the demand of the traffic, the crews were excavating another channel, like an airport adding an extra runway.

Timothy wondered how much of the cavern was natural, how much constructed by the civil engineers who designed the systems required by the populace, and how much had been artificially created by this brutal industrial enterprise. Timothy and Jessamyn couldn't take their eyes off the hive of activity, and yet there was an island of calm within the busy chamber that was also a literal island directly across a channel from the *X-tra Large*, underneath a small balcony leading to what must have been a second story to the cavernous installation. The island was connected to the other islands by means of slightly bowed wooden bridges made from two-by-twelve pieces of lumber that were raised and lowered as needed by an elaborate series of ropes and pulleys. The place felt like a cross between the backstage of a theater and an ant farm.

Two people crossed the bridge to the island. The first was the man who'd gotten off the boat that Timothy and Jessamyn followed, be it a ferry or water taxi or water limo. He was a dapper middle-aged man wearing a gray three-piece suit, a sharply knotted tie, gleaming black shoes, and golden cuff links. He was so tall that he made Jessamyn look like a midget. The second was either a genuine midget or a porcelain doll wearing a white gown and jeweled tiara. Both of them exuded an air of ownership.

The doll spoke to the giant.

Jessamyn raised her chin to Timothy, and he knew what she meant. She wanted to get closer, to hear what the people who seemed to control the bizarre situation were talking about.

He considered the idea for about half a second. Then he nodded. "But," he added, "I don't think you should go in that outfit."

Jessamyn glanced down at her muck-matted orange shorts and Hawaiian shirt. "You're right. But you're not dressed for the occasion, either."

"Yeah, but I've rented some clothing for both of us."

"What?"

"Unfortunately, the agency doesn't make deliveries." And before he could think of fifty excellent reasons not to act, Timothy stepped into the open, walked about twenty steps, lifted up the nearest garments from the heap on which You had deposited his coat—careful, however, to avoid You's own coat, whether out of concern for the frightened creature or fear of the fleas or lice or bedbugs that probably infested it—and returned.

Jessamyn approved of both his moxie and the camouflage gear. Donning a huge, stained raincoat and a shapeless felt hat, she looked like an army tent. "Nice."

"Yeah, I got it at Tramps Like Us."

It was a Jersey joke, so she laughed, then stepped forward.

For a quarter of a second, You and several members of his work detail glanced in the intruders' direction, but none of them noticed the sneakers beneath the shabby raincoats. They weren't able to conceive of a stranger willingly entering their domain.

135

From the platform, however, a keener, more suspicious eye shifted. It was that of the doll, too distant to have possibly heard Jessamyn's inadvertent laugh. She gazed across the endlessly replenished North American Styx, knowing, just knowing that something was amiss.

Timothy and Jessamyn might as well have been butterflies pinned to a mat. Maybe they could flap their wings, but they could not escape, and so they continued forward, closer, hoping to look like they belonged, when the tall man next to the doll declared, "So when will we have it?"

His voice seemed to break a spell. The small figure turned her attention to the man, and Timothy and Jessamyn were released from her pitiless scrutiny. They continued to approach the island until they were close enough to hear the conversation.

The tall man continued. "You said that we'd have it today."

The doll clasped her delicate hands together and rubbed her palms. Then she snapped a finger at one of the guards, who immediately hastened over the bridge. The man wore leather pants and an armless T-shirt. A crudely executed tattoo of a snake extended from his wrist to his shoulder.

Jessamyn nudged Timothy in the ribs as they slowly sidled forward. "It's him."

"Him?" Timothy had been looking elsewhere when the man who stole the *X-tra Large* crossed his companion's line of vision below DUO's workshop.

"And she's the one who told him to take the boat."

"Lobo," the doll said, addressing the man. Her voice was strange: high-pitched, yet mellifluous, even hypnotic. "Tell Dr. Pym-Gordon that we are working as fast as we can. Of course, we'd prefer the work to go faster, but delicate excavation may entail unexpected delays."

The adjutant named Lobo remained in place but turned his head and repeated the "request" verbatim.

"No one ever works as fast as they can," the "doctor" stated as if musing on a sorrowful truth.

Then, for the first time, the doll addressed him directly. "Do you, Allan? Is curatorship a precise art?" The tall man now had a full name, a title, and a job.

Dr. Allan Pym-Gordon—a curator of what?—said, "I try."

"Maybe you don't try hard enough. My men all try hard enough. That's because they know that if they don't, I'll feed 'em to the rats." She laughed. "Lobo, do you remember that Brazilian gentleman who used to work for us, stole some of our food?"

"Yeah, we caught him trying to go up top."

"What did we do with him?"

"We fed him to the rats."

Timothy sensed the wheels turning in Dr. Pym-Gordon's head. If he ignored the comment, he might seem humorless if it was supposed to be funny; but if he laughed and the comment was intended to be serious, he'd seem foolish in the face of danger. On the other hand, laughing at danger was also a sign of toughness. So he emitted an unconvincing chuckle. "Hah."

The doll did not join him. Instead, she gazed intently at a weird mural on one of the chamber walls. Timothy thought he had seen the mural before but couldn't identify it. It showed a crowd, in motion, hustling forward. Most of the individuals were carrying things, a large chandelier standing out above.

What made the image especially difficult to identify was that it was a sketch done in the soft, swooping neon colors of graffiti and therefore more clearly DUO's than . . .

"The Arch of Titus," Jessamyn said, identifying the image.

Timothy should have known. The original frieze was featured

in his previous year's art history textbook. He'd been thrown off by the form and the coloring and the contemporary objects in the painting. Instead of hauling the loot of the ancient world, DUO's marauders carried a pair of tickets to who knew what sold-out concert or ball game, an iPad, a flat-screen TV, and a tray with a cornucopia of foods spilling over as if into a hungry viewer's mouth. The chandelier took the place of conquered Jerusalem's sacred candelabra in the original.

And directly in front of the painting, the homeless men re-enacted DUO's imagery by carting all sorts of goods from one boat to another.

The doll demanded, "How did that get here?"

"New since last night," Lobo answered. "He sneaks past everyone and is gone by morning."

"What about the guard?"

"We were watching the other side because that's where he—"

"Get rid of it."

Just then, maybe made hasty by the scrutiny, one of the laborers tripped and dropped his box, which hit the rough stone with a crash and a clatter. Judging from the look on the doll's face, whatever was in the box wasn't cheap.

At a benign moment when the sun shone—well, maybe not literally, but surely there were good times, even in the sewer—the doll might have waved a magnanimous hand over the error and made it disappear.

Less providentially, she might have wistfully shaken her head and docked the malefactor a meal or decreed a day in confinement. Some token to maintain discipline.

Today, however, was not a day for forgiveness. Yes, the harbor was busy, but her crew could not stop DUO's incursions. Yes, the cremblers had obtained a fine vessel in the *X-tra Large* as a present for their mistress, but along with it came an unpleasant police investigation. Then there was the delay in some project involving their finely clad visitor, who wanted what he wanted today. The doll's baleful eye alit on the oaf who'd dropped the case of breakables. He sat in the midst of shards, rubbing his ankle. Everyone in the cavern paused to watch the doll watch him: the overseers, the workers, the tall, well-dressed doctor/curator/dandy.

She looked at the irritating Dr. Pym-Gordon and then smiled. She had an idea. She stood and stretched, and walked forward as calmly as if intending to take a refreshing dip in the ever-flowing underground waters. Indeed, she paused at the arched wooden bridge separating her from the accident as if contemplating the effort it would take to cross the bridge or the symbolism of the crossing. She turned to Dr. Pym-Gordon and said, "Come with me, Allan. I want you to meet my babies." Then she asked Lobo, "Where are my babies?"

"Some are in the coop," he replied.

"And the rest?"

"They're still attached to the boat we hauled in a while ago." He pointed to the *X-tra Large.*

"Of course. Of course," the doll murmured as the group walked over to the captured vessel. "How nice of my babies to bring me such a gift. They work so hard and never get what they really deserve."

The brutal environment did not seem to include anyone who could possibly be deemed a baby, but the doll bent toward the prow of the boat, with a hand extended toward some creatures impossible for Timothy and Jessamyn to discern. "Here they are. Tahiti, is that you?" she cooed, her voice gentler. "Bali, boy. Want a nibble?"

She reached into her pocket and then extended her hand to

some of the animals that had presumably drawn the *X-tra Large* south from 145th Street. Was it a team of trained dogs? Fish? If the animals were larger, visible, and she'd been removing lumps of sugar, they might have been horses.

The doctor glanced at the incongruous 12½-foot-long sailboat. "Nice sloop."

"Yes, I just got it."

"Have anything to do with that little to-do in Washington Heights?"

"I don't know what you're talking about."

Timothy nudged Jessamyn in the gut and mouthed, "Bull."

Up close, Dr. Pym-Gordon appreciated the boat. "It's a real beauty."

"Yes, I suppose so. Every time you think you know the extent of the gifts of the netherworld, you're surprised. How much do you think this might fetch up top?"

It was the third time Jessamyn and Timothy had heard that phrase. "Up top" seemed to be down below's vernacular for any world other than its own—any place with sun.

"Oh, I have no idea."

"And how about your own gift from below? The one we are working as hard as we can to obtain."

Dr. Pym-Gordon shrugged. "Prices vary."

The doll laughed again. "All of my clients are the same. The only thing you care about is money. Doesn't make a difference if it's Madison Avenue antiques or the pretty white powder our friends over there prefer." She gestured to the men exchanging their different-sized envelopes. "All of you think that you're cheating silly, little Malomi."

Now Timothy and Jessamyn were sure who she was. The doll had repeated the name mentioned in the tunnel.

"We've got—"

"A deal, Doctor. 1 know that we have a deal, and we will fulfill our part because we are honest and you are the kind of man to violate your employer's trust. You don't have to pretend that we like each other, because as far as I'm concerned you're all just . . ." She paused as if trying to think of the most disdainful term possible. "*Topsiders*. Now for some entertainment."

The doctor nodded agreeably.

"All right, 1 want the whole archipelago," she ordered Lobo. "Saints first. Bart, Croix. Whoa! Whoa!" She stood upright as if her eager babies were about to knock her over. Most every island in the world was a part of the system here. Malomi knew geography.

Timothy and Jessamyn watched Dr. Pym-Gordon watch his host, his forehead creased with a combination of wonderment and disgust.

"Ah, the babies are hungry," Malomi announced. "Feeding time is not until later, but a snack is in order because they worked so hard today."

Several cremblers hastened to provide morsels for the hard-working animals named after sandbars and volcanic outcroppings around the globe.

"Still not enough," Malomi tsk-tsked. Then she turned to the worker who'd dropped the box and lay splayed out on the floor amid the shattered glassware. "You, come here and help us."

"I'm Kelp, ma'am." He stood up and approached the doll.

Timothy and Jessamyn glanced at each other with the same thought: Not all underground workers called themselves "You." Kelp retained a vestige of his topside identity.

"Kelp, then," mused the doll as if she had the same thought as the intruders. Unfortunately, she was not pleased by his display of individualism. She wanted an army of Yous. "Do you happen to know where Majorca and Minorca are?" she asked.

"Minorca's back in the cage. She's about to give birth."

"Again?"

Perhaps the conversation led the fumbler to a false sense of security. His eyes creased with pleasure and he answered slyly. "She's a fecund little breeder, she is."

The doll lashed out and up with a tiny fist and hit Kelp in the head. A welt appeared across his brow. "Don't you ever speak like that about my babies. Now apologize to Minorca's friends."

"I'm sorry." Kelp glanced from Lobo to another guard to Allan Pym-Gordon.

"Not them, you idiot."

Kelp looked confused.

"Them." Mistress Malomi gestured to the creatures she had been feeding. Every eye in the cavern was glued to the show.

Kelp looked down and said, "I'm sorry."

"That is insufficient."

"I'm very sorry."

"That's better, but they require proof of your regret."

Kelp appeared baffled. He couldn't imagine what proof she had in mind.

Malomi sighed with exasperation. "Give them your hand."

The worker blanched.

"I said, give them your hand, Kelp."

The guards turned ominously, and Kelp understood that he could do this by himself or he could be helped. If he was helped, the ordeal was bound to last longer, and it might involve more than a hand. He plunged his fist into the channel.

Immediately, the water—even at a distance—appeared to commence boiling.

Kelp twisted his body, but kept his hand steady. A sound like a hissing teakettle came from his mouth.

"Shh," whispered Malomi.

Kelp grimaced.

Slowly now, clarifying the sin and the punishment, Malomi asked, "Are you saying that you're sorry for giving offense?"

Kelp gritted his teeth and moaned, "I'm sorry. I'm sorry." He squeezed out individual words between gasps. "I'm . . . I'm . . . I'm as . . . as . . . suh-sorry . . . sorry . . . as I can . . . be."

"Then you may remove your hand."

He yanked it out of the water. It was bright red with the blood only washed half-clean by the ongoing current.

Timothy whispered, "Barracuda?"

Jessamyn shook her head in horror.

Slashes and gouges on Kelp's hand indicated where he'd been bitten. Immediately, the wounds refilled with blood.

Malomi was pleased. "You are dismissed."

Kelp wrapped a rag around his hand. He staggered back to his work detail and the doll turned to her guest. "Would you believe that these babies were once feral?"

Allan Pym-Gordon shook his head.

Malomi continued. "Just a little bit of love, that's all it took to domesticate them. Of course, they've got to work for their keep just like everyone else. Don't you, Oahu? He's my favorite. What a brute. C'mon, boy. Out of the water. They just love the wetness. C'mon."

A brown snout with silvery whiskers popped out of the water and started sniffing. Then a single, slippery paw appeared, then another, and finally the creature emerged. Oahu was a rat, but he was the size of an overstuffed dachshund, and he shook like a dog, too, spraying water over everyone in sight.

Timothy stared at the tube of pure muscle that had a tail as long and vicious as an unfurled whip as he felt Jessamyn's fingers digging into the soft flesh above his elbow.

The visitor stared, too.

Oahu looked at the doll and the doll stared at him with pleasure. "You know what he's thinking, don't you? He's thinking, *I'd like to eat that person.* Yes, he is. Yes, you are, my baby. *Oocha, boocha, boocha.* Don't deny it. But don't try it, either, because I have sharper teeth. Well, not really, but I've got to make him think so. Otherwise, watch out. You know why he's named Oahu?"

Clearly unhappy to be playing this guessing game, the proper doctor ventured, "Because you like islands?"

"Well, I do. That's obvious. Isn't it, Bali boy?" She addressed another rat that was not as extraordinary as Oahu. "But that's only part of the truth. Oh, *O-ahhh-huuu.* That's the sound that the first person he ate made."

The doctor's face tensed as he struggled to avoid responding to the performance. Changing the subject, he calmly replied, "You should get out more."

"Maybe when our exchange is concluded, I'll take a vacation."

"Hmmph." Pym-Gordon coughed. "Can't imagine why you'd ever want to leave this place."

Malomi, on the other hand, returned to business. "Doesn't look it, but the hard part's done. We have the locations to the inch, and we've gone far enough underneath that alarms can't be triggered. You're sure there's no further protection in the storage room?"

"Positive, but I'm worried about privacy. The papers say that the police are crawling all over the sewer like earthworms."

Malomi leaned against her latest acquisition and stroked its brass railing. "Do you really think they can bother us here? Here?!" She lifted her arms to encompass her domain.

"I heard they weren't more than twenty blocks away."

"Allan. Allan. Relax. Twenty blocks is a universe."

"And by now it may be ten."

"I don't care if it's two. Vishnu!" She called to an Indian man with a thin gray beard.

"Yes, Your Majesty."

So she was not a doll, not a midget, not merely a mistress: she was a queen.

Jessamyn's eyebrows rose at the title.

Timothy shrugged.

"Raise the wall," the little royal commanded.

Vishnu signaled to the traffic controller in a booth in the center of the arena. A minute later, the wall that Timothy and Jessamyn had swum beneath began a slow and creaking ascent. The wall was composed of a thin veneer of genuine stone mounted on thick sheets of plywood. It was large enough to accommodate any traffic the sewer could bear.

Malomi nodded, and the gate once more enclosed her kingdom.

Water obviously continued to flow underneath it, but any sightseer or cop would cruise on by into the labyrinth under Central Park.

Content, Queen Malomi said, "I'm not worried."

"And yet," Pym-Gordon insisted, "I am taking a risk."

"You are being rewarded."

"True," he acknowledged.

"And I won't even be invited to your retirement party."

"True."

Three long blocks wide, fifty-one short blocks long, Central Park was designed by Frederick Law Olmsted and Calvert Vaux to simulate an urban Eden. Neither a tree nor a boulder was planted or placed in the so-called lungs of the city without their explicit approval.

Containing over a hundred statues ranging from international liberators to Alice in Wonderland, a band shell, a zoo, an ice-skating rink, a memorial to John Lennon, dozens of ball fields, Belvedere Castle, and an outdoor theater, the park has scores of physical and cultural amenities. On summer nights, performances by the New York Philharmonic and special events featuring rock stars draw as many people as live in most midsize cities.

There's the Ramble—a several-acre thicket once known for anonymous romances—and a croquet court for Anglicized gee-zers. Meandering through the greenery are roadways for cars and bridle paths for horses, though the sole public stable closed years ago. There are also various waterways, independent or connected; a shallow, oval pond where children sail motorized boats; a deeper pond for real rowboats; and a billion-gallon reservoir.

Malomi took pride in her hideout. "You can't do this anyplace else in the system because most of the sewers follow directly beneath the streets. But here, where there are branches and dead ends, we can hide anything. We can hide riches. We can hide ourselves. We could even hide your dead body, Dr. Pym-Gordon."

Several of the skells, including Kelp, grinned as the man in the suit paled.

"Of course," Malomi continued, "what with Oahu and the rest of the islands, there wouldn't be anything worth hiding." She gestured toward the "islands," and several of the workers began to scoop the enormous rats out of the water.

"Dinnertime?" the well-dressed client asked sarcastically.

"Later," the queen answered.

The cremblers prodded the furry mass in the direction of a large wire cage that was set into an alcove in the middle of the perverse Grand Central Terminal. The cage was the rats' home out of the water.

"Ummm . . ." Timothy turned to Jessamyn. "You know, I really don't care what these weird people are doing. I just want to get the boat and get out of here."

"So what do you intend to do, waltz over and set sail?"

They peered across the cavern. Jessamyn's suggestion was almost plausible since everyone was busy with some task, loading, unloading. And yet one idle glance would be sufficient to doom them. And they knew—just knew—that would not be a good thing.

"No, I don't think I'd waltz."

"What then, boogie down?"

"In a way." He explained how one could swim or slide beside the surface of the ledge to arrive at the boat unnoticed.

"And then?"

It wouldn't take long to untie the rope holding the *X-tra Large* to a metal pipe and hook up the sail and pick up speed. But if they were spotted too soon, one of the guards could outrun the boat and leap onto the deck.

"A distraction," Jessamyn declared. "We need a distraction."

"Yeah. At the opposite end of the space, to draw attention." He pointed to a ladder standing beside an untended barge near the rat cage. "I can knock that over while you start the *X-tra Large*. Then I can hop on while we head for the exit. Good?"

She thought of her partner's dancerlike movements earlier in the journey. Left hand loosen the sail, right hand tighten the pulley, left foot shift the boom, right foot doing something or other, every limb operating together in perfect harmony. "Except for one small thing."

"What's that?"

"I'll create the distraction while you get the boat."

"Don't be ridiculous. It's too dangerous."

"For a *girl*? Uh-uh. My plan has nothing to do with danger. There's no way I could get the *X-tra Large* in motion quickly enough by myself. And if one sail gets tangled, I won't be able to do it at all."

"I . . ."

"Just shut up, will you. This is not a subject open for discussion. You get the boat and I'll get you the time. That's all there is to it."

For a quarter of a second, he remembered his mother, and how he had resented it when she gave orders, even the stunningly mild "Clean your room." There was comfort in obeying an order from a strong female. No doubt Jessamyn was right. Each of them had particular skills appropriate to particular tasks. Besides, the giantess with the even more gigantic ego was a natural distraction.

He relented. "OK, give me a couple of minutes to swim over to the boat and free the ropes. It will depend on how they've tied it. After that, I'll take the easiest, most direct route, going with the current, which is heading in that direction. Also—"

She put a hand to his lips. "Trust me."

Just then Dr. Pym-Gordon's cell phone rang.

Jessamyn noted, "Good reception."

# CHAPTER

# 13

**U**P TOP, THOMAS MURPHY COULDN'T STAND THE TEN-sion. The air in the trailer was dank with sweat and frustration. Half-empty coffee cups and sticky doughnut wrappers and Chinese food cartons littered every surface in sight except for one small desk reserved for the schematic plans and blueprints of Civil Engineer Cass Wainwright, who seldom ate and never complained. Unlike NYPD Captain Walter Mullane, who growled at anyone who opened the door or called on the perpetually ringing phone.

"Well, go eastward then," he ordered the first of the police boats in the sewer as he sent the second boat west.

"Can't you move any faster?" he snapped at the individual officers wading south toward 125th Street.

"What do you want?" he barked, biting the head off a rookie who tried to ask for a bathroom break.

And the whole miserable SDJ was made worse by the grotesque error of the night before. "Yes, sir," he replied to the commissioner. "We're doing as much as we can. Yes, sir," he repeated, while scratching at his toupee as if it was inhabited by a colony of lice.

The commissioner kept him on the phone for fifteen minutes, complaining that the press was claiming that the NYPD wasn't able to find a pair of teenagers on a broken boat slower than a three-legged dog.

He was right. Journalists were insatiable. Along with reporters for the daily tabloids came a stringer from *Le Monde* and a sophomore from the *Columbia Spectator*. And the late-edition papers were crueler than the initial reports, focusing less on the pathos of the lost children than the incompetence of the police. "Still Missing!" cried the *Post*. "Sewer Madness," chuckled the *Daily News*, whose reporter had to be evicted from the trailer for badgering the grieving mother for a quote.

Miranda Hazard looked haggard, now a mere shadow of the lively young widow who'd set out for a nautical jaunt with her new boyfriend. She cast daggers at Tom Murphy every time their eyes met in the confined space, and occasionally gazed out the windows of the trailer with undisguised loathing for the crowd—diminished by now but still substantial—that found thrills in her suffering.

"Are you sure we can't get you a hotel room, ma'am?" Mullane asked.

All she did was shake her head.

Mullane sympathized. After the hours it had taken to find, transport, and lower the two motorboats from Brooklyn into the sewer, the department was squarely behind the eight ball. It hardly made a difference that Johnny Angel had also located a fleet of Coast Guard vessels that were entering the system at the 145th Street outflow, per Cass Wainwright's suggestion. Nonetheless, Mullane tried to act confident. "We'll get them now, ma'am. For sure."

"Sure," she echoed dully.

Mullane looked at Murphy, who offered no help but instead said, "I'm going to take a walk."

Outside the trailer was another beautiful summer afternoon. Tom skirted some local kids shoving each other into the yellow tape. Once upon a time, he might have been one of those kids, though the most dramatic event he could remember from his childhood involved a pet-store fire. Before abandoning the premises, the manager had opened all the cages so that puppies and kittens, rabbits and ferrets, lizards and hamsters, and, as youthful rumor had it, a single poisonous rattlesnake roamed upper Broadway for weeks.

Automatically, he turned on Wadsworth Avenue and continued north until he found the six-story redbrick apartment building his family had lived in. Gazing up to the fourth floor, he saw the fire escape of the once Murphy living room. Three clay pots filled with blooming geraniums provided a cheerful welcome.

The flowers sent Tom into a reverie as he wandered around the neighborhood, finding the building where his best friend used to live with his German-speaking mother and aunt. He remembered the taste of their schnitzel. He also remembered doo-wop girls with big hair who hung out in the lobby.

Nothing looked quite the same, least of all the people Tom had seen through teenage eyes, until he turned a corner, hardly aware of his destination, and there was PS 192. The schoolhouse was as noble and as decrepit as ever: red brick, white columns, graffiti. Only a ramp for wheelchairs was new. It led up to the familiar double doors. Then Tom started crying.

A woman wheeling a child in a stroller circled around him with a nervous motion.

He cried because the school brought his son to mind. Timothy attended school. Timothy went sailing, loved reading, enjoyed visiting his father at the factory. Timothy was unutterably, unbearably lost.

Somehow he returned to the trailer. The police captain looked at him and so did the woman who—he'd believed, for a moment—might replace Timothy's mother. If Miranda Hazard had initially cut him off after the *X-tra Large* fell through a hole in the ground, she looked at him differently now. She even spoke to him. "Is something wrong?"

The question was so stupid, he almost smiled. Then he answered, "No, something isn't wrong. Everything is wrong. And it's all my fault." He started gasping.

"No," she said quietly. "It's not anybody's fault."

# CHAPTER 14

**T**HE CREW THAT STOLE THE *X-TRA LARGE* KNEW NOTH-ing about sailboats. All they had done was use their creepy team of rats to tow their plunder away from the spot where they'd found it. Here, on the perimeter of their hub/harbor/ware-house, they'd merely tied one of the shredded ropes in a bow—the kind used on a pair of sneakers—to a random pipe jutting out of the city's foundation wall. When the sail fluttered, they loosened it from the boom rather than the mast. That, too, was lucky, because Timothy could easily set the vessel in motion again by hooking the grommets in the sail over pegs in the boom. Within seconds, he ought to be able to catch the sewer breeze and head downstream.

Likewise, Jessamyn's task was simple: knock over the ladder, raise a ruckus, and run to the agreed-upon meeting point thirty feet from the tunnel. After that, *Bon voyage.*

No problem. Yet the plotters' timing had to be perfect. So just as Timothy arrived at and untied the boat, which began a gentle glide away from its dock, he was disconcerted to see Jessamyn moving past the ladder.

He wanted to cry out, *What are you doing?* but he knew. The foolish girl had decided to create a bigger, noisier distraction than tipping over a ladder. Unfortunately, this would take her farther away from the boat. *No, please*, he begged silently.

She approached the cage into which the cremblers had herded the . . . um . . . herd of rats.

Timothy had to slow the motion of the vessel he'd been doing everything in his power to hasten. He shoved the boom starboard to thwart rather than catch the breeze. Still, the boat moved relentlessly in the direction of the tunnel as Jessamyn slid free the bolt that locked the cage and flung open the mesh door. A gray mass burst out of confinement, running helter-skelter in every direction.

She started running, too.

He tightened the sail.

"The rats are loose!" one of the cremblers shouted.

"What?"

"Hey!"

"Get them!" commanded Lobo, and everyone went wild.

Everyone except for one person. In the midst of the pandemonium, Malomi remained calm. Lobo was correct that the situation had to be rectified, but what had caused it? Her eyes swept the premises for a clue.

Five skells were already running toward the cage; one, in a stained raincoat and droopy felt hat, was running away. Then the hat flew off and a head of bright red hair shone like a sun in the sunless cavern. Malomi had sensed that something was wrong earlier, but she'd been distracted by her business.

She also saw the *X-tra Large* unmoored with a boy at the helm. The two intruders were both heading toward the spot where several minor channels met and the current picked up speed.

Understanding immediately, Malomi made the necessary change in orders. "Get *them*!" she yelled, pointing.

In a flash, three skells who had cornered Staten, a bruiser with one eye and a scar down his cheek from a fight with a German shepherd, veered away from the rat as if they were remote-controlled by Malomi's will.

Jessamyn was half a dozen steps from the stern of the *X-tra Large* when she heard their footsteps and turned her head, and because she was so tall her shoulder bumped into the curved ceiling and she lost her balance in the mud and slippery rat droppings and fell to her knees.

"Get up!" Timothy called.

She yelled, "Go. *Go!*"

The captain, who'd been a good but not great math student in his previous identity, made an instant calculation. If he paused, they'd both be caught. Therefore, the only way he could save her was to abandon her now and return later. He shifted the boom twenty degrees in the direction of the breeze, and the *X-tra Large* disappeared into the tunnel.

Jessamyn saw the sail blink around the corner just as two of the slovenly creatures leapt onto her. "Too late!" She laughed as if a part of her had gone free and there was nothing they could do.

Moreover, there was plenty *she* could do. When one of the skells loosened his hold for a second, she jammed her elbow smack-back into his face, a move she'd perfected on the Montclair basketball court. Odd, but she hated basketball because she'd been forced to play it due to her height; it felt like a freak show. *Come one, come all. Watch the battle of the Amazons!*

Worse, boy players were local heroes whom cheerleaders flashed their panties for, whereas girl players scared the pants off adolescent males, turning them into intimidated babies—except perhaps for Timothy Murphy, the sailor. She was glad that he had made it into the tunnels. Now he could contact the police and rescue her. Before that, however, Kat Hazard wasn't going down without a fight.

With the first of Jessamyn's would-be captors rolling backward, yowling about his broken nose, the second was easy to shrug off and the third she booted into the channel. Unfortunately, a dozen more had captured the loosened rats and were now converging.

As if dribbling downcourt along the foul line, she led a group of four skells to a path by the channel, then faked left and ran right. Amazingly, the entire group bought the fake. They bumped into each other like cartoon characters. She realized: *They are truly dumb.*

If there hadn't been so many of them, she might have enjoyed the game. It was like playing string with a kitten who'd fall for the same trick over and over again. Alas, that was the key; as slow-witted as her pursuers were, they were tireless. As athletic as the Montclair Junior Varsity Girls Team's starting forward was, she was exhausted.

No substitutions allowed.

From the initial accident, to the perilous chute under Edgecombe Avenue, to this evil grotto, Jessamyn had been in constant motion. She outran and outmaneuvered a few more groups of the skells until she finally noticed one potential escape route that might bring her to the police before Timothy. She smiled at the thought of him bursting into some precinct only to find her sitting in the captain's office, sipping tea and nibbling a glazed doughnut.

The path to freedom was a crevasse between two walls just

out of sight of the two other crews fast approaching her. She slipped into the narrow aisle that angled upward.

Once or twice, she stumbled over a stone outcropping but regained her footing. The thought of freedom gave her strength. At the end of the ramp was a faint light—not the artificial glimmer of the bare bulbs strung throughout the cathedral but the milky glow of the sun.

Jessamyn sought the light as instinctively as a plant curling skyward, yearning for sustenance. In fact, the crevasse came to a blunt dead end, but there was a kind of a flue, perhaps four feet wide, below a catch basin on the surface. The light was filtering down from ten or twelve feet above. She could see branches with bright-green leaves and the edge of a bronze statue. The ramp had brought her within sight of Central Park.

Jessamyn considered the situation. Since she'd lost the quasi-zombies, she could climb the flue at leisure by alternately pressing her feet off opposite surfaces. She'd never been interested in the climbing fad that had swept Montclair Junior High a year earlier, but if her classmates could do it, so could she. She wasn't sure what obstacles she might encounter at the top, but she'd cross that catch basin when she came to it. After her adventures of the past two days, she was more confident than she'd been on the morning of a pre-PSAT exam.

And by the way, she'd scored a perfect 2400, thank you very much.

Sure enough, most of the deadly dullards were now circling the entrance to the crevasse, as if muttering to each other, "I don't know. She used to be here. Do you know?"

She wedged her foot into a gap in the stonework on the left, pushed against the right wall with her palm, and lifted her right leg a few feet higher. Then she reversed direction, finding a rhythm, like a pendulum swinging higher with each motion. And with each swing, the light grew brighter. Her fingers inched upward until at last she reached the heavy cast-iron grate that opened onto a city street.

She felt the underside of the metal, flakey from rust and wet from a constant dribbling from the gutter. Leaves caught between her fingers, but those fingers were free now, out in the air.

"There she is!" a voice shouted.

Jessamyn looked toward the opening of the crevasse. A dirty finger extended from a dirty sleeve, pointing.

"No!" she cried.

The skells bumped against each other in their eagerness to enter the narrow defile. Eventually, one of them squirted between the others and appeared at the base of the flue.

"Found her. Found the topsider!" the voice called out, and feet trooped behind him.

She looked down, and the glow of freedom illuminated a familiar face. She looked her betrayer in the eyes and nearly sobbed. "How could You do this?"

You looked behind him and begged, "Do I get an extra portion?"

The high-pitched voice of the mistress of the underground kingdom said, "Yes, You does."

Jessamyn's fingers struggled with the grate, desperately trying to shove it off its mooring and to hoist herself the few inches to freedom.

Indeed, she thought she heard a sympathetic voice from somewhere above. "Look. Myra, over—"

Malomi climbed onto You's shoulders. "Hello," she said. The voice was soothing, but also emotionless. It wasn't suggesting that things were going to be OK; it was declaring that nothing was going to change. It was saying, *Give up.*

An icy hand gripped Jessamyn's ankle. The hand was soft and small and unshakeable. Still, Jessamyn clutched the metal grate, hanging from it and kicking wildly. "Help me," she cried to the thick municipal bars that refused to budge. "Help me!"

Yet the ring of thumb and forefinger began to exert a downward pull and Jessamyn's fingers began to loosen from the metal grate. She looked beneath her and for the first time saw the doll up close. Her crimson lipstick shone. Her bright, black eyes glittered at the thrill of the capture. Her royal glass tiara twinkled.

Jessamyn gave one more futile call for help into the world of light and then she stopped kicking, like a hanged man who had finally become a corpse. Her body fell.

# CHAPTER

# 15

**I**'M TELLING YOU, I SAW A HAND."

The park officer squinted at the girl making the report. Her eyes weren't bloodshot; she didn't slur her words; and she was neatly dressed in a pink cashmere cardigan and skirt, but you could never tell these days. If she wasn't under the influence, perhaps she was naturally loony. He murmured, "Hmm," while his pen hovered an inch over the pad.

"And I heard something."

"Yes?"

"Right here."

They stood on the concrete sidewalk above the rusty sewer grate and looked down at it. Could the indentations in a mat of leaves be finger marks? Unlikely.

"I'm not positive about this, but I believe the person was calling for help. I mean, it makes sense, doesn't it?"

"Of course."

They stood awkwardly for three or five seconds, until the girl extended her neck toward the officer, like a turtle. "So what are you going to do?"

"Do?"

"Like, yeah. Do. I mean, if you've got someone who's in trouble, isn't that sort of your job?"

The officer turned to the girl's companion in a bud-green cardigan, who was drawing her fingers through long blond hair. "And you saw this, too?"

"No, I was occupied."

Off to the side, two teenage boys sat on a bench and flipped pieces of gravel at a street sign. *Occupied.*

"But Shelley thought it was, like, really important to report this," the second girl added, tepidly supporting her friend.

"I was just doing my civic duty," Shelley announced proudly.

"Well, thank you."

Again they paused, until Shelley declared, "You're not going to do anything, are you? I mean, what if it's those kids who got lost in the sewer?"

The officer yawned. "A hundred blocks from here."

"So?"

"So I'm going to report this just like any other incident." That was true. Park duty was as easy as it got. The officer castigated litterers and confiscated cans of beer from drunks.

Shelley's friend tugged at her sweater and the two boys rolled their eyes. There were plenty of other girls around if these two insisted on hanging out with the police.

"Well, I'm going to watch you report this." Shelley crossed her arms over her chest.

The policeman couldn't help but smile, which infuriated Shelley even more, but what the heck. He pulled a walkie-talkie out of a kind of holster at his hip and pressed the talk button.

A crackling response from park headquarters answered, "Dozie. One-one."

"Dozie. Three-six here. I've got a report of . . . um . . . some-one . . . um . . . stuck in a sewer."

"What's that, Dozie three-six?"

The officer repeated himself, and was going to make this obnoxious girl feel entirely foolish, when the operator interrupted. "Your location, Dozie three-six. Imperative. Immediate."

His eyes widened, and he answered as best he could since they were hardly on the city grid. "North Drive, approximately ten blocks south and east of the Lasker skating rink."

"Maintain your location. Detectives will be there within five minutes."

Shelley smiled.

Word was reported to the command post in Washington Heights that there had been a sighting in Central Park.

From 184th Street, Captain Mullane immediately called the two motorboats and slightly larger Coast Guard cutters that were now in the system to determine which was closest to the sighting.

"Weird down here," Mosolino in PB-2 was saying to Reynolds when their radio began beeping.

"PB-2 here."

"Mullane here. And here's where you've got to go." The captain snapped directions. "Make it fast."

"Yes, sir," Reynolds at the helm replied, happy to oblige. "Hold tight," he said to Mosolino as he throttled up the motorboat, which reared like a bronco and made waves.

In fact, this was the coolest duty either of them had been assigned to in ages, better even than Yankee Stadium during the play-offs. Reynolds cornered hard where Lenox Avenue reached the park and the sewer began echoing the long, looping drives instead of the straight lines of the uptown gird. Once, he scraped the side but the boat held, the motor roared, and all that was missing was sunshine.

Up top, Mullane dispatched two cars to Central Park, where they soon came sirening up to stunned park officer Bart Partensky and smug Shelley, but nothing more could be gleaned from them.

They radioed the precise coordinates to Reynolds and Mosolino, the latter of whom, relegated to communications, radioed back, "I do believe that we're right underneath you." He and Reynolds observed but paid no attention to a narrow alley beneath a catch basin in their search for an enormous—well, miniature out in the world but enormous in the context—sailing vessel.

# CHAPTER 16

**H**EL-LO." THE VOICE SOUNDED MECHANICAL, LIKE AN old automated operator, cobbled out of inflectionless pre-recorded syllables. It was high-pitched and slightly nasal.

Then, as if to prove that the speaker was human, her eyes blinked, but the black circles revealed as little expression as the voice.

As for body language, there was none. The speaker sat motionless on a stained red satin pillow on a high-backed wooden chair that looked as if it belonged in a church. Behind her stood snake-tattooed Lobo and Kelp, with a rough bandage swathing his left hand.

Jessamyn sat on a theater-size Oriental rug on the floor in front of the chair, guarded by three more cremblers. She replied, "Hello."

"My name is Malomi, or perhaps you already know that."

Inadvertently, Jessamyn's eyes signaled the truth of this.

"And who might you be?"

There was no point in lying. "My name is Jessamyn."

"And a fine name that is, but I'd imagine you with a somewhat tougher name, something like . . ." Malomi paused.

Hardly knowing what impelled her, Jessamyn declared, "Friends call me Kat."

"Yes." Malomi smiled winsomely. "That's more like it. Welcome to my home, Kat." She extended the tiny hand that had been like a steel ring around Jessamyn's ankle.

Disdaining assistance, Jessamyn rose to her feet. Now she loomed over Malomi, who had to look up to make eye contact. Then, Jessamyn understood why she'd been able to discern Malomi's expressions across the length of the chamber when everyone else's faces were barely visible. Her eyes were out of proportion to the rest of her features, gleaming black disks above a dot of a nose and a bow of a mouth. She looked like one of those sentimental paintings of cute children and clowns.

Except she wasn't cute. The enormous eyes again read her captive's thoughts and ceased twinkling as if the electricity had been cut. "My, you are quite large."

It was perhaps the one statement that made Jessamyn feel self-conscious. She shuffled in place.

"And your friend?"

"I don't know who you're talking about."

"The one who stole my boat."

"It's not your boat. It's Timothy's and—" She stopped abruptly.

Malomi's lips twitched. It wasn't a smile but the mean-spirited grimace of someone watching a trap spring. "Everything down here is mine. Everything and everyone. You who break into my home. You who steal my boat. You!" she called as she lifted her miniature feet straight out in the air, looking more like a doll than ever.

Immediately, You bent over and crawled forward until the pudgy calves rested on his back.

She spoke again to Jessamyn. "If you wished to keep your toy, you never should have brought it into my house. You are a foolish

**165**

girl who's gotten herself into more trouble than she can handle. You and your brave little friend . . . Timmy."

"You'll never catch him, and he'll—"

"Come back to rescue you? Well, it is nice to know that dreams still exist up top, but they don't exist in Undertown, my child," the doll declared.

"It was an accident."

"Accident-on-purpose?"

True enough, but how could Malomi know? Jessamyn's mind spun in search of an answer. Briefly, she feared that Timothy had also been captured and told them everything, but then Malomi wouldn't be asking questions. Could the cremblers have captured the police searching for the *X-tra Large*? That, too, was impossible. Maybe they knew what the police were doing by monitoring their communications. Maybe not. In any case, there was no point in lying. "Yes, but I didn't understand the consequences."

"Silly, silly girl. There are always consequences, and then there are always further desires. Now, what do you want?"

So much for pleasantries. Jessamyn replied, "Nothing."

The child queen considered this for a moment. She nodded at a lugubrious, bearded man in a plaid overcoat. He stepped forward and smacked Jessamyn across the cheek.

Jessamyn toppled sideways but halted her fall with a palm flat on the rug. Compared to what she'd seen at the harbor, a slap wasn't so bad.

Blindfolded, she'd been force-marched for maybe fifteen minutes, out of her crevasse, into the great chamber, up the staircase from the cavern, up and down several ramps, left, left again, right, until she had no idea which direction she'd gone. Why? Because they didn't want her to know her location. Because the location mattered.

This room, also spacious though empty of anything besides the throne and rug, was different from the rest of the underground spaces she had seen. It, too, was lit by long strands of tiny bulbs, but there were no catch basins. There wasn't even a possibility of someone in Central Park hearing anyone down here.

"Ahem," coughed the finely attired visitor to the cavern. Jessamyn hadn't noticed him standing motionless against the wall, gray on gray, unperturbed by the furor that interrupted his business. He spoke to Malomi as if nothing unusual had occurred. "I really must be going."

"Of course. My men will escort you out."

"And when shall I expect to receive my purchase?"

"Tomorrow," Malomi declared. "Isn't that correct, Lobo?"

"Absolutely," he replied.

They stood silent for a minute and then the doctor glanced at Jessamyn and asked, "What are you going to do with her?"

"Do you really want to know?"

"No."

Malomi addressed one of the cremblers. "Take him up top."

Jessamyn couldn't help but feel a pang of despair to see Dr. Curator Allan Pym-Gordon leave. He was en route to the world they once shared. That world consisted of the slice of park she'd glimpsed through the sewer grate and the green trees that fed on sunlight. It was a world of shops filled with lovely things, and of movies and museums. It was a world in which her mother woke her for school and dated Tom Murphy and set out for a Sunday sail and a picnic lunch. She was starved.

"Thank God he's gone. I really do not like that man. He's so . . . unsavory."

Jessamyn nodded.

"What do you want?" Malomi repeated.

Jessamyn knew that she would be smacked again if she gave the wrong answer, but she couldn't imagine what other answer Malomi wished to hear. "I mean it, I don't want anything."

Again, Malomi mulled over the response, as if it had been delivered in a foreign language that required translation. She nodded to the crembler, who smacked Jessamyn again. Harder, but it hurt less because she anticipated the blow, a swat to the top of her head.

"What do you want?"

Jessamyn answered before she could think. "Food."

The cremblers tensed with anticipation. Even You, the human footstool, perked up at this announcement. Then Malomi smiled in an entirely different manner and replied, "But of course. How could I have been so rude? You must be starved."

Did this mean *You are hungry, so I will feed you*, or *I must starve you to make you talk*? Jessamyn didn't know.

Malomi lifted her feet off You's back and he scrambled away. Then she gave another order.

To Jessamyn it sounded like "Tablemen." For a moment she expected the rest of the cremblers to arrange themselves in the shape of a human table with human chairs. Instead, they rushed out of the chamber and allowed Jessamyn a few seconds alone with her captor, who reached out—not down, because Malomi was no taller standing than Jessamyn was sitting on the carpet—for her hand.

Again, their eyes met. Jessamyn knew that she was being tested. Given an opportunity to attempt escape, would she take it? No, that was a fool's game. Surely, cremblers were stationed at every exit. Surely, she'd be punished. Also, her request had clearly surprised Malomi, whose bright eyes showed a faint sign of humanity for the first time. She accepted the hand.

# CHAPTER 17

**W**HAT?"

*"Did you . . . ?"*

Officer Mosolino put his hands to his ears and shook his head to show that he couldn't hear anything. Nor could he see much, despite the big lamp mounted on the hood of PB-2 to illuminate the passages. Nor were they helped by the rectangles of light at the catch basins, some about ten feet up, some much higher, depending on the topography.

Officer Reynolds cut the engine. "What did you say?"

"I asked if you heard anything."

"All I heard was noise. Damn, it's loud down here. You think it could be another boat?"

"If it is, it's not a sailboat. Maybe PB-1 is in the vicinity." They swiveled the lamp and looked around, seeing nothing but walls, dark and gleaming. The radio crackled.

Mosolino hit the talk button. "PB-2 reporting. PB-2 . . ."

"We have you, PB-2. What's the score?"

"We are at the site."

"And?" Captain Mullane's voice communicated his eagerness.

"Nothing, sir."

"Nothing?"

"Sorry, it must have been a false report."

If so, it wasn't the first. People as far apart as Pelham Bay in the Bronx and Belle Harbor in Queens claimed to have heard voices emerging from their local sewers. Every dumb one had to be investigated, and more often than not it turned out that the claimants also heard little people in their bathtubs.

Some sightings found the kids together, some apart. There was Timothy working in a pizza place on St. Marks Place and Jessamyn atop a Japanese tour bus on Wall Street. According to one report by a "reputable source," they were playing soccer in the East River Park. And that wasn't counting the old lady who saw them on the Staten Island Ferry.

Still, Walter Mullane attributed greater urgency to the claims of Shelley, the teenager in Central Park. She wasn't too far from the area where Wainwright believed the *X-tra Large* might drift if its two passengers were unconscious.

Oh, they knew a lot more about the two kids by now. They knew that the girl was the smartest kid in Montclair, New Jersey, as well as a three-letter athlete, and the boy an underachiever who essentially lived in fantasy literature.

A police psychiatrist had spoken with the parents, both to calm them and to find out anything that might be helpful. All he had come up with was that they were "bright, inventive kids."

Recalling the shrink, Captain Mullane said, "Remind me to never get mentally ill."

"What's that, sir?" Mosolino asked from PB-2.

"Nothing. Keep searching. What? Wait a second."

Wainwright had made a silent "T for Time" sign with his hands.

The captain addressed the engineer. "You have an idea?"

"I have a hunch."

Mullane smiled. The man was getting the hang of the local vocabulary. "As good as any. What is it?"

Still looking at his maps, Wainwright suggested, "How about we spread the net a bit wider?"

"Where?"

"I'd say a sweep around the park."

"Ten four," Mullane said in agreement. "Did you hear that, PB-2?"

"Loud and clear, sir. We're on it."

And though Reynolds and Mosolino had a sincere desire to find the missing kids, they weren't above enjoying their extraordinary assignment. "My turn," Mosolino said as he choked up the throttle and the small boat roared past the gate camouflaged with stonework. Eyes focused straight ahead, except for the tangents that the *X-tra Large* might have taken, the two subterranean policemen knew what they were looking for and didn't look for anything else.

Gradually the channel widened at the confluence of two sewer streams. The combined flow was swifter and the banks farther apart. It was the beginning of a great loop around the reservoir set amid the park's greenery.

Light travels faster than sound, but light doesn't bend around corners unless there's a black hole nearby. Timothy knew this from his leisure reading. And even though the entire New York sewer system might be considered its own kind of black hole with a perverse magnetism that drew the likes of You and DUO and the awful, demented dwarf Malomi—and maybe, now that he thought about it, two unhappy suburban teenagers—it

171

didn't have the power to alter the laws of the physical universe. He heard the motorboat before he saw the light on its prow.

He did his best to boost his own speed by unfurling the sail to its maximum extent, shifting the boom an inch to the starboard or port every other second to catch every minuscule change in the wind, and taking advantage of the additional width of the channel, but someone was gaining on him. Who else could it be but cremblers? They knew he had the *X-tra Large*. They knew which direction he'd gone. They didn't like it, and they had motors.

Hoping for a turnoff, Timothy prepared for an encounter. His pursuers had the advantage in terms of speed and manpower, but any nautical engagement could be won by a lesser force armed with intelligence and surprise. He considered the pathetic weaponry that lay ready for use on the deck just as a headlight illuminated the raggedy sail of the *X-tra Large*.

"Cripes!" Reynolds shouted over the roar of the police boat. "Thar she blows."

"Eyes on," Mosolino at the wheel replied. "Get a message to the cap."

"PB-2. PB-2. Urgent. Urgent."

Having spoken to the feckless crew less than fifteen minutes earlier, Mullane was in no mood for their kind of fun. But "urgent" meant he had to respond. "Better be good, guys."

Reynolds's first reply was inaudible over the boat's motor.

"What? Speak clearly."

"Sighting, sir." He repeated himself, breaking the word into syllables. "Sight-ing."

Mullane snorted. "Another ghost ship?"

"No, sir. It's got a sail, and it's definitely in motion."

"Sighting!" the captain shouted to the various officers and city representatives poring over sewer diagrams and eating doughnuts in the trailer. "Everyone shut up! Proceed, Reynolds. What's going on?"

"We're closing fast, sir. It's no more than a block away."

"Have they seen you?"

"Can't tell, sir, but they ought to have heard us."

"Go get them, man."

"Yes, sir." Mosolino revved the throttle as high as it would go until PB-2 came within hailing distance of the young teenager visibly piloting the *X-tra Large*.

And the PB was obviously visible to the kid. Occasionally, he glanced back and then tightened the sail, almost ostentatiously ignoring the crass motorboat entering his wake.

Reynolds couldn't help but admire the kid. His boat was beaten to pieces and yet he sailed it along the sewer water as smoothly as an America's Cup contestant. "Pull over. Police!" Reynolds shouted into a bullhorn.

*Police?* Timothy knew there was a municipal boat in the system, but it was too coincidental that it would happen upon him minutes after he'd escaped from the cremblers. The men in the motorboat were indeed wearing some type of uniform, but he couldn't identify it in the dim light. "Prove it," he shouted.

The man with the bullhorn took out a wallet and flashed something. It could have been a badge. It could have been tinfoil.

"C'mon, Timothy!" the man shouted as the motor approached at a wide point in the tunnel. The cremblers didn't know his name. The man looked like someone from topside, too, buff and clean-shaven rather than scrawny and scruffy. Timothy was tempted.

"Where is Jessamyn?" called the officer as PB-2 tailed the sailboat like a road hog on the Jersey Turnpike.

That's when Timothy realized that he still had to escape,

173

because no one would take him seriously. The police would barge into the cremblers' lair and get Jessamyn hurt. Only *he* could free the girl he'd put in harm's way.

"Slow down!"

The policeman was tensing his muscles for a leap onto the deck of the *X-tra Large*. If the boy was going to act, he'd have to do so immediately. But he needed time. Or timing. "All right. Give me a second."

He slackened the sail, and almost immediately the boat lost its windborne impetus.

Unfortunately, the police boat slowed, too.

"Good boy," the policeman behind the wheel called. "Now, make room. I'm coming aboard."

Well, that would not do. It would not do at all. Timothy drew back the sail, and the *X-tra Large* pulled ahead.

Reynolds called in to command, "Suspect not cooperating. We're giving chase," and Mosolino revved up PB-2. *Good.*

Timothy gathered the mass of rope that Jessamyn had coiled during their inventory of the boat's assets and waited until the PB was several feet behind, closing the gap to the *X-tra Large*, to take careful aim and toss the armful of ropes into its path.

Mosolino was enough of a boater to understand exactly what effect the ropes would have and tried to veer away, but the channel hemmed him in, and the ropes slid underneath the hull to the stern like a colony of eels.

One rope was chopped to pieces by the turning blades of the outboard motor, maybe the second one, too, but the third or the fourth or the fifth coil wrapped itself around the engine stem, and the blades froze. Mosolino slammed down the throttle to keep the engine from overheating. Too late. Without airflow, the motor sputtered and choked. A burp of smoke emerged from the water.

PB-2 sat in the channel, incapacitated, amid soggy ropes floating on the surface like noodles in chicken soup.

Once again, the *X-tra Large* was alone, its mast inches below the tunnel's curved ceiling, its sides barely squeezing between banks that again shrank. It was, Timothy thought, a bit like the channel that led from the Albanese Brothers Marina out to sea between stone jetties.

No, it was nothing like that. He was in a sewer, being hunted by police and cremblers. Yet he, too, was on the hunt.

That thought brought the idea of food to mind. In fact, he was so hungry that he experienced weird olfactory hallucinations in which the aroma of butter and garlic and brine and lime was palpable beside the hatchway to the cabin and its empty larder.

He shook his head, knowing that he could do nothing to satisfy his craving except bring the voyage of the *X-tra Large* to an end. There were two ways to accomplish that, and he'd just chosen to eliminate the wiser alternative by eluding the police officers and incidentally destroying police property. He looked back to see the two men with badges standing in the sewer, extracting tangled skeins of rope from their disabled vehicle.

Oh well, add two more strays to the population beneath Manhattan. Unfortunately, these two would surely receive reinforcements and be all the more diligent and far less sympathetic in their subsequent pursuit.

Timothy knew that he had to strategize, but without a morsel in his belly he couldn't focus on anything but the teasing, tormenting, imaginary scent of food. He set course and climbed down the ladder into the cabin.

Everything below the surface was pitch-black, but the igniting gizmo from the lantern was still in his back pocket. He'd shoved it in there after losing the lantern on the Edgecombe rapids.

He lit a candle to search for anything that was left in the pantry—a block of raw ramen, the dregs of a jar of mayonnaise, a packet of duck sauce from take-out Chinese food.

Now he really thought he was losing it, because the olfactory mirage became visual.

Dominating the galley's foldout table were a pair of enormous lobsters, four-pounders by the look of them. One brick-red claw drooped over the side of a platter filled with chips of ice, as if the creature was considering escape. And that wasn't all. The lobsters were surrounded by heaps of clams and mussels and shrimp and calamari and every other kind of seafood imaginable. Magically, a cornucopia had been delivered, complete with silverware and bottles of fancy Italian sparkling water.

He didn't know what else to do but what he'd seen in movies; he rubbed his eyes. The food remained. But if he wasn't crazy, then who had brought the feast? And where were they? He started, and yet there was absolute silence. He was the only guest at the festive table.

Tentatively, he took one of the pink-and-white-striped shrimp and was about to lower it into his mouth when he caught a glimpse of a single pat of butter that ought to have gone with a slice of bread and noticed an impression, difficult to read in the faint light from above. Finally, he was able to discern the calligraphy. It read *Les Tuileries.*

The cremblers must have stopped at some Upper East Side restaurant after Timothy and Jessamyn lost sight of the *X-tra Large.* No, he could hardly imagine You ordering a seafood feast to go from a restaurant fancy enough to emboss its own butter. And yet the food was real.

Finders, keepers. Finders, eaters.

And yet, despite the bounty spread before him, he felt sad. He thought of his father, surely worried, and Jessamyn's mother, surely frantic. But then he imagined them cuddling on the big leather couch by the slate fireplace in the Murphy living room in Montclair. He could almost hear Miranda's soft voice cooing, "At last, they're gone."

"Yes," Tom Murphy said. "And we're alone."

No, he wasn't giving them credit. He was the only one who was alone, and he had no idea how he was going to rescue Jessamyn. He didn't know if he could even find her in the underground labyrinth. He took the great tray of food up to the deck, where he was about to heave it overboard in a statement of ultimate surrender, when a voice came out of the darkness. "I wouldn't do that if I was you."

He'd heard that voice before and his belly must have known something that his brain couldn't register, because he felt a sensation of warmth or comfort. And the comfort turned to instant joy once he saw on the tunnel wall a great mural of a gleaming plate crossed by a heavy silver knife and fork, like a medieval coat of arms identifying the owner. "DUO!"

"Hey, man," said the young artist, sitting on the ledge under the mural, backpack on his shoulders, can of spray paint in his hand. "I hope you're not planning to get rid of that. Lobster's a lot better than potato chips. Least as I've heard, though I've never had the pleasure."

Timothy positively bubbled. "Great to see you."

"So, you planning to invite me up for a taste?"

Timothy grinned. *"Mi casa es su casa."*

"Well, then . . ." DUO quickly sprayed his name under the still-wet mural and stepped on board.

"Have a shrimp?" Timothy held out the platter.

"Soon, but I'd recommend putting a little mileage on this vehicle. Bad guys behind."

*"What?"*

"Don't overreact. You left 'em walking in chest-high water. We just need to get out of this channel. So take a left at the corner."

While DUO directed and Timothy steered, the artist explained the layout of the place.

"See, the channels are straightening, so we're out of Central Park and into the grid. That's good news and bad news."

"Tell me the bad news." It was Timothy's nature to confront evil tidings first. Yet before he heard them, he wondered if Jessamyn was a good-news-first kind of girl.

DUO said, "Well, anyone who's on our tail can see us."

Yep, that was bad all right. "What's the good news?"

"Cops too far back to catch up with us on foot. And if another boat is coming, you'll hear it before it appears. You can totally lose them if you hightail it out of here."

"But I've got to stay near Jessamyn."

DUO grew serious. "I was afraid to ask. Where is she?"

"They caught her when we tried to steal back the *Xtra-Large*."

"Say no more. I figured that's why you didn't want to get the fuzz involved."

"'Figured?' I thought you knew everything."

"Malomi's estate doesn't have a crawl space, so I can't tell what's happening there except for when I sneak in to do a wall. But the little lady's never met anyone like Jessamyn. I doubt she's going to act in haste."

"So I've got to get back there."

"Not with a hundred cremblers crawling over the place, you don't."

"And half of them are after me. I need a plan."

"They don't have speed boats like the cops, and if they're searching, most are on foot, so still way back there in the maze." DUO pondered the dilemma. "About a plan. You know, I think a lot better with a full belly. Is that a lobster?"

Henry VIII never had such a feast. Timothy and DUO cracked the big claws with the all-purpose hammer from the tool chest and pried out the flesh with a screwdriver. They slid tiny clams from their half shells. They tore the bulk of shrimps from their translucent casings. By the end of the meal, they were so giddy that they tossed calamari rings across the deck to see if they could catch them in their mouths like seals in the Central Park Zoo. When neither could eat another bite, Timothy carefully placed the leftover food into plastic bags to keep its smell from luring rodents and put the utensils back in the galley closet next to the igniter, where they belonged. He could almost hear his father saying with approval, "Everything in its place." That reminded him of something tickling at the back of his brain. "Say, DUO, how'd you know where I was?"

"Hang out here long enough, you know everything."

"But it's so big. How do you get around?"

"I swim."

"Nooo!"

"Of course not. I surf."

"Really?"

DUO opened the backpack that Timothy had assumed carried painting supplies, which it did, along with one other item the boy removed: a curved sheet of bright red plastic with four small wheels mounted on the bottom. "Least I got my own board. The top of the tunnel beats those half-pipes in the park any day."

That was the moment Timothy realized that his fate—and Jessamyn's—was in the hands of the solitary boy with the dual iden-tity. He knew approximately how far behind he had left the PB-2 and how much farther behind them Jessamyn had been captured by the cremblers. What he really needed to know, however, was what to do now. Fortunately, he had a mate who knew the lay of the land better than all the cremblers, the scary petite queen, and the cops combined. "So . . . you mentioned a plan?"

The boy who typically thought in color and form more than in ideas or information jumped up. "Two birds, one stone. You just have to make everyone who's after you think you're someplace else. Then you backtrack and rescue your damsel in distress."

"I wouldn't let her hear you say that! And you'll help me?"

DUO paused.

"Right?"

DUO looked worried, and despite their previous camaraderie he took on a suspicious air. "Why should I?"

Timothy considered the question. There were several possible answers. First, he was bigger than DUO and could threaten him. Second, he could beg. Either alternative might have worked up top, but the boy knew every inch of the sewer and could easily slip away.

Timothy could try to get DUO excited about the adventure. Unfortunately, he'd already had too much adventure and couldn't muster the necessary enthusiasm. Then there was the solidarity card. DUO obviously didn't have much use for Malomi and the cremblers; as enemies of the same enemies, the boys were natural allies.

Timothy opened his mouth and said, "Because I like your work."

DUO blushed, his deep-brown cheeks turning browner. "I don't like getting mixed up with them."

"Neither do I."

"But you're leaving. You won't ever have to see them again."

Timothy nodded. "That's true."

"If they find out I helped you, they'll go ape."

"True again."

"So you see, there's really only one thing to do."

"Which is . . . ?" Timothy waited for the final negative.

From far away came the putter of a single outboard motor. DUO jumped to his feet and declared, "Time to sail."

"Where?"

"Anywhere. But you're gonna have to do it yourself. It's time for me to leave."

"Why?" Timothy nearly moaned. But it was an unfair question. He couldn't ask anyone else to share this horrendous situation.

But DUO wasn't abandoning ship because he was afraid. As far as he was concerned, Timothy had asked an honest question and deserved an honest answer. "Homework."

"But . . ." Timothy wanted to scream. There were thieves and kidnappers. How could DUO be worried about homework at such a time?

"My mom doesn't care for excuses," DUO told him, answering the unasked question.

Timothy remembered what DUO had said earlier. "So where should I make everyone think I am?"

"If you need help with that, then we both have problems. That's the easy part. Now, thanks for the grub, and how about you let me out over there?" He gestured to a nearby ledge.

Timothy pulled the X-tra Large to the side of the channel, and DUO hopped off. "See you later, alligator."

"Bye," Timothy said sadly.

"Hey, don't be so doleful . . . Jake."

# CHAPTER 18

HAT DO YOU MEAN, THEY GOT AWAY?"

"Strictly speaking, *he*, sir."

It took a second for Captain Mullane to absorb this information. "Are you telling me that the girl wasn't with him?"

"I'm saying that I did not see her, sir. Maybe she was below-decks, but the boy was operating the boat by himself."

*Belowdecks.* Since when did New York City police officers speak in nautical lingo? The man practically ended his sentence with an *Aye, aye.* "And he got away?"

"Yes, sir."

"You're telling me that a kid on a sailboat managed to elude two police officers in a motorboat? Or should I say *former* officers about to become beat patrolmen who can't be trusted with a *scooter*?"

"He disabled the PB, sir."

"I'm getting impatient."

"He threw ropes into the blades. They got caught in the motor. It burned out."

"What is he, the Jack Sparrow of the sewer?"

Mosolino didn't have an answer. Neither did Reynolds.

"I'm putting Officer Bosco on the line. Give him your precise location and then come in. We'll see if we can find someone else who can handle a thirteen-year-old."

"Yes, sir. But there's one thing, sir."

"What now?"

"Since the boat doesn't work, we . . . um . . . I don't know how we can come in."

"I do."

"Yes, sir?"

"Walk, Mosolino. Swim, Reynolds. Do the doggy paddle. Just watch out for the crocodiles." Mullane threw down his walkie-talkie and looked at the crowd outside the trailer. It had grown. Broadcasting vans from the networks joined the local journalists covering the story as the lost children became national news. A crew of foreign reporters following a soccer star from São Paulo took advantage of their presence to show their Brazilian audience the dangers of New York. A Facebook page was set up for *Subterranean Homesick News.*

The only good thing to happen all afternoon was that the captain finally managed to get the children's parents out of the way, into a hotel near Times Square where the city regularly rented rooms for sequestered jurors. Tom and Miranda hadn't wanted to leave, but Mullane insisted that they needed a rest. He swore that he'd contact them the moment he received any further information.

Alone now with the city engineer, he asked, "What's up, Doc?"

Cass Wainwright was sarcasm-proof. His finger moved apparently of its own volition—like the marker of a Ouija board—across one of his maps. "Obviously, the boy has managed to use both the

183

currents and whatever winds are in the system to maneuver the boat."

"Yeah?"

"That means that he should be able to travel anywhere the tunnels are wide enough and tall enough to accommodate him."

Again, the captain said, "Yeah?"

"So, he might have a destination."

"And what do you think that may be?"

The engineer shrugged. "I suppose it depends on what he wants."

The man was a genius, which, as far as the captain, who'd put his share of geniuses in jail, was concerned, meant exactly nothing.

# CHAPTER
## 19

**ALONE, TIMOTHY STEERED THE** *X-TRA LARGE* straight on for hours, mulling over the plan he'd started thinking about the moment DUO had left. The sounds of the outboard motor had long since puttered out. He continued until dusk arrived in the New York City sewer system. Instead of life-nourishing sun filtering down from the catch basins, the tunnel was lit, to the extent it ever was, by the glare of artificial lighting above. Also, the city was louder than it had been under Central Park. Timothy heard car horns and the squeal of brakes and the hum of communal humanity.

He pulled in the sail and grabbed a metal hook protruding from the stone wall next to some sort of cable box, to halt the boat's forward motion. About ten feet directly above him was a catch basin. Perfect.

He examined the box of tools he'd last used as eating utensils, then went back down the three steps to enter the head that was just big enough for a toilet and a small sink with a mirrored medicine cabinet. Again, perfect.

Back on deck, he took a roll of duct tape from the box and secured one thin section of broken mast to another to a third. Each was about four feet long, so together they overlapped the front and rear of the Herreshoff 12½ like an enormous pool cue. Then he took a wrench from the toolbox and returned to the bathroom.

He peered at himself in the mirror, an act he'd always avoided when brushing his teeth in the bathroom at home in Montclair. There, he'd fretted that he was too short, his shoulders too thin, his expression fearful. Here, the image was a far cry from anything he'd seen before.

To begin with, he was utterly filthy, hair matted, grime covering nearly every inch of his skin. Likewise, his clothing was stained and torn. And that was only the surface.

The expression that met him was calm and set, the eyes no longer those of a typical suburban boy who hadn't been able to do anything but cry when his mother died several years earlier. *Yeah,* they seemed to declare. *I'm here. You got a problem with that?* They were the eyes of a Jake.

Meeting Jake's look straight on, Timothy wrapped his left fist in a bath towel and pressed it to the corner of the mirror while his right hand picked up the wrench and smashed the exposed glass with a single sharp rap on the nose.

Most of the mirror clattered into the bowl of the sink, but the section behind Timothy's toweled hand remained in place. Carefully, he extracted two shards of glass from the frame, each about six or eight inches square. Then he brought the mini mirrors to the deck, rubbed them clean with toilet paper, and attached them to the end of the spar with duct tape, keeping as much silvery glass exposed as possible. One mirror aimed upward, the other down.

Who said geometry was mysterious? Timothy lifted the long spar toward the catch basin and adjusted the angles of the mirrors so that the topmost glass reflected the bottom, which reflected upward. He felt like a U-boat commander scanning the ocean with his periscope.

Shoes, he was seeing lots of shoes. He twirled the rod in his hand and the mirrors swiveled on their wooden axis.

Cars, lots of cars. Bright yellow taxis and a bus with wheels that looked as large as planets.

He was on an avenue, not a street; that's where most buses cruised. He turned the mirrors again and saw a hydrant, two parking meters, and a doorman in a braided uniform reading a newspaper.

Too bad he couldn't read the not-so-fine print, because he was fairly certain that he'd find his own name. He'd also learn what the police knew about his and Jessamyn's whereabouts.

He spun the axis once more, but the slightest wobble made it difficult to get a clear image. He had to hold the heavy periscope absolutely still, shifting it no more than a quarter of an inch. The effect multiplied along the length to the mirrors, one of which had loosened when it hit the bottom of the basin. There, atop a steel pole on the corner, were two rectangular signs. One read "5 AV," the other "E 68 ST."

The Upper East Side, traditionally New York's toniest neighborhood, is also one of the city's largest, stretching approximately two hundred square blocks from 59th Street to 96th Street, and from Fifth Avenue to the East River. It has as many great institutions as most international capitals: the Metropolitan Museum of Art and Mount Sinai Hospital as well as the Whitney and Guggenheim museums and Cornell Medical Center and a slew of other medical facilities and cultural repositories. Attached to these, thriving in their shadow, are scores of private galleries and thousands of individual doctors' offices. Bloomingdale's department store anchors the southern border, but there are innumerable other places to shop, from Barneys to boutiques selling men's clothes or women's wear. There are bridal salons, and children's clothing stores where the navy blazer with brass buttons a lad of the carriage district will outgrow in a year costs more than a businessman's suit. Of course there are food stores and bookstores and hardware stores and newsstands and every form of specialized commerce necessary to serve the area's fifty thousand or so residents.

The people vary, too, but even though hundreds of student nurses live near the hospitals and taxi drivers of every ethnicity on earth inhabit fifth-floor walk-ups off York Avenue and senior citizens rely on Social Security, the Upper East Side is best known for the elegant co-ops along Fifth and Park Avenues, built primarily between the First and Second World Wars.

At 1040 Fifth Avenue, seventeen stories of symmetrical limestone designed by Rosario Candela, the preferred architect of the American aristocracy, are twenty-seven units that currently cost a cool eight figures each—and please don't even consider a mortgage, since the board frowns upon the vulgarity of debt. Shifts of doormen protect the building's entrance twenty-four hours a day. It is occupied primarily by New York's anonymous wealthy: bankers and real estate moguls and heirs to fortunes, who call themselves "investors." It was also home to one of the most famous women of the latter half of the twentieth century, Jacqueline Kennedy Onassis, who moved in after the assassination of her first husband in 1963 and lived there until her death in 1994. Jackie's former home on the fifteenth floor overlooks the park and the reservoir posthumously named for her.

Suburbanites aren't familiar with every inch of the city, but Timothy Murphy had a keen sense of Manhattan geography. He brought down his jerry-rigged periscope, carefully laid it lengthwise along the deck, and let the current carry him downtown. The street was busy enough, but his plan required a crowd. Also, he still needed to put more distance between himself and the cremblers. He knew precisely where to go.

Fifth Avenue took him straight down past the Pierre and Plaza hotels and Tiffany's and Rockefeller Center to the big public library at 42nd Street, where two noble marble lions guarded the entrance. He turned right, starboard, westward—the three directions he thought of simultaneously, like someone who speaks multiple languages.

The roar of a subway beyond a shared wall reminded him of DUO's mural. There was no graffiti down here. Less access? Less ambition? But just as the subway tunnels split and joined, merged and diverged, so the sewer lines had to accommodate them, as well as the up-top scissoring of Seventh Avenue and Broadway that created Times Square.

Fortunately, the triangle gave the captain of the *X-tra Large* room to make the seafaring equivalent of a three-point turn, so that he could amscray from the Crossroads of the World as soon as he'd completed his mission. First things first, he hammered a nail from the toolbox into the tip of his twelve-foot-long periscope. Then he bent the nail into a hook with a pair of pliers. He made his final preparations and lifted up the duct-taped mast topped by the opposing mirrors along with one more item draped over the hook: an uninflated, pancake-flat, bright-orange life vest with *X-tra Large* stenciled across the back.

He thought of what Jessamyn might have said: "It's not as if we're going to drown in two feet of water." Precisely. That's why the vest was expendable in the service of a greater goal. Still, the timing of its delivery had to be impeccable or it might get lost in the crush of pedestrian traffic.

An eddy of paper scraps signaled the beginning of what sailors called "weather" above. Timothy would not have been pleased if he'd been out on the waves. Nor was he pleased below the earth. If it was about to rain, people were less likely to linger. If they were in a hurry, they might miss his message. But there was no point in worrying about things you couldn't change.

Delicately, he used the tip of the mast to poke and nudge the rubbery vest through the bars in the grate at the corner of 45th and Broadway. So there was an orange plastic obstruction in a gutter in the center of the center of the world. It didn't merit a second glance. People saw more remarkable things in Times Square every day.

No problem. With the help of his trusty mirrors, Timothy inserted the hook of the nail into the tab of the vest while keeping an eye on pedestrian traffic.

The aim was to put evidence of the *X-tra Large*'s presence into the hands of the police at a point on the grid that would deflect them from the area in Central Park where Jessamyn was actually being held. Furthermore, he assumed that the cremblers would follow the police, getting them off his back, too. How much time this would buy him, he wasn't sure, but he needed every minute.

Sneakers, Doc Martens, and flip-flops walked on by. They didn't interest him. Nor did saddle shoes or red high heels, though the red fishnet stockings that accompanied the stilettos might have merited a second glance. *Summer in the city,* Timothy thought. Everyone was at play, except for him and a pair of clunky black leather shoes.

He nearly pulled the hook, but above the shoes were a pair of distinctly civilian argyle socks.

And above, to the east, sharing the Square with theaters and burnished-glass office towers covered with dozens of brilliantly illuminated neon and LCD signs, was a quaint four-story building, once upon a time l. Miller's Show Folks Shoe Shop with its fabulous logo, Dedicated to Beauty in Footwear, spelled BEAVTY in the limestone frieze etched in the 1920s. Below the motto were niches with statues of famous performers of the era, including Ethel Barrymore (as Ophelia) and Mary Pickford (as Little Lord Fauntleroy), by Alexander Stirling Calder, father of the better-known abstract sculptor whose daughter's husband operated the downtown Manhattan Scientology franchise during the 1980s. Oh, and Andy Warhol used to do illustrations for the store's catalog. Oops! The ladies' statues were now hidden by a sign for a franchise burger joint opening on the first floor.

Timothy remained in place, eyes glued to the mirror, waiting, wondering if the time he was wasting would equal the time he hoped to gain. Finally, he saw the right shoe, the right deep-blue pants leg, the regulation thin black hose, and, for a moment, a glimpse of a leather holster.

Either one of New York's Finest was standing directly above him or someone was going to a costume party dressed as a policeman. Timothy yanked the mast down and the nail pulled the tab marked INFLATE on the life vest, which immediately blew up, obscuring his view from below while grabbing attention above.

"Hey!" someone called.

"What's that?"

Even with the fully inflated orange vest blocking Timothy's view, he could tell that a crowd was gathering.

"Step back," ordered a voice that most likely belonged to the black shoe and holster.

"What's going on?" someone asked.

"Is anyone down there?"

Mission accomplished, Timothy Murphy pulled the sail taut, shifted the boom, and felt the *X-tra Large* set off against the wind.

# CHAPTER
# 20

**J**ESSAMYN WALKED BETWEEN THE FILTHY, MISSHAPEN homeless men who flanked the entrance to the chamber like guards at a royal palace. Some of them, like You, trembled at the sight of Malomi, while others, like Lobo, were stiff, emotionless automatons whose last home had probably been a jail cell. Bingo! She remembered You's conflation of her name and Timothy's to form "Jessathy." In his mind, the tremblers and the criminals together formed "cremblers." They were the two castes of a unique underground species, like drones and workers in a queen bee's hive.

They led her to another chamber with a baronial, mahogany table—why didn't anyone ever call such furniture dukish or earlesque?—lit by a dozen tapering candles on a silvery candelabra. When Malomi commanded "Tablemen," she actually meant "Set the table, men!"

The power Her Tiny Highness wielded over her subjects was absolute. And yet the girl/woman—even up close, Jessamyn couldn't tell if she was a child or a very small adult—ought to have been playing in a yard with a dog instead of training rats in the sewer. She ought to have siblings instead of servants. In fact, Jessamyn ought to have had siblings, too, but that future had been foreclosed when her father took a wrong turn onto a one-way street.

Jessamyn was a prisoner, but she pitied her warden. She looked around. Everything about the hewn-rock chambers, the silver and crystal, was ancient. The only thing that was new under the earth was the *X-tra Large*.

"A very attractive vessel," Malomi said as she nodded to an attendant to pour a syrupy red liquid over ice into a couple of goblets.

The queen at one end of the table then lifted her glass in a toast toward the large girl seated at the other end. "We don't get many visitors down here and we never get females. To your company," she declared.

Jessamyn nodded politely and took a sip, and nearly choked because it was so sweet.

"Good?" Malomi asked.

"Mmph, I mean *mmm*, very," Jessamyn replied.

"We get it from a special kosher place on the Lower East Side."

The dinner arrived moments later, and it was as fine as the liquid goop was awful: strips of carpaccio, "from an Italian deli in Chelsea," Malomi said, and a large, rare roast beef, "from Lobel's" she informed her guest without further identifying the fanciest butcher in town.

Jessamyn was ravenous and took the information in stride as long as the food itself—all meat, no starch, no vegetables—kept coming.

"More?" Malomi asked with the pleasure of a host who sees that her guest is satisfied.

"Please."

Malomi nodded to the server to cut another slice off the roast with a long, gleaming knife. "Zai-chin, available only at Zabar's. They made samurai swords for six hundred years and recently went into the domestic market. Do you like to shop?"

In fact, Jessamyn didn't particularly enjoy shopping. On the infrequent occasions when she was invited to accompany other girls on an expedition—*odd word*, she thought, *as if they were trekking the Himalayas*—to a winter sale, she tended to bow out with a vague excuse. Eventually, people stopped asking. It was one of the things—along with her brains and her height—that separated her from the other ninth-graders in Montclair. Now, however, it was clearly best to placate Malomi, who was so proud of her purchases. "Oh, yes," she enthused.

"Where?"

"Well, um, the Willowbrook Mall."

"What's it like?"

"Like every other mall, I suppose."

"I've never been to a mall."

Although Jessamyn eschewed the pleasures of her tribe, she was astonished to hear anyone say that they'd never had such a basic human experience. "Then where did you get all this?" She gestured to the array of consumer items laid out on the table, most of which had white price stickers attached. Even the great table had a tag dangling below its lacquered surface.

"Stores, I suppose. They have them up above."

She *supposed*?

"Tell me about the mall."

For a second, Jessamyn wasn't sure if she was the object of a curious joke, but Malomi's eyes shone with eagerness. "It's a huge shopping center with about a hundred stores. There are big department stores at the ends and small boutiques in between. You usually enter through the big stores, from the parking lot."

"You have a car?"

"No, I'm too young."

"Too young?"

"I'm only fourteen."

"Hmm."

"Do you have a car?"

"No, because I don't have any streets, but I once *sold* a car. Of course, that's the business I'm in."

"Selling cars?" Jessamyn asked, though Malomi had said "once."

"Selling things, like . . ." She gestured to the table and its settings and the trays of food. "These."

Now Jessamyn was fascinated. "To who?"

"Whoever wants to buy them."

Jessamyn couldn't help asking the unpleasant if obvious question. "Here?"

"Where else?" Malomi replied with utter sincerity.

Jessamyn remembered the groups of men checking inventory lists against crates at the informal loading docks. The light went on over her head and she gasped. "Are these things stolen?"

For the first time, Malomi acted like a kid. She emitted a cartoonish tee-hee giggle. "Of course they are."

"But . . ."

"How do I obtain the merchandise?" Malomi provided the unspoken question.

"Yes." Jessamyn's curiosity got the best of her.

"Look around you."

At the end of the dining room, another subterranean canal gurgled under the arched ceiling strung with pipes and cables, one of which was patched into the room's wiring.

Malomi was enjoying the kind of game she seldom had a chance to play. She offered another hint. "How did you get here?"

Jessamyn made a hesitant guess. "Water?"

Malomi nodded like a teacher to a bright student. "Precisely. Every building needs water and needs to get rid of water. The up-tops think it's magic. They never question where the utilities they rely on come from. It all connects here in Undertown. Up top there's Uptown and Downtown and Midtown. But Undertown is as big as all of them put together, and there's a path into every building in the city. You just have to find where the building is and then probe for the soft spot between the service connection and the basement. That's where we get food and knives and dishes and whatever they have above. Once, we got a Ferrari from the basement of a garage. Of course, we had to take it apart first, but it's not much harder than a Lego set. We have one of those, too, a great big castle with a thousand pieces from FAO Schwarz."

"And you've never . . . ?"

"Gotten caught? Not by the up-tops. They always look up top. Sometimes we assist them by leaving a misleading clue, like breaking a lock or cutting a hole in the ceiling. That way, the police will suspect the sky instead of the water. No, I guess we've never gotten caught . . . until now."

Jessamyn gulped.

"But you wouldn't tell anyone, would you?" Again, Malomi's eyes took on a shellacked gloss that was impossible to read.

"Of course not."

"And you wouldn't even know where you were. Would you?"

"Not the faintest idea."

"And besides, no one would believe you anyway."

"I'm just a kid with a vivid imagination."

"Dessert?"

Again, the way Malomi changed subjects in a heartbeat left Jessamyn uneasy. But she was pretty certain that she was being offered something sweet, and remembered her manners. "Yes, please."

A nod from Malomi sent her minions dashing off into some kitchen off the cavern within the underground realm to fetch their mistress and her guest an enormous tiered chocolate cake set on a Steuben crystal cake platter bearing a price tag in the low four figures.

Jessamyn's eyes rose.

Malomi shrugged. "Fifth Avenue's the easiest. They can't believe that anyone would dare steal from them, so they attribute any losses to inventory errors. The cost of doing business."

While Malomi continued to explain her modus operandi, Jessamyn looked at words iced in pink onto the cake's topmost plateau. *Happy 20th Anniversary, Karen & Michael.*

Malomi shrugged and said, "Sometimes you get whatever you can," and cut the cake.

It was about the most delicious confection Jessamyn had ever eaten, a crisp outer layer of shaved chocolate barely hiding a cherry cream center. "Oh, my," she exclaimed.

"Good?" The hostess was happy that she'd pleased her guest.

"Oh, yes. It's delicious."

"I sent out for it. While we were eating dinner. It's a little tricky to get into the back room of Greenberg's while they're open, but this is a special occasion."

Indeed it was, and Jessamyn perceived the nature of the occasion. Not exactly a tea party among friends. She was the prisoner of a dangerous, potentially lethal adversary who showed no mercy.

Actually, the situation was worse than that, because Malomi had no mercy to show. It was a quality that a supreme monarch had no reason to learn. Jessamyn had to kill time—the expression in her

197

mind gave her a jolt—while waiting for the police to rescue her. She tried to make conversation. "Soooo . . . how did you get here?"

Rather than answer, Malomi stood abruptly. Jessamyn half-expected her to snap, "Off with her head." Instead, she announced, "Time to feed the babies."

Jessamyn remembered the babies, and wondered whether it would have been better to have her head cut off.

"This way." Malomi ushered her into a procession led and followed by pairs of cremblers carrying lit torches that gave the underground passageways out of sight of the blessed catch basins a darker, more medieval atmosphere than the sewer. Obviously, the queen had decided during dinner that there was no longer a need to blindfold her guest, but there were so many turns in the labyrinth that Jessamyn wouldn't have been able to find her way around without a map. Still, she did her best to impress minor landmarks in her head: a rusted telephone box that must have been used in the 1940s, a former doorway where bricks were laid directly atop each other rather than staggered.

The earth beneath Central Park was different from land in the rest of the city. Elsewhere, foundations were dug for residential and commercial structures; and the miles running below avenues were reserved for trains and sewers until newer utilities from telephone to cable to fiber-optic lines became necessary for civilized urban life. Beneath the park was barely tamed.

Olmsted and Vaux's masterpiece included the only lakes and open watercourses on Manhattan Island. They required a unique drainage system that either compelled or allowed for the honeycomb that the cremblers claimed as their own.

In fact, the harbor was closer to Malomi's private quarters than Jessamyn imagined. Escorted by the guards, she rounded a corner into the vast arena, where torches were snuffed in a red pail filled with sand (stolen from PS 138 on 128th Street) and set into a rack on the wall. As before, the space was a hive of activity. The men she'd seen earlier were gone, but a new crew was loading about a dozen large rectangular boxes into another boat.

"July Fourth," Malomi explained. "Whenever there's a big holiday coming up, people's minds turn to television. Personally, I think it's all rot, but what do I know?"

It was a rhetorical question, so Jessamyn didn't answer but merely watched the transaction. The man accepting the boxes from the cremblers was muscular and wore a T-shirt. A large T-shirt. Extra-large. That evoked her former vessel and Timothy. Whatever happened to her, she hoped that he would be OK.

Then the extra-large man took a wad of bills out of his pocket and handed it to a surprisingly young and well-dressed crembler whom Jessamyn hadn't seen before. At least he was comparatively well-dressed, in a frayed three-piece suit. It struck Jessamyn as odd that the cremblers didn't bother to steal new clothes. Then again, she considered her own begrimed shorts. Maybe the suit had been new, straight from Brooks Brothers' basement, two days ago.

"Ivan is my comptroller," Malomi said, continuing her tour. "He collects all our money. His parents brought him here from Russia about seven years ago, but he couldn't make it up top because he never wished to leave Communism. That's why he joined us."

"And . . ."

"Believe me, the only one you can trust with money is someone who thinks it's filthy. Besides," she whispered in a mock aside, "he knows what would happen to him if he tried anything tricky. Let's feed the babies."

Of course, Jessamyn knew where the island rats were kept caged. After all, she'd released them to abet her aborted escape.

"Shh," Malomi whispered for real this time. "They're sleeping.

Usually they don't sleep until after dinner, but they've had unexpected . . . exercise. Tsk-tsk. Naughty girl."

If Jessamyn hadn't been frightened out of her wits, she might have let loose with a healthy "Awww." The rats lay curled into each other's bellies like kittens. One of them pawed in his sleep, dreaming perhaps of his mother. The cuteness wasn't helped, however, by a slick coating of rat poop that covered the floor of the cage. Cleanliness was not a virtue here.

Malomi lifted her heel and stepped down smartly. At the click, the rats awoke and scrambled to right themselves. One hurled itself at the metal cage, bounced back, and charged forward again. Drool flowed over its coarse pink lips.

"Would you like to feed them?" Malomi asked.

Jessamyn didn't dare refuse what was apparently quite an honor. She could tell because the skells had been shouldering each other for the opportunity. "Sure," she said.

"You." She pointed to an elderly vagrant who wasn't You. "Give it to her."

Resentfully, he handed over a sagging black plastic garbage bag.

"There's the feeding slot." Malomi tapped the chicken wire near a mail-size opening about four feet off the ground.

The rats leapt toward the slot and tumbled back over each other and leapt again in their eagerness.

Jessamyn reached into the bag, and instantly recoiled when her fingers came into contact with some sort of cold and slimy flesh.

"Go on," Malomi said. "They're quite hungry."

Jessamyn's hand felt like it was wriggling among dead worms. Intestines? Timothy's intestines? They had found him, caught him, killed him, and were going to make her feed him to the awful rats gnashing their teeth and salivating. And surely she was next. The feast Malomi had provided in the dining hall was a condemned person's last meal. But she wouldn't go quietly. No one who aspired to the name of Kat would ever go quietly. If poor, lost Timothy was in the loathsome bag, she'd strangle the lousy little queen before anyone could stop her. Steeling herself, she plunged her hand into the bag of flesh, grabbed the first thing she could, and brought out . . .

A fish?

She looked at the thing in her hand. It was an uncut slab of smoked salmon.

"If you don't toss that in soon, they're going to gnaw through the cage and get it themselves."

Jessamyn didn't know how long she'd been staring at the rats or the fish. She felt as if she had been roused from a heavy sleep. Unfortunately, it wasn't her mother who'd woken her. Today wasn't a school day.

"Oh, right." She wedged the salmon into the slot until it flopped over the edge and dropped into the cage. One rat grabbed it and another bit into the first rat's back. A third rat squirmed between the first rat's legs to rip out a chunk of the fish flesh from below. Jessamyn slid more pieces of fish into the slot as fast as she could pull them from the garbage bag. Some were red and some bone white, some skinned and some with heads with glassy eyes staring at her in mute recrimination.

Finally, the bag was empty and her hand and arm were as slick with fluid as if she'd inserted them into a tub of oil.

None of the mass of flesh she'd given to the rats was visible. It had all been devoured as swiftly as it was delivered. The creatures settled down, their little tongues cleaning their paws.

Jessamyn looked at Malomi and asked a single-word question. "Fish?"

"We get it from Russ and Daughters on Houston Street, the best in the city."

Though nothing in this bizarre world ought to have surprised her, Jessamyn still couldn't grasp the reasoning for anything.

Malomi continued. "Personally, I hate the stuff. Anything that comes out of the water gives me the creeps. Won't touch it. But the babies can't get enough. Sometimes the skells steal it from local restaurants when they think I won't find out." She shrugged and started to say something else when another boat arrived and another crembler with a thick mat of beard and straggly hair that covered his forehead approached her with an apparently urgent message.

"Yes?" she said to him.

He looked at Jessamyn suspiciously and leaned down to whisper something in Malomi's tiny ear.

Her eyes brightened, and she said, "Really? So soon?"

"It was easier than we expected. Seems there was another tunnel leading out into the park. To the Needle. We found it while following the line from a fountain. Blocked off, of course, but forgotten. Two sledges and it fell to pieces. It's huge down there. Maybe bigger than under Grand Central."

*Fountain?* Jessamyn thought. *Needle?* What basement could be as big as a train station?

"You found your way inside, all right?"

"The directions were perfect. Everything numbered exactly. Like a Walmart."

Of course, he'd referred to Cleopatra's Needle, the seventy-one-foot-tall Egyptian obelisk that had been brought to New York in 1881 and erected behind the Metropolitan Museum, whose founders and directors and curators and millions of visitors would not appreciate the comparison to Walmart.

"And?" Malomi insisted.

"Row 552—EU—19—T—1808. We had to go past a mile of aisles, but we found it."

"And you took nothing else?"

He raised his hands. "Nothing. Though there was this beautiful—"

"Did you take it?"

"No."

*"No?"*

"I swear."

"Good. It will take them years to discover that anything is missing. Contact Dr. Pym-Gordon immediately. Tell him that the merchandise is here and he can collect it tomorrow at noon. I want to get it off my hands."

"Yes, Malomi."

Malomi turned to Jessamyn. "As you can see, we're branching out. One stupid object will net more than a year's worth of television sets. Even more than the usual shipment of drugs. Ivan won't know what to do with the money." She laughed.

"And what . . . ?" Jessamyn began.

"Yes?"

"What *do* you do with the money?"

"I keep it in case . . ." Malomi's eyes grew misty.

Now Jessamyn prodded her to go on. "Yes?"

"In case the worst thing in the world happens."

"What's that?"

"That I have to leave. And go . . ."

"Up?"

Malomi shuddered. "It's time to sleep."

# CHAPTER

## 21

**E**XHILARATED BY THE SUCCESS OF HIS PLAN TO LEAVE a big fat orange distraction in the single most public spot in the city—also the most complex in terms of underground systems; also the farthest he dared travel from the bizarre cavern in which he'd left Jessamyn—Timothy began to move out. A natural navigator, he had a fairly good sense of where he'd come from: somewhere in Central Park, near the Metropolitan Museum of Art, which must have been the cause of the detour he'd had to take to escape the cremblers and elude the police.

And yet Timothy Murphy's navigational skills weren't quite as honed as he'd thought. Maybe he wasn't as brilliant as Columbus; or, as preferred by Mr. Hayes, MJHS's ponytailed history teacher, Leif Eriksson crossing the Atlantic; or Captain Cook crossing the Pacific (or half of it, until he was eaten in Hawaii); or Magellan circling the globe; or Captain Kirk boldly leading the *Starship Enterprise* where no man had gone before.

Instead, Captain Murphy needed landmarks like the Barnegat Lighthouse and the Manhattan skyline to—horrible word—*timidly* sail precisely where he and his father had sailed before. For nearly two days he'd flattered himself into believing that he was master of the subterranean domain, maintaining the tiller through the Edgecombe rapids, slipping past both cops and robbers. He'd been so clever that he was entirely alone, entirely lost.

How had he gone wrong? Immediately after depositing his life preserver in Times Square, he'd headed straight up Broadway to Columbus Circle, counting catch basins, two per block from 46th to 59th Streets. Then he rounded an arc in which the curvature of the sewer wall was ornamented with a painting of three sailing ships. The ships were the *Niña*, the *Pinta*, and the *Santa María*, the style indubitably DUO's.

For all the young painter's vigorous color swipes—not strokes, because he used a can instead of a brush—there was something literal about his subject matter. Timothy remembered the magnificent subway mural within spitting distance of actual subway tracks, the sly fresco of the looting of Jerusalem inside the den of thieves, and the empty plate awaiting dinner. Unlike the science fiction writers Timothy read, DUO found inspiration in the real. If he drew Columbus, he was in Columbus Circle. Unless this was Genoa.

Why then, fifteen blocks away from the traffic circle, hadn't Timothy encountered any of Central Park's distinctive loops? Why wasn't he anywhere near the home of the cremblers, somewhere in the vicinity of Cleopatra's Needle?

The intersection of Broadway and Amsterdam Avenue at 72nd Street creates two acute triangular islands, like an hourglass. Both provide access to the number 1 local and numbers 2 and 3 express subway lines, but the larger, northern triangle also contains plantings and benches and a statue of the Italian composer Giuseppe

Verdi. An urban oasis set between two major traffic arteries where buses and taxis and trucks and plain-vanilla automobiles cruise past twenty-four hours a day, Verdi Square was a major heroin distribution hub nicknamed Needle Park in the late sixties.

The area had gone a long way down since its pre–World War II heyday. Back then, the Ansonia Hotel, a bulky Beaux-Arts wedding cake of a building, stretching along Broadway from 73rd to 74th Streets, was home to, among others, Enrico Caruso and Babe Ruth, while German-Jewish immigrants sipped mocha in the Café Éclair around the corner on 72nd. By the 1970s, however, the spa in the Ansonia's basement had become the Continental Baths, a gay bathhouse where a zaftig chanteuse named Bette Midler performed.

But New York real estate that falls one day is bound to rise the next. The Ansonia became chic, and several new apartment buildings opened down the block. Values jumped with the thermometer on the palazzo-style Apple Bank for Savings building, a neurotic gauge that stayed relatively accurate into the mid-80s of an August day and then reflected what the citizens really thought, jumping immediately to 103 and refusing to budge until the actual temperature returned to 84.

The area was unfamiliar to Timothy Murphy since it wasn't the locus of theaters or museums or his father's personal history. Yet he could tell that he was underneath a busy intersection because of the multiple catch basins that angled off the standard grid. He could also tell from the tone of the traffic and the sound of pedestrians that he was in a residential neighborhood rather than a park district. The regular hum and rattle of wheels and engines meant that he was near a station for both local and express trains. All this information would have made it easy for him to pinpoint where he was if he only had a map.

Reluctantly, he drew in the sail and parked the *X-tra Large* beside one of the sewer ledges, hoping to figure out where he had gone wrong. He peered both up- and downtown, seeking a clue, like a subwaygoer craning his neck over the edge of a platform.

"Rats," he muttered as he pulled the boom ninety degrees astern and prepared to make a U-turn to retrace his path.

"Rats," he said again, more loudly.

Faintly, the sewer seemed to echo "Rats."

At least he had company. More pointedly, Timothy called out, "Rats to all the . . ." What did he want to curse? "Motorboats."

". . . otorboats," the sewer replied.

Timothy liked that. Once more, he shouted, "Rats to all the hospitals!"

The sewer replied, "When are you going to stop playing games?"

Timothy didn't jump the way he would have forty hours earlier. He'd grown accustomed to the unexpected. He merely scanned the arched ceiling of the tunnel. Half a block north, one light looked different than that coming from the other catch basins. They all pulsed with the pace of the nighttime traffic, but this one held steady. He pushed off the wall with a spear of broken mast and oared about a hundred feet, until he was directly beneath an open hatch. "DUO?" he called. "Hello?"

In response, the cheerful painter's head popped into the opening, backlit by one of his improvised lighting systems. "I'm ba-a-a-ck."

"Homework done?"

"Exhausting. But I had a chance to dig up some information. You are seriously getting around, bro."

Timothy shrugged.

"I mean, the Undertown news is about nothing but the *X-tra*

*Large* and its crew twenty-four-seven. And you're pretty big news up top, too."

Standing on the battered vessel, holding on to the splintered mast under the torn sail, it seemed entirely natural to Timothy to have this conversation. "What did you hear?"

"That you are one slippery eel." DUO laughed. "Man, those cops are still sloshing home, and they are pissed, but you got about a dozen more boats looking for you."

"Really?"

"Yeah, it's like Fleet Week, but for some reason the navy's heading to Times Square. Any idea why?"

Timothy nodded modestly. "What else?"

"You want to climb up and have some tea?"

Timothy considered the invitation. "Hmm. The last time you invited me up, I lost my boat."

"Sorry about that. It's not like we get much company down here, so I didn't think the cremblers would notice. Anyway . . . ," DUO continued in a friendly manner, "there's a nook about three blocks up where you can park the vehicle and you won't get a ticket. C'mon, I'll meet you there."

Timothy shoved off against the side of the tunnel, his arms feeling like strings, palms blistered. But after ten minutes and six basins, he still didn't see any nook that DUO might have been referring to.

"Hey!" a familiar voice called from behind him. Holding aside a curtain of canvas painted to look like stonework, the grinning artist said, "Not bad, huh?"

The thought of reversing direction one more time was almost too much for the captain of the *X-tra Large*.

DUO registered his guest's exhaustion and said, "Just let go and the water will bring you in."

Indeed, the top of the truncated mast slid beneath the scrim into a hidden channel that flowed into the distance. DUO dropped a chain ending in a mountain-climbing carabiner from above, and Timothy clipped it to the rail. After that, he climbed up the mast into the sewer's attic.

The space wasn't as comfortable as DUO's Harlem digs—it was more of a camp than a home—but there were a few chairs and a mattress salvaged from up top. There was another mini fridge and a hot plate and a few cups and utensils and, of course, a plastic milk crate filled with cans of spray paint and several rolls of canvas and the shiny skateboard DUO used to get around.

Like Malomi entertaining, DUO started boiling tea for his guest. "You're safe here, but you're a long way from home."

Absurdly—or inevitably—the word "home" reminded Timothy of one thing—or person. "I've got to get to Jessamyn."

"Not here you won't."

"Why not?"

"Because you managed to get lost between 57th and 59th Streets, that's why."

"How?"

"Took an extra fifteen degrees around Columbus Circle. That's why you came up Broadway instead of entering the park. Must have been admiring the paintings."

"Something like that."

DUO poured hot water from the kettle into a pair of cups, each with its own teabag. "Milk? Sugar?"

"Both, please."

Sitting in a broken-armed, wooden rocking chair with a chipped mug of hot tea warming his lap, Timothy felt as cozy as if he were swaying back and forth in a hammock. "It's nice here."

DUO shrugged off the compliment. "Just a place to hang my hat when I'm downtown."

All references are relative. Seventy-ninth Street, approximately, was downtown for a Harlem dweller. Timothy asked, "So where exactly are we?"

In response, DUO unfurled one of the rolls of canvas that had been sitting in the milk crate. It was a pencil drawing of a vast plain inhabited by a dozen dinosaurs. Tyrannosaurus rex loomed ominously over a sullen brontosaurus, while a stegosaurus grazed in a meadow and a pterodactyl soared overhead.

Timothy answered his own question. "Museum of Natural History."

DUO said, "Well, about two blocks away, but this is what I'm planning."

"Nice."

"Yeah, there's a good wall under the 77th Street entrance where this should fit."

Timothy sipped at his hot tea and nodded. Even with its broken arm and springs poking through the bottom, the rocker was the most comfortable chair he'd ever sat in. He was so bone-tired he didn't think he'd be able to summon the strength to rise.

DUO said, "Go to sleep. You can't do anything now. And you've got a busy day ahead."

# CHAPTER 22

**F**OR THE PRESS, THE PIT ON 184TH STREET WAS THE GIFT that kept on giving. "X-tra Large Still at Large" read the *Post*'s morning headline, while Channel 5 sent a crew to the City Island Marina for comments on sailboats. Other reporters harassed Con Ed for unsafe working conditions and covered a candlelight vigil that was held on the grounds of Montclair Junior High.

Even the reserved *Times* led off its Metro pages with a story that began, "In the most unusual manhunt in years, scores of police officers have been joined by the Coast Guard in the search for lost . . ."

The article was accurate up to a point, though the word *joined* probably should have been in quotes because the various officials hardly communicated. Unfortunately for Captain Mullane, the NYPD held jurisdiction beneath the streets of Manhattan, so he was in charge of the nautical force whether he liked it or not.

He stood in the waiting room of the George Washington Bridge Bus Station that had been commandeered once the increasing troop strength grew too unwieldy for the construction trailer at the site. Though it was apparent that the *X-tra Large* had crossed the police cordon at 125th Street, the field operation center remained in Washington Heights rather than waste time by moving elsewhere. On an easel in the front of the room was a transparent street map of Manhattan with another map superimposed over it.

"As you can see," Mullane informed the room of cops and cadets, "the storm sewer basically follows the pattern of streets. Basically, but not exactly. There are places where it's much wider due to the underground springs that were here before the island was settled. There are other places where subway lines force detours. There are places where information is incomplete. And there are places where the information is wrong."

A voice from the rear said, "You mean the kids may be in bed in New Jersey?"

The captain surveyed the room, but no one acknowledged speaking. "I'm glad that someone here has a sense of humor. You want to share that with your superiors in case bad stuff happens to these kids because of us?"

There were no takers.

"Now, I've asked Civil Engineer Cass Wainwright here to give you more specifics. He builds new sewers when necessary, repairs old ones, and basically knows the system better than anyone."

Wainwright smiled and said, "Except the rats."

An appreciative chuckle rose from the room.

"Gentlemen . . . and women, Manhattan's storm sewer is over six thousand miles long with a capacity of more than two billion—that's billion with a *b*—cubic feet of liquid, and the fact that you've never seen Central Park underwater proves that it does its job surpassingly well. If that much water was collected and set into a depression in the earth, it would make a nice-size lake.

"Now, once you get down there, some of it's going to be surprising and some is going to be surprisingly familiar. I've seen supermarket carts, garbage cans, car fenders, enough chairs to seat everyone in this room, and a six-foot brocade sofa that created a blockage near the 59th Street Bridge. Got that?"

The engineer looked around at the roomful of nodding police officers.

"Now, let's think about rain. Or drizzle. You can put your hand out and it will hardly get wet, but the accumulated moisture from every square inch of street or sidewalk or roof or awning, any horizontal surface whatsoever, is flowing into a catch basin at the corner in front of your home or office. It's like automobile traffic. One car can drive thirty miles an hour, but ten thousand going into the Lincoln Tunnel at the same time means an hour-long jam. Half an inch of rain can look misty outside, but it's a torrent underground.

"Add to this the water from springs, as well as the fact that the sewer has its own microclimate. Things grow there that don't grow anyplace else in the city. Fungus. Mold. In places, the water's eroded the tunnels and carved new paths into the bedrock. Places that were once level have been changed by housing and civic construction. There's even some uncharted territory in Central Park that we've tried to map, but it seems to shift on us. In recent years, several lines have simply disappeared. Finally, we decided that as long as it wasn't broke, we weren't going to try to fix it. OK?"

Again, the officers nodded. They didn't get it at all, but they would once they went down there.

"At this point," Wainwright declared, "the *X-tra Large* can be anywhere."

A diligent officer in the back row asked, "But we have had sightings?"

"Correct. There was the encounter with two policemen in Central Park and the event in Times Square. Both are good signs. They show that the kids are healthy and trying to get our attention."

Strictly speaking, Wainwright's statement wasn't entirely true. First, the plural "kids" was an assumption rather than an observation. Only the boy had been spotted. Second, Timothy did indeed attract police attention but only in the process of escaping from the police. In fact, his flight was the opposite of a good sign. It meant that the boy had a reason to avoid the authorities. To explain this, Mullane took the podium again and said, "I've asked Dr. Salman Singh to speak to us. He's an expert in child psychology at Mount Sinai Hospital. He's going to give us some insight into the kids' state of mind that might help us to help them."

Dr. Singh set directly to the task. "Of course, there is no certainty without interviewing the children themselves. But it is likely that they feel some element of guilt and are afraid to be caught. The longer this condition lasts, the greater the guilt. I can virtually guarantee that they are afraid of the dark and the isolation, that they have no resources and cannot control their situation. That is why they sent that life vest up into Times Square. It is a cry for help. They are paralyzed and will not make any particular decisions. They may be fighting with each other, blaming each other as well as themselves."

Mullane never had much patience for shrinks, but he was covering all bases. "Thank you, Dr. Singh. Anyone out there have any questions for the doctor?"

"Yeah, how can I get my kid to clean his room?"

Normally, the captain might have gotten angry, but a moment of humor alleviated the tension. Besides, Dr. Singh took the mocking question with good grace. "Alas," he said, "there are some mysteries that are too great for the psychiatric profession."

After an hour of further briefings from transportation and sanitation and the utilities, the public relations director of the commissioner's office at One Police Plaza entered the room, glancing anxiously at his BlackBerry. Without mentioning the devastating coverage in the press, he declared, "Let me be clear. At this moment the department has no greater priority than finding these children." He looked around the room and didn't say another word.

"Um, is that it?" the captain asked.

"Let me be clear," he repeated. "At this moment the department has *no greater priority* than finding these children."

"That's clear. Any questions?"

No one in the room had any questions.

"OK, people. We've got rubber jackets and about a hundred pairs of wading boots in all sizes that will be distributed to you along with waterproof flashlights and communications devices. Go out there and be heroes."

# CHAPTER

# 23

**J**ESSAMYN ASSUMED THAT IT WAS MORNING WHEN SHE awoke, even though the only light in her chamber came from the hallway. And yet the atmosphere was . . . different. Most significantly, no one was guarding the cell that she'd been escorted to the night before. She walked out and crossed the dining chamber in which she'd feasted, and felt hungry, but continued to the barracks room where the inhabitants slept. Forty feet long, fifteen wide, filled with racks of triple-decker bunks, it reeked of sweat and musk. One ancient skell gave her a suspicious glance and then pretended to sleep.

She passed an open door to another room, in which the comptroller, Ivan, sat at a desk, hunched over a tall ledger with columns of figures. Unlike the cremblers, he met her eyes. "Help you?"

"Um, sure. I'd like some croissants and fresh-squeezed orange juice, and I'd like to have it served on the deck of the boat you guys stole and, oh yeah, let's do all of that in Raritan Bay."

He smiled at her sass and answered, "Sorry. No can do."

"Why not? Are you afraid of some made-up pipsqueak?"

"If you're referring to our exalted leader, the answer is yes, but that's not the only reason I can't serve you in the sun."

"What other reason could there possibly be?"

"The sky's overcast. But I can probably send someone out for the juice and croissants."

She sniffed.

"Also, I'm busy. Big deal today. Did you sleep well?"

"As well as could be expected."

"Better than that. It's almost noon."

"What?"

"You must have been tired."

Jessamyn supposed that was true. Who wouldn't be tired after her ordeal? But rather than repeat the obvious, she returned to something Ivan mentioned a minute earlier. "What sort of big deal?"

Why she pried, she couldn't be sure, but any information might be helpful. Of course, Malomi and the cremblers might think it dangerous for her to possess such information, but so what? That bridge had been crossed. And demolished. Crushed into rubble. Sent off to Jersey for landfill. Worse, the elapsed time made her certain that Timothy was not returning. Either he'd been captured or hurt elsewhere in the sewer. If she was to escape, she was going to have to do it by herself.

The accountant remained silent.

"Or maybe your deal is not so big."

"Oh, yes it is. After this, we can forget the televisions for the mob, the drugs for the pushers."

"Just Ferraris?" she asked.

He smiled. "So Malomi told you about that. We didn't make too much money, maybe ten thousand. It was just for the fun of it. Now, however, we leave the vulgar American-consumer society behind."

"And work with people who respect culture?" Jessamyn mused, thinking of the doctor in the three-piece suit.

"Perhaps."

His eyes glittered; he was aching to brag. All she had to do was give him the opportunity. Row 552–EU–19–T–1808. What structure had 552 rows? At the minimum, if there was no 553. A customshouse, perhaps. An airplane terminal. But the cremblers were limited by the confines of Manhattan Island. A library. The public library on 42nd Street. "You're stealing a book. A rare book. A precious book."

"Ah," Ivan the accountant sighed. "If this was Russia, there might be such respect for learning. In Moscow, they know what to do with the intelligentsia."

Jessamyn couldn't help it. She scoffed. "Kill them."

"Precisely. Assassination is the greatest sign of respect one can offer to an author. All Americans care about are possessions. But I'll admit, the library was not a bad guess, my little cherry blossom. And I cannot say another word. Now, scoot. I have work to do."

Thwarted, Jessamyn ventured on alone. She found a storeroom filled with boxes of computers and sneakers and Rolex watches. She also found a kind of galley with a long table and mismatched chairs under metal shelving lined with cases of food probably stolen from a supermarket. Malomi ate the best; her men survived on oatmeal.

Finally, she found a ramp that seemed to connect the dry upper level of the installation with the actual tunnels. The air smelled damper; the light was grayer. She rounded a corner and stepped onto the balcony overlooking the harbor.

A meeting was in progress down below. The well-dressed doctor from the day before was back, in a navy blue pinstripe suit with

French cuffs and a patterned red tie, but he also had an enormous canvas duffel bag at his feet and was accompanied by two younger men wearing unseasonable leather jackets. A third guard stood behind the wheel of the taxi barge that had brought them in.

Malomi and Lobo and a half-circle of cremblers faced the delegation.

Jessamyn leaned over the balcony and eavesdropped.

The doctor was eager. "A bit of luck, you say?"

"We knew that we were underneath the museum, but the breakthrough saved days of excavation," Malomi said.

*The museum.* Not the library but another cultural repository. The cremblers had engineered the theft of some object from the vast storerooms of the Metropolitan Museum of Art. Stolen to order by Dr. Allan Pym-Gordon, who was either a collector or was commissioned on behalf of a collector to steal one single object. She remembered that he'd been called a curator. He was stealing an object entrusted to his care. That was how the cremblers knew the precise storage code.

"And when," the doctor interrupted, "will it be here?"

"Any minute. My men were just sealing up their entry point. No one will miss your precious masterpiece for another century. Now, as for the payment . . ." She peered down at the duffel bag.

"First the painting."

Jessamyn recalled the code. EU probably stood for Europe. And 1808 was the year. Jessamyn tried to recall the painters she'd studied in an art history class.

"It's coming."

"So is the payment."

Simultaneously, You reached down for the duffel and the two young men reached into their jackets, but the doctor raised a hand and they halted. Standoff.

The doctor shrugged and said, "As long as it's not going anywhere."

You tugged the heavy bag toward a table that had been set up on the island.

Malomi said, "This isn't going to explode or give off some signal if we open it?"

"Of course not," Pym-Gordon replied coolly. "You've been watching too much television."

"Television," Malomi repeated disdainfully. "We sell the sets. We don't watch them."

Ivan must have followed Jessamyn when she left his alcove, because he appeared directly beside her. He whispered, "That's just one of the reasons why I love her."

Malomi and the doctor negotiated quietly while Jessamyn and Ivan conversed as if they were mingling at a cocktail party. "How long have you known her?"

"Three years, two months, two weeks."

"Does she ever go . . ."

"Up?"

Jessamyn nodded, as if she couldn't repeat the word, as if it was dirty.

"Never. Not while I have been here. Before that, I think not, but can't for certain say."

"But how did she get here?"

"It is legend."

The legend glanced up at the couple on the balcony. "Ah, my dear," she called up to Jessamyn. "Sincerest apologies for the accommodations. We're not used to visitors. I hope that you slept well."

"It was fine."

"Ivan, will you please join us," she called, summoning her

221

financial manager. Apparently, a truce had been arranged. The money could be counted, but it could not be taken elsewhere until the art object arrived.

The skells and cremblers stood silent as Ivan walked down the stairs and tentatively reached for the duffel bag. Lobo was unable to avoid staring.

Malomi saw the hunger in his eyes and asked, "Do you have a question?"

"No, ma'am. I was just . . ."

"You were just hoping that we might divide up some portion."

"A small portion, because the rest must be saved."

"Correct. And what would you do with your portion of the portion we might conceivably divide?"

"I might visit some friends in . . ." He was trying to be careful. "Different places."

"But then you'd come back?"

"Of course."

Of course, he was lying. Malomi asked, "Why bother if you have enough money to live well up top?"

Lobo knew the catechism. "Because I could never live as well as I do down here."

"Is that true?" She turned to You.

He nodded.

Malomi looked at the comptroller, who'd just come down from the balcony. "Ivan?"

"If I never see those pigs again it will be too soon."

"Spoken like a true old-timer," she said, congratulating him.

Jessamyn could tell that there was a divide between the elderly vagrants and the younger thieves. The first group stole because they were homeless; the second were homeless because they were criminals.

"It's coming!" shouted a hoarse voice from the far side of the cavern.

Everyone—Malomi and Ivan, Dr. Pym-Gordon and his hired hoodlums—looked toward the entry, where the camouflaged gate rose creaking. Even the babies in their cage seemed to sniff in the direction of a new barge floating in with a box so big that four skells were required to unload it onto the concrete island.

"Shall we check the merchandise?" the doctor asked.

"Must we?" Malomi replied.

"Must we count the money?" he rejoined.

Malomi nodded, and the cremblers set to prying off the corner supports and external structure with a crowbar. Whatever was in the box, it was well packed. The doctor winced as a piece of lath cracked off and a corner of a canvas was exposed.

It was a painting, and it was held in place as securely as the bombproof case in Washington, D.C., held the Declaration of Independence. Inside the box, the painting was further protected by a layer of baste cotton. And until an hour earlier, it also had protection from heat and moisture and, so thought the security personnel at the museum, thieves.

The gentleman purchaser grimaced as the skells' grimy fingers peeled away the cotton. "Watch it," he blurted.

"We will," Malomi answered coolly. "And the money."

Before more than the upper-left quadrant of the baste covering had been removed, Jessamyn could identify the painter if not the painting. Distinctive whorls practically burst off the canvas, and a greenish tinge with white highlights announced it as an abstract seascape created by the inimitable hand of J. M. W. (Joseph Mallord William) Turner. EU–19–T stood for a nineteenth-century European painting by someone whose name began with *T*.

Jessamyn had no idea how many Turners the Met owned,

whether on display or kept in storage, but it was hard to imagine that *Dawn at Rose Point with Trawler* could be overlooked. It was about nine feet wide and six feet tall, and only in the lower-right-hand corner was the vessel of the title visible. The commercial fishing boat was a smudgy triangular blur amid the clash of elements. The storm-laden air was full of moisture, the exploding waves filled with air.

Dr. Pym-Gordon was in a trance. He stared at the canvas and started to breathe heavily as inch after inch was exposed until, at last, a strip of cotton was peeled off an etched-copper plaque at the bottom of the frame that read *1808.*

Malomi interrupted his reverie. "I presume the goods are acceptable."

"Oh, yes." Dr. Pym-Gordon took a step closer and peered intently at what seemed to be a random square inch. Unconsciously, his tongue lolled outside his mouth as if he was about to lick the brushstrokes. Then he snapped to attention and said in agreement, "Fine."

"Then . . ." Malomi gestured to the bag held by You, guarded by the two galoots.

The doctor nodded, and they stepped aside.

Jessamyn also gazed at the painting. It made her think of her own tiny voyage of the last few days, but even more it made her sad. Waves of grief washed over her like the waves that tossed the trawler as she thought of the existential voyage her father had taken several years earlier. Would the men on the unnamed fishing boat survive their journey, make it to harbor, to see Turner's exquisite rendering of their peril?

Where was Jessamyn's mother? Everything about Miranda Hazard that had driven her daughter crazy—the constant hectoring for her already brilliant child to do her homework, the contradictory suggestions that Jessamyn get out more, and the way Miranda dressed like a teenager on her dates with Tom Murphy—was suddenly endearing, in the face of the fact that it could all be lost forever.

And where was Malomi's father? Dead, like Jessamyn's own dad? Had she been kidnapped by the cremblers, their first great theft? Perhaps. But how then had she come to rule them?

Maybe her parents had been homeless. They could have sought refuge in the warm sewer during some brutal winter and been killed in the kind of accident that could occur only in this wild, watery domain. The kind of "accident" that might yet befall Jessamyn, which Malomi would surely arrange in order to prevent her from revealing the secret kingdom.

She would drown; that was obvious. She looked at the murky water, a bit higher in the intertwining channels than it had been the day before. The moment Malomi gave the word, You or Lobo or any of her servants would push Jessamyn's head under the surface and count to one hundred.

Bubbles would rise, small pockets of air escaping from her constricted lungs, as she tried to thrash free. She'd lose strength first, then consciousness, then the spark of life. They would drag her dead body someplace where the water emptied out, perhaps the Hudson. She wouldn't feel the sun on her skin, or the flies.

Unless they chose to make her body disappear as surely as the soul.

Several homeless men hoisted the duffel bag onto the table for the count as others set the exposed canvas on the deck of the barge. Ivan sat in a chair behind the table and cleaned his wire-rim glasses on the lapel of his jacket.

Dr. Pym-Gordon announced, "One and a half million dollars in used hundreds."

Ivan unzipped the bag and took out the first wad bound with rubber band and flipped the bills back one by one.

"You don't have to count."

Ivan looked up.

Malomi met his eyes straight on and he kept counting.

"They're all there."

Ivan kept on.

The doctor smiled. "You don't trust me?"

Malomi replied, "No, sir, I surely do not."

"Well, ma'am, I guess you've got your reasons."

If Jessamyn Hazard wasn't going to simply give up and give in to despair, she needed to know more about her adversary—immediately. No one was watching her, because most eyes were on the money, except for the few that were on the painting, and some that never left Malomi. The latter were vulnerable to persuasion.

Brazenly, she walked down the stairs and crossed the plank bridge onto the island, until she was almost next to Malomi. She was about to speak when a low rumbling came through the sewer, as if a dragon was waking in the center of the earth.

All of the cremblers looked up. Only the doctor remained focused on the large canvas. Where the barge would go with it was a mystery. There must have been another access point into the system beside the great hole at 184th Street. Or perhaps they'd just follow a tunnel to the Hudson to a pier like any other pleasure boat that happened to be carrying a stolen masterpiece.

Jessamyn leaned down and asked the only thing that came to mind. "Where can I go to the bathroom?"

Malomi met her eyes. Was she suspicious? No, the question was so mundane that it couldn't be contrived. Besides, another boomlet drove the thought from her head. Money was on the table

**226**

and a storm was coming. She gestured back up the stairs to the chambers.

Just what Jessamyn hoped for. She walked over to You and said, "Malomi said that you should take me up there."

He'd seen the conversation, seen the gesture, and had no reason to believe that anyone might lie, because no one ever lied in Undertown. He led her up the staircase.

As idly as possible, simply making conversation, Jessamyn asked, "When did she come here?"

"It was a great day."

"Yes, she said that she remembered you . . . um, You."

The homeless man's pleasure at this comment was so evident that Jessamyn couldn't help but feel sorry for her lie. Still, her resolve held. "Of course, even the memory is a miracle because she was so young."

"Just a baby. The doctor said that she couldn't be more than two weeks old."

*Pym-Gordon?* "Yes, she mentioned the doctor."

"You misses him."

*Not Pym-Gordon.* "She does, too."

"He couldn't heal himself."

Jessamyn nodded sympathetically and allowed You to tell the story. It turned out that a small colony of homeless men had found their way into the sewer system through a hole from the subway tracks in Union Square. The sewer was warmer than subway platforms, and hygiene easier to maintain. Also, the system was better suited for getting around the city than the limited tunnels of the transit department. Subways had routes. Every street required a sewer.

The doctor was a former citizen of up top; they all were. Most panhandled on the sidewalk or foraged through garbage cans during the day, but the more they obtained, the less they wished to return to the world that shunned them.

"He had some problem. You doesn't know what it was."

Jessamyn nodded kindly. Yes, a doctor who chose to live in the sewer had a problem.

"But we didn't talk to each other. Not much. Maybe to say that the cops were sweeping the tunnels under Grand Central or something. That's it."

"And then?" Something changed in the underground mutual help society.

"There's this nice ledge in Union Square, extra wide, near the steam pipes, so it's cozy in the winter and private. You didn't tell anyone about it, but You didn't chase anyone away, either. About five of us were there, minding our own business . . ."

"Yes?"

"And there she was."

"Go on."

"Stream was thin, water slow. Everyone says that Zeke saw her first, but You was looking uptunnel and spotted the basket. About so big . . . So small." He extended his rough hands two feet apart. "With a white cloth over the side, and an itty-bitty baby hand rising up. Coulda knocked me over with a baseball bat."

Jessamyn smiled. "You mean a feather."

"No, nobody ever knocked You over with a feather."

Everyone had their own frame of reference. "Oh."

"Zeke reached out and pulled it in. Thing was made well, You can say that. The space between the twigs was patched with tar so's it couldn't leak nor sink. There was a soft blanket under her so she'd be comfortable. And that white blanket covering her. We gathered, first time so close to each other, or anyone else, in . . . long time. And . . ."

"And?"

"There she was."

"Yes."

"You got responsibilities when You has a baby. You got to get food and clothes and stuff. Doc said she couldn't have been more than two weeks old."

"Yes."

"He also said that she couldn't have been in the water for more than a day. If that basket hadn't come to Union Square when it did, poor child would have been a goner. It touches You's heart."

It touched Jessamyn's heart, too. She glanced down toward the vicious empress of the underworld and tried to imagine her as a newborn. "And you never found out—"

"Nope," he interrupted her, talkative now about the subject that mattered most to him. "You also guesses that her folks were playing with her in a river in the park and she floated away."

Jessamyn's guess was more cynical. Malomi had been discarded by some idiotic mom who couldn't handle an infant and literally flushed her away, albeit with the sentimental gesture of the woven basket.

Leave her fate up to chance.

Some fate, to land among the forlorn.

But hadn't the exact same thing happened to Jessamyn two days earlier, at fourteen years rather than fourteen days of age? Both were females in a male world, and both arrived underground on an exotic vessel.

The difference was that Malomi had shaped the world that Jessamyn discovered. Perhaps the mysterious doctor had shaped her education, and her disdain for the upper world. She grew up with fear and hatred and a ravening desire for vengeance, and the homeless men who worshipped her became her first victims.

229

She wanted. They provided. Then, perhaps, rumors of the skells' initial thefts spread to criminals, who realized that the sewer was a perfect place to transport and exchange hot merchandise. Of course, it couldn't have been easy for a person of such diminutive stature to wield control. On the other hand, she and the homeless men had a unique knowledge of the system. Then, somehow, they obtained boats—perhaps like the Ferrari, piece by piece. The fleet gave them an unassailable advantage. Business grew.

Malomi had intelligence. Jessamyn wondered what might have happened if both of *her* parents had died and she'd been cast into the waters. Then rescued into a life with no friends, no books, no distractions, and one single purpose: domination.

That's why Malomi kept stealing. She craved everything that the up-top world considered valuable. She wouldn't stop until she had everything and the world above was utterly barren.

But that wouldn't happen. The scale was too disproportionate. Poor Malomi had lost the battle before it started.

Which brought Jessamyn back to her own concerns. She remembered Malomi's eagerness to explain and to entertain her guest. Was it possible that she saw Jessamyn as the older sister that she'd never had? Or the mother who'd abandoned her?

Was she seeking to impress Jessamyn? Or was she preparing to avenge herself on the up-tops by means of the girl who'd fallen into her den?

Either way, it was imperative to get out.

"So w-w-what does Jessamy want?" You stammered, perhaps worried that he had spoken too much by communicating the single great joy of his life.

It was almost a shame to take advantage of him, but then, Jessamyn told herself, Malomi had been taking advantage of him for years. "A gun," she said.

"You d-d-doesn't have a gun."

"Of course you don't . . . You. But those men do, and Malomi is worried about them. She doesn't trust them."

You nodded.

"She told me that she was afraid they would hurt her."

Indeed, there seemed to be tension below as Ivan counted stack after stack of cash from the bottomless duffel bag.

"Just in case," Jessamyn said.

You's eyes widened.

"You know . . ." She was about to say more, but another fabrication was unnecessary as long as she placed the emphasis in the right place. Instead of a meaningless prefatory "Y'know," it could be taken as an absolute two-word declaration: "YOU know."

Indeed, the poor vagrant assumed that he must know. He considered the scene below. Rather than a familiar, if unusually profitable, commercial exchange, it seemed fraught with danger. He nodded and said, "You'll take care of it."

# CHAPTER

## 24

**T**HERE." THE ENGINEER NODDED SADLY TO THE FRONT of the trailer.

"Where? What?" All Captain Mullane could see was the jolly crowd of media and thrill seekers, fewer perhaps than several hours earlier when the NYPD had finally managed to dispatch the latest surge of manpower into the sewer. Then again, Mullane could barely see through the blurry window because he'd gone sleepless for the now forty-plus hours since the children disappeared, the longest he'd stayed awake since a psycho on 190th Street took a postman hostage some ten years back. "Rubberneckers," he scoffed.

"That's not what I meant," the engineer said in an ineffably sad tone.

"You know what, Wainwright, why don't you tell me what you meant?" Despite his gruffness, Mullane had grown to appreciate the engineer. For starters, the man had kept vigil even though no one had ordered him to stay. Around three A.M. the previous night, the captain had asked him why he was sticking around and all

Wainwright said in reply was, "I guess that if I don't have a life, I might as well save two others."

Now the engineer stood up with a sigh and placed his fingertip on a spot on the window.

The captain squinted to make out what the engineer was pointing at.

"It's a drop, Mullane. A raindrop. The first. Clock's stopped ticking. You've got to pull your guys."

Sure, Wainwright had tried to explain the danger of precipitation to the assembled troops at the GW Bridge Bus Station, but he had seen their eyes glaze over during the briefing. To them, scientists were academics with theories that seldom bore any relationship to reality.

Unfortunately, the damn drop on the window meant that a new element had entered into the elaborate game of hide-and-seek. Nature had its own agenda.

Another drop appeared.

Wainwright looked up at the gray sky.

Mullane voiced the engineer's forecast: "It's raining."

According to the National Weather Service, the worst kind of rain was expected—a hard, swift summer shower. The more common, slower-paced rains posed no difficulty for New York's sewer system; as steadily as the water arrived, so did it depart through the myriad underground channels, eventually flowing into one of the rivers that surrounded and defined Manhattan Island. But this kind of storm meant that all of the precipitation that fell onto the hot roofs and sidewalks and streets of the city would flow simultaneously into the catch basins that people above never noticed and that people below occasionally used as a source of light. It would inundate the sewer, where scores of police officers on foot, eleven police and Coast Guard vessels, and two teenagers—along with anyone else who happened to be underground—would experience nature's wrath.

"What do you suggest?"

"Call back the boats."

"What about the kids?"

"The men in those boats won't be able to help them."

Police were used to putting themselves in harm's way to protect citizens. Indeed, as long as there is a minimal chance of success, risk must be taken. But suicide is not a public servant's mandate. When there is zero chance of success, retreat is mandatory.

A police captain placed his men in jeopardy every day of the year. A police captain never asked the impossible.

Mullane picked up the phone to give the order to halt the mission even as he realized one slim exception to Wainwright's nearly absolute statement. "All units report." He spoke clearly as his eyes met the engineer's.

If the rain didn't materialize, he'd be slammed like a golf ball by everyone from the commissioner to the writers of the editorial pages. His career was on the line. Another drop fell on the window.

"PB-6 here."

"PB-5."

One by one, ten out of the eleven boats scouring the system called in.

The captain acknowledged each one and told them to stand by for an announcement. They waited for five minutes, ten, and still one last boat didn't respond. Mullane called out, "PB-8? Do you copy? PB-8. This is command. Copy. Stat."

Several minutes later, a huffing voice answered, "PB-8 here, Captain. Sorry, we were on foot, investigating."

"What sort of investigation?"

"Well, it's the damnedest thing, sir. We were cruising along and nearly passed this wall when it sort of rippled."

"Rippled?"

"Yes, sir. Turned out to be a curtain painted like a wall. You could pass it a million times and not notice the difference, but a breeze caught it just as we approached. It hides another tunnel going into—"

"What's your location, PB-8?"

"Approximately 77th Street and Columbus Avenue, sir."

"Hold on." Mullane put his palm to the walkie-talkie's mouthpiece and asked the engineer, "What's going on?"

"Central Park. It's where the wild stuff is, but I've never heard of a curtain before."

"You think the kid did it to hide from us?"

"He seems to be a pretty impressive tyke, I'll grant you that. But I doubt he's Michelangelo."

"Who then?"

"I don't have the faintest idea, but I don't think that makes much difference. Not now."

The window was speckled with a dozen drops.

The captain thought for a minute and then made the necessary decision. "Come in, PB-8. Come in, everybody. Search is canceled for now."

The deed was done, consigning two teenagers to whatever fury loomed in the sky. Mullane put down the walkie-talkie, but he couldn't let this go without considering every last option—not even for the duration of one summer storm that the weather service assured him would blow over within hours. He turned to the engineer. "You said that the *boats* couldn't do anything. You think something else can?"

"I'm not sure."

"What is it you're not sure of?"

"Well, by all rights, these kids should have been found ages ago. Or *caught*, if that's the right word. I mean, it's hard to hide a twelve-foot sailboat in an open sewer."

"Unless Timothy Murphy is an alias for David Copperfield."

"Yes. And if they went too far from the center of the system, the pitch would have carried them out into the Hudson or East River by now."

"So . . ."

"What that last boat said made sense. Central Park is the most confusing portion of the system because it's not on a grid. It's also the nearest to level because it's close to the axis of the island. That makes it easier to maneuver in. And that's where the other boat saw the *X-tra Large*."

"What about the life preserver in Times Square?"

"Yes, I've been thinking about that. Did you notice that it was the next thing that happened after the sighting in Central Park?"

"Yes."

"Well, if Timothy was able to signal his location, why didn't he do it on 79th Street or 72nd? Why did he wait until he got to Times Square to provide us with that vest?"

"Because . . ." Mullane played out the logic. "He wanted us to think he was *in* Times Square."

"We also know that the kid is smart. So why did he want us to think such a silly thing?"

"Because we already knew he was in Central Park and he wanted us to leave the park so—"

Wainwright slapped the desk with his palm. "So he could return! *That's* where they've got to be."

"You think I should have let PB-8 continue?"

**236**

"No. Absolutely not. Like I said, it's too dangerous for a boat. Could get slammed around when the storm comes."

"On the other hand . . ."

"What?"

"You tell me."

"Are you sure there's another hand?"

"There's always another hand, Wainwright. What is it?"

"I don't know. It's a long shot."

"WHAT is it?"

"Two guys with appropriate gear. Scuba."

"They wouldn't get knocked around?"

"Not as much as a boat in a channel that wasn't built for boats. Also, there'd be a rope or a chain, the kind of thing divers use. That way, if they got into trouble, they could be pulled out on a moment's notice."

"Where would they go in?"

The engineer looked at the map. "The sighting by the girl yesterday was here." He pointed to the east side of the park around 100th Street. "PB-8 found the curtain here." He pointed to the west side of the park in the 70s. Then he split the difference, and pointed to the center of the park in the 80s. "Here."

"Just open a basin and drop in a badge like bait?"

"Easier."

Mullane's eyes widened.

Wainwright shrugged. "We have our ways."

"So . . ." The captain was exhausted. He thought how a certain kind of underground silence with no mayors or commissioners or journalists or citizens of the greatest city on earth might be a relief. "When do we start?"

# CHAPTER

# 25

**K**IDS." **TOM MURPHY PUSHED AROUND THE EGGS** congealing on his plate. The unhappy couple sat in the dismal restaurant off the lobby of their hotel after a poor night's sleep and another frustrating call to Captain Mullane.

"Yes."

"Timmy's been a pretty easy person to live with. I mean, except when . . ."

"Yes." Miranda Hazard understood. A dead parent was no blessing.

"He always had a vivid imagination, but it never got him into any trouble. I thought it was a good thing. I can't imagine what's gotten into him . . ." After a pause, he hastened to correct any misimpression. "Not that I'm blaming your daughter."

"I know."

"She seemed like a perfectly—"

"Perfect," Miranda interrupted. "She's a perfectly perfect young woman. Head on her shoulders."

"From what Timmy told me, Jessamyn is smarter than anyone

in the school . . . including the teachers. But they're doing more than thumbing their noses at authority here. What got into them?"

If each was a paragon, perhaps there was something explosive about the combination of the two, like baking soda and vinegar.

Miranda choked back a sob: for herself, for Tom, for Jessamyn, for anyone who suffered. Only one thing gave her minor comfort. She looked out the restaurant's streaked window at the gray sky and said, "I used to love a gloomy day."

Tom's head, hanging dolefully over the uneaten food, rose to meet her eyes. "Really?"

"I know it's silly, but I always felt my best when everyone else was moping because of the weather."

"Then let's get out of here." He slapped a bill on the table, enough to cover the uneaten meal and a generous tip.

Together, they exited the restaurant and crossed the lobby to the revolving door onto Tenth Avenue. People were bent against the wind, hair and light summer jackets waving behind them. Some carried umbrellas and an elderly man pushed a cart filled with umbrellas in the direction of Times Square.

Miranda looked at the opportunistic vendor and suggested, "Shall we give the guy his first sale?"

"You bet. In fifteen minutes, they'll cost twice as much."

Without thinking, Miranda looped her arm into the crook of Tom's elbow, while he purchased a cheap black umbrella as the first drops of rain fell. Silently, comfortably, they walked for nearly thirty blocks, until Tom caught sight of a wedge of green at the end of a row of brownstones and said, "Park?"

Miranda smiled briefly. "Sure."

# CHAPTER 26

**T**IMOTHY AWOKE FEELING BETTER THAN HE HAD IN ages. Maybe it was because he knew where he had to go—approximately—and what he had to do—exactly. There was a comfort to this certitude even as there was anxiety about whether his action would have any effect. He was like a soldier set for battle. The great decision had already been made. His role was merely to triumph or die.

Some thoughts for a suburban teenager, imagining how he might explain himself to his father if—no, that was negative, *when*—he returned. "You see, there was this demented underground queen. She was about three and a half feet tall. Yeah, really dangerous . . . and she had this army of homeless guys who were scared of their own shadows, but there aren't any shadows in the sewer, so they were totally fearless . . . and . . . and . . ."

That reminded him of something. "DUO?" he called, but of course the boy was gone. Fortunately, he had left breakfast—a New York bagel for fortitude.

Timothy set sail and poled his vessel along the channel,

humming "Paddlin' Madelaine Home" as if he hadn't a care in the world. Standing proud near the prow, the captain of the *X-tra Large* could do as he pleased, at ease in his surroundings.

The water level was a bit higher than usual, the current swifter and the breeze brisker, but he was able to catch the wind off the curved walls as deftly as any athlete catching the ball of his sport: pigskin football into the gut, orange nubby basketball on fingertips, leathery baseball in a mitt, hard rubber ball in a jai alai player's basket. In fact, he was more masterful because those other players could respond only to people who set the balls in motion; Timothy was playing with, or against, forces of nature.

Back propped against the mast, he spread his legs wide, nearly spanning the narrow boat, and stretched his hands toward the sides of the tunnel, feeling as if he was gliding over the inky surface of the water, pulling the *X-tra Large* behind him. In some way that he couldn't define, this was true. The boat had been battered far beyond its manufacturer's expectations, and it looked like it. Sections of flooring were gouged; the rail, where it remained intact, was dented, bent, and wobbly. And every inch of once-glowing teak and gleaming brass and glossy white trim was covered with a thick coating of loathsome sludge.

Maybe it wasn't as rank and organic as the stuff that ran through the city's so-called sanitary sewer, but it wasn't the Upper Montclair municipal swimming pool, either. Timothy made out sodden newspapers plastered onto the side of the *X-tra Large* like papier-mâché and semisolid blobs that he preferred not to examine. These he let flow past, but occasionally they left a smear on the side of the boat.

He'd gone a ways, perhaps three or four blocks, though it was difficult to measure distance in the maze-like labyrinth, until he came to one of the park's distinctive forks, unlike the perpendicular intersections where streets met avenues. He was considering which fork to take, when he saw an image painted on the mottled gray stonework. About a foot square, it was the outline of a hand made into a fist with its thumb extended, like that of a hitchhiker.

How Timothy even knew what a hitchhiker was, he couldn't say; he'd surely never seen one on Valley Road or along Route 46 to the Willowbrook Mall and the Minnesauken Octoplex. Hitchhikers existed in some earlier Americana, maybe the same era as Katznelson's Luncheonette, where the old lady's egg creams might have been dodo-bird omelets.

He looked at the outline of the fist and thumb on the wall. Something about it was odd. Besides the hitchhiking symbol, it could also be a thumbs-up sign. In either case, it was definitely pointing toward the left fork of the tunnel. DUO had marked the route.

Silently, Timothy gave thanks to his invisible trailblazer and sailed left. As soon as he made the turn, a gust of wind came up from behind him to hasten the *X-tra Large* on its designated path. A good omen.

Aware of potential lookouts from Malomi's enclave, he slackened the sail and was cautious to avoid making noise with his pole. And as he hushed, the tunnel hushed along with him. There were none of the skitterings he'd heard before, and he'd long since left behind the city grid, where the rumble of a subway might vibrate through the waters.

The atmosphere was abnormally quiet because the air pressure up top had dropped abruptly in the last ten minutes when a hot front moved in to the metropolitan area, drawing a bank of clouds in its wake. Timothy couldn't tell that the first few drops were falling, coalescing and starting their communal drive toward the sewer.

Was it possible that the sewer was *too* quiet? Timothy listened carefully, but beyond the gentle sloshing of the current and a faint pattering from the catch basins, there was nothing.

"DUO," he whispered. "Are you there?" He looked up at the ceiling of the tunnel, but the earth's surface was too close for there to be room for one of the graffitist's crawl spaces.

"You," he whispered. "Are you there, You?" He didn't really expect the homeless man to answer. Still, it was best to check.

"Jessamyn. Jess." Of course, she didn't answer, either, but it was theoretically possible that the resourceful girl had effected her own escape from the cremblers. No such luck.

He'd see his father soon enough, but he couldn't imagine facing Jessamyn's mother without her daughter. How selfish was that: dwelling on poor Timmy's feelings? What about Jessamyn herself? His mind refused to imagine her fate if his mission failed.

He'd resented Miranda's appearance in the Murphy house because he didn't want anyone to take the place of his mother. But didn't his father have the right to basic human happiness? Wouldn't his mother have wanted that for her husband? Wouldn't she have wanted a woman to help take care of her son? Miranda was no threat to Timothy.

At this point, he might not have minded encountering a few rats—preferably not the grotesquely huge ones that had hauled away the *X-tra Large* but some baby rats, with whiskers that twitched cutely—just to show that Timothy Murphy wasn't the sole living creature in this dark, wet world.

He was tempted to light the propane tank to provide himself with something that flickered, that danced, that could keep him company until he finally found the company he feared. Alas, he dared not. Even the whispers had been foolish, and he knew he was fortunate they hadn't been heard. Revealing his presence prematurely would ruin any element of surprise that might help him.

Surprise was vital because he didn't have much else on his side.

Then he heard a gunshot.

# CHAPTER
# 27

**O**N ONE SIDE OF THE CONCRETE ISLAND WHERE Malomi and Dr. Pym-Gordon conducted their business was a single large rectangle of tightly woven cloth dense with pigment, primarily gray and blue, with streaks of shocking white and glittering specks of gold and pocks of red splashed across its surface. On the other side of the island were—presumably, pending Ivan's final count—fifteen thousand small rectangular pieces of paper, each bearing the same identical image printed in green ink. The former reflected individual consciousness, the latter communal norms. One was unique, the others mechanically reproduced; one art, the others commerce; yet nearly all of the attention in the arena was focused on the vulgar, fungible commodity.

No, it wasn't quite so simple. Both the Turner and the Franklins were constructs, their value a function of social agreement rather than intrinsic worth. Jessamyn wondered if Benjamin Franklin had encountered the finger paintings of the preschool J. M. W. Turner while he was the United States ambassador to France.

But what did have intrinsic value? Diamonds were only compressed carbon, gold and silver and platinum but a few of the basic elements forged in the blast that created the universe. Elephants didn't think that gold had value. Trees were not impressed with platinum. But an elephant's ivory was also valued by humans, as were the trunks of teak and mahogany trees. Finally, it came down to what people *decided* had value.

No crowd follower, Jessamyn would have agreed with most of her species a month, a week, or three days ago. Now, however, she realized that there was a world of difference between want and need. The ability to pursue wants was a luxury reserved for those who had already satisfied needs.

What was a need? That which is required prior to the consideration of a want. Food was a need. So was shelter. And Malomi shared those with her special guest. Yet there were further needs Jessamyn had never noticed before.

Light, to start with. A flash seemed to burst from the center of the canvas. It was so bright that Jessamyn was surprised it didn't blind everyone in the chamber, yet no one else blinked. Oddly, it helped reassure Jessamyn that in the midst of life's storms there was a chance to behold something luminous, numinous, glorious.

Let the men stare at the little bills of currency. She would have traded all the cash in the world to return to the world of light that she'd never fully appreciated.

Where was her mother? And who exactly was Thomas Murphy, maker of T-shirts and also maker of Timothy Murphy? She was glad that her copilot on the *X-tra Large* had escaped from this dungeon. She hadn't thought of her move earlier as a sacrifice, but so be it. She'd saved a life. Someplace, a light was shining.

Glancing to the side of the canvas that had briefly permitted her to forget her actual situation, Jessamyn saw You sidling along the wall toward the group of men waiting for Ivan to finish his count of the packs of hundred-dollar bills taken from the duffel bag. The poor, gray man's attempt to be inconspicuous was so ludicrous he might as well have rented a klieg light.

Perhaps he hadn't been the best choice for an ally. You could squeal. You could fail. You could screw up everything. Perhaps Malomi would release Jessamyn after this deal was consummated.

Then she saw the look in Malomi's eyes as Dr. Pym-Gordon pointed out that the count of random bundles was accurate so far. "Frankly," he said, "I'm in rather a hurry. The weather is quite inauspicious."

The malignant queen shook her head and replied, "Not till every single bill is counted."

Of course, Malomi didn't care about money. Millions must have been cached away in her treasury, even as cremblers foraged through the basements of the bakeries of New York to steal a bagel. Instead, Malomi examined the painting she'd been commissioned to steal. She showed no response to the flash of light in the swirl of darkness that Turner's genius conjured out of a stormy night centuries earlier.

Art may not be as necessary as eating, but it provides another kind of nourishment.

Malomi's eyes looked enormous, maybe because they reflected the light of the painting. Or maybe, Jessamyn decided, she was like those fish that live twenty thousand feet beneath the Pacific Ocean, the ones that evolved in response to their radical environment. They were blind because eyes are useless in depths that light cannot penetrate. Also, their innards exerted enormous outward pressure to keep from being crushed by the weight of the ocean, so much so that none could come to the surface; if they did, they'd explode.

Were Malomi's eyes so huge because they'd never—or not since some first week or ten days or two weeks ago—been exposed to natural light? Was she under a kind of emotional pressure that couldn't survive in any other environment?

Smarter than the fish, sadder than the fish, Malomi must have understood that there was a life above that was forbidden to her, alone of her species. That was why she didn't care about the money, even though she made Ivan count every bill. Watching her watch both the painting and the money, Jessamyn understood: The tiny queen's project was not acquisition but destruction. She wanted to extract as much as she could from up-top circulation: food, electronics, the car she'd fondly recalled heisting, and now fine art. She wasn't stealing from individuals or institutions; she was stealing from the entire illuminated world. Of course, she'd resell her stolen goods, but she'd do so in a gray market that undermined all commonness and decency. What she really wanted to do was to flush the world's possessions down her own personal drain. Just like she had been flushed down the drain by her parents. She adjusted her jeweled tiara so that it reflected the lights of the chamber into a dozen dancing prisms.

Then Jessamyn heard a gunshot. At least she thought it was a gunshot, but no one in the tableau seemed to move, and You was still a good twenty feet from his objective.

Another shot followed the first and she realized that both were thunderclaps from above. Any earlier atmospheric rumblings had been muffled by the earth, so only the last two blasts were audible in the sewer.

That's when Jessamyn noticed that the water had begun to rise. When she'd seen it last there was a foot between the channel level and the concrete. Now the water was inches below the lip, and some lapped over the edge to form a small puddle at the base of the table where Ivan sat, reciting, "Ninety-three, ninety-four, ninety-five, ninety-six, ninety-seven, ninety-eight, ninety-nine . . ." He licked the tip of his left index finger and turned over the corner of the last bill in the stack. "One hundred. That's six hundred and forty thousand. Or is it six thirty-five?"

Dr. Pym-Gordon tapped his foot and rolled his eyes. "Six forty."

"Are you sure?" Ivan asked with apparent naïveté, but his eyes broke for a quarter of a second to look at his mistress, and Jessamyn realized he'd been coached to go slowly.

"Yes, I'm sure."

"Hmm."

"Can't we get this over with?"

"Well," Malomi mused, "I suppose we could keep half of the money and cut the painting in half."

The doctor started to object. "Who do you think you—" But then he stopped, because he, too, understood. She would have been delighted to slit the precious canvas in half. In fact, Ivan's delay was meant to await the storm that might destroy the painting Pym-Gordon had purchased. Malomi's tiny, crimson-painted toe made idle figure eights in the water flowing over her feet. Her tiara sparkled.

"That's it. You have your fee and I've had enough," Pym-Gordon declared. "We're out of here." He placed one foot onto his boat, and three cremblers stepped forward. In response, one of the doctor's thugs pulled a gun out from under his leather jacket.

If You had been the slightest bit uncertain about Jessamyn's "message" from Malomi, he no longer had any doubt. Moving faster than seemed possible for his age and condition, he leapt out of the shadows and grabbed for the barrel of the gun.

A third shot rang out, this one different from the thunderclaps.

Quantities of money effect qualitative change. On the road from mere prosperity to dynastic wealth, new creatures evolve. Rain works the same way. Sometime after the delicate patter of pointillist drops have become thundering hooves, a shower becomes a storm. A million drops are more than the sum of their splatters. They are voluptuous and deadly.

Water splashed against the prow of the *X-tra Large*, which cut straight through the flow. The storm was now as much of a given as the air, and then more thunderclaps echoed like bowling balls rolling down parallel lanes at the same moment. The walls shook.

Above, Timothy saw a gray square of catch basin blocked by translucent plastic—an umbrella torn from its user's hands—and yet the water must have soaked into the earth nearby because it spurted out from cracks in the sewer walls in half a dozen miniature waterfalls.

Ahead of the boat, he saw the paw of a dog carried by the strengthening current and reached over the side to save the creature, a stuffed animal with a patched belly. Maybe it had been swept out of a stroller-bound toddler's hands and washed into the sewer. Up top, the parents were probably rushing their baby to safety.

The water started foaming where it gushed down from open basins and where the previously calm channel met any minor obstruction. Still, the *X-tra Large* was able to maintain its course with a little help from the generous—or capricious—winds.

Timothy knew that he was heading in the right direction when the boat entered a wide channel underneath the great lawn spanning a half dozen ball fields and picnic grounds in the middle of Central Park. He'd been there before, when the *X-tra Large* first entered Malomi's kingdom, but he wasn't sure which way to turn. He gazed upward, hoping for a little advice.

Clearly, no help would be forthcoming from that quarter. Instead, he was granted a vision in compensation. About the most beautiful thing he'd ever seen. Angled across one corner of the arched ceiling was a spiderweb. The moisture in the air had condensed onto its strands so that it looked like it was illuminated from within by a million tiny diamonds. Timothy Murphy was in a hurry, but he couldn't resist pausing to appreciate the unexpected loveliness. And as unexpected as the jeweled web was the thought that came immediately to mind: He wished that he could show it to Jessamyn.

That was when he heard the gunshot. Unlike the thunder above, it originated nearby, somewhere in the underworld. In comparison to the constant clamor of the storm, the shot was like a finger snap; short, sharp, and commanding. *Come!*

Where? A green hand painted on the wall showed the way to the wide opening that he and Jessamyn had swum under the day before. All he had to do was pick up where he'd left off.

Timothy obeyed.

You lay on the floor in a puddle of sewer water pinkened by blood seeping from a bullethole in his thigh. It was impossible to tell how bad the wound was, however, because his torn skin was nearly the same color as his torn pants.

"Back!" shouted the man with the gun to two other skells who'd jumped toward their hurt companion.

Tall, elegant Dr. Allan Pym-Gordon considered the situation and made a decision. "It's unfortunate," he said, "that we cannot conclude our transaction in an amicable manner, but if that is to be the case, then I believe that we should not attempt any transaction at all. Now, sir . . ." He addressed Ivan, still sitting at the table, trying to maintain his concentration.

"Eighty-six . . . eighty-seven . . . eighty-eight . . . eighty-nine . . ."

Pym-Gordon interrupted the count. "If you would please return my money."

Ivan looked at Malomi. The cash itself was irrelevant to her, but more than money was at stake. There was pride. And reputation. If word got out that Malomi had been had, other customers might try to take advantage. Besides, the Russian wanted to make sure that Pym-Gordon hadn't been planning to shortchange the cremblers from the get-go.

Of course, it was possible that the art thief had never intended to cheat anyone—except the museum. He could have made his decision on the spur of the moment, after You's lunge toward his man's gun.

In fact, You's grab was curiouser than the curator could know. The ancient vagabond, now writhing on the floor, hadn't acted out of personal volition once in all the time Ivan had known him. Some idea, perhaps the first he'd had since he abandoned whatever up-top life he'd once led, had gotten into him. The money counter looked at the mistress of Undertown, and like him, she appeared more surprised than offended at the turn of events.

"Ahem." Pym-Gordon coughed as politely as if he was at a cocktail party. "The money?"

Still, Ivan couldn't relinquish his train of thought. What was wrong with the picture?

Only one person in the great space could provide the solution to the problem. He looked up to the balcony at Jessamyn.

# CHAPTER

# 28

CIVIL ENGINEER WAINWRIGHT SAW WITH NEW EYES THE ancient diving suit he hadn't worn since his days as a college student fascinated by the physics of moving water. Rather than a sleek James Bond–style wet suit, the clunky-looking metal apparatus with a bulbous glass globe resembled astronauts' garb. Wainwright had carried the thing, along with a suitcase filled with a portable winch and several hundred feet of rope, down the stairs from his apartment. There, double-parked at the curb, Mullane greeted him. "What'd you do, steal this thing off the set of *20,000 Leagues Under the Sea?*"

"You have a problem with that?"

Mullane raised his palms. "No, but if I'm going to wear that contraption, I'd sort of–"

"You?"

"Who else?"

Together the men wrestled the heavy suit into the backseat of the car, where it sat like an alien passenger waiting to be chauffeured to its destination. Wainwright slammed the door and raised his own palms. "Me."

"Sorry," Mullane said, serious now. "But a police captain cannot put the life of a civilian in jeopardy." Wainwright started to object, but Mullane wouldn't hear another word. "No, really. This is my duty. Now, I'll be glad to accept your advice. So tell me, which side of that thing goes up . . ."

In the minutes it took to drive to the park and circle around the barrier that kept cars out of the way of bikers and hikers and birders and dog walkers during the day, Wainwright conducted a massively abbreviated seminar on diving safety. "You're going to have a rope attached to your belt. It will be attached to a winch strong enough to lift a refrigerator. If you get into any trouble, tug twice, and I'll get you out of there. But just to be on the safe side, I want you to tug once every three minutes."

"Ten."

"Three."

"Eight."

"Three."

"Six."

"Three."

"Four minutes."

"OK, four, but one second more and I'm going to hit the winch. Agreed?"

Mullane nodded. He wasn't reckless. He knew that a good man on the ground might save his life.

"Ahead. Left." Wainwright directed him to a dirt road that led to the reservoir.

The engineer chose the location for several reasons. It was between the mark on his map where the teenage girl had seen a hand rise from the sewer and the mark where PB-2 had lost the *X-tra Large*. It was also the densest, most convoluted part of the system, the best place to hide or get lost. Last, it was one of the few entrances to the system that didn't require a backhoe to lift up a grate and dig a trench.

By the time they arrived, the rain had started, initially as a drizzle, then as a steady, undramatic pour. Wainwright looked at the sky and shook his head.

Mullane said, "What's the matter? Doesn't seem like such terrible weather to me."

"It's going to get worse." Wainwright pointed to a deep gray wall of clouds gliding in from the west. "We'd better hurry." He took a jangling keychain out of his pocket and opened the door to a small stone-faced building just as another thunderclap boomed overhead. "After you." He ushered the captain in like a host welcoming a visitor.

"Nice house," Mullane said. "Could use a window or two."

"Maybe," Wainwright replied. "But the front yard can't be beat."

The building consisted of a single fifteen-foot cube of a room containing a machine so large that the walls must have been constructed around it. Ten, maybe twenty tons of greasy brown metal gears and wheels spun and whirred. Wainwright explained: "Helps aerate the reservoir. Otherwise you'd have algal scum within seventy-two hours. It's also connected to the sewer. That's why I have keys. Now for some prep work . . ." He unpacked the winch and wedged it between two steel beams on which the large machine sat. Then he took one end of the spooled nylon rope and gestured to a door that Mullane thought might have led out to the park. "Ready?"

The door creaked as Mullane drew it open, revealing a dark stairwell that led down to a narrow ledge overlooking inky darkness. Even with the light from his headlamp, it took Mullane several seconds to grasp the sight. A river with perfectly parallel banks extended in both directions, though it curved away at the edge of his vision. For all the sleepless hours Mullane had spent directing the search for the lost children, he'd never imagined the actual sewer.

Wainwright knelt and dipped his hand into the current and shook his head. "The level's higher than I'd like. That means that the earlier rain has already saturated the ground. Whatever comes out of those clouds next, it's going to run through here like the cheaper paper towel."

A thought struck the captain. "How many places like this are there?" he asked, changing the subject.

"You mean entry points?"

Mullane nodded.

"Maybe a dozen in Manhattan. More in the boroughs."

"Could the kids have simply found one, maybe this one, and walked out on their own?"

Wainwright considered the possibility. Finally, he concluded, "Yes."

"Then—"

"But there are two problems."

"That's all?"

"First, if the kids left, they didn't take the *X-tra Large* with them, and we haven't found it."

Mullane nodded.

"And then," the engineer who was speaking like a detective added, "there's the psychological component." Cass Wainwright wasn't speaking of syndromes or complexes. He was speaking about human nature. "By now I'll bet you think you sort of know Timothy and Jessamyn. Right?"

"Right."

"Do you think they'd *want* to leave?"

Captain Mullane looked at his accomplice. In fact, Civil Engineer Wainwright was the one who didn't want to leave the sewer. He loved this place.

Another thunderclap rattled the sky and shook the earth.

It was time for Mullane to don his diving outfit.

# CHAPTER 29

**T**HE GUNSHOT WAS LIKE A LIGHTNING BOLT—IT commanded instant attention. On the northern periphery of the cremblers' encampment, Timothy Murphy urged the *X-tra Large* forward with every tool at his disposal. Farther west, Captain Walter Mullane declared, "Gun about one, two hundred yards away. I'm moving in."

All business now, Wainwright agreed. "Let me clip you." He attached the end of the nylon rope to a carabiner on the belt of the diving suit. "Remember, I'll be upstairs at the winch. Keep the cord taut and give me a tug every four minutes, or I'll hit the rewind."

"Gotcha." Mullane started trotting along the ledge beside the sewer channel. He hoped that the shot did not involve the missing kids, but that was like hoping an empty gasoline can at the scene of an arson wasn't connected to the fire. A gunshot meant only one thing. On Sunday there had been an accident; now, on Tuesday, there was a crime.

On a park bench next to the toy-boat basin ten blocks away, Tom Murphy and Miranda Hazard both glanced out from under their shared umbrella in the same direction. "Did you hear something?" she asked.

"Probably a car backfiring."

"You know, it's not that I can't see the problems."

"The car's?"

"The kids'. I mean, at least Jessie's."

"Oh," Tom said. "Tim has problems, too."

"But it doesn't make a stick of difference in the way I feel."

He agreed wholeheartedly. "Not at all."

"Why do you think that is?"

He shrugged. "We're built that way. Evolution, I suppose. Take care of the young. Protect the gene. If we judged them the way we do other people, we might be tempted to abandon them."

"Of course," Miranda said, "it doesn't work in the reverse direction." She looked over at the shallow pool, the rain spatters racing across its surface like miniature sailboats on a sunny day. "It's nice here."

He said, "Be nicer when we can bring the kids. Problems and all."

"Yes," she murmured, finally convinced that everything would be all right.

🐀

While the couple on the bench drifted into reverie, everyone else who'd heard the shots at Ground—make that Subground—Zero was instantly alert. In the eye of the man-made storm, all attention was riveted to the small island that was gradually disappearing under the rising waters.

Ivan still sat in his chair, holding a packet of hundred-dollar bills.

"Ohh. Ohhh, it hurts," You moaned as the flowing rainwater washed the blood from the wound in his leg and covered his torso with pink foam.

"Want another?" growled the thug with the gun as he stepped forward to sweep the heaps of cash on the table into the open duffel bag.

Smiling at the turn of events, Dr. Pym-Gordon said, "My esteemed colleague asked a question."

The question, however, was rhetorical. At this point, the good doctor had the upper hand. Gently, he reached out and shifted the angle of his colleague's gun a few inches, so that it was aiming at Malomi rather than the wounded man on the floor.

The lights hanging throughout the chamber flickered due to a storm-related electrical short. For a second, the effect evoked a disco for Jessamyn—even though she'd never been to one.

"Let them keep it," Malomi ordered the three cremblers who stood poised, ready to leap at Dr. Pym-Gordon and his men.

The doctor nodded and said, "I thought you'd be reasonable."

Unfortunately, water had soaked into the duffel bag while no one was looking, and some of the bills began to drift off with the current. A few hundreds could be glimpsed entering the main-stream and swiftly rounding a corner.

Several cremblers waded into the stream to collect the errant bills. So did one of Dr. Pym-Gordon's hired thugs, but he slipped, and more cash spilled out of the unzipped, overstuffed bag, and a rush of wind from uptunnel blew additional, uncounted bills off the table. Some hit the water and floated; some hit the water and sank; some were caught in the gust like confetti at a ticker-tape parade down lower Broadway.

Ivan tried spreading his arms over the rest of the bills yearning to fly off the table and cried, "What should I do?"

"Put them on the deck," Dr. Pym-Gordon ordered, even though the crembler was asking Malomi, not him.

Lobo replied, "They'll get wet."

Jessamyn almost laughed.

But just as Lobo answered Pym-Gordon's question, the doctor answered, "Then we'll just have to dry them out. Now. Here." He pointed to the barge holding the enormous, unboxed canvas, the craving for which had set the entire operation in motion, and then stopped abruptly. "What the . . . ?"

Like a vision out of a folktale, an enormous clipper ship floated into the cavern. Well, actually, it was the tiniest possible sailboat with a single torn sail strung from a barely upright half-mast, but it loomed extra-large in the cavern.

Also, the vessel didn't merely float, like a rubber duck, like a Styrofoam cup, like driftwood or hundred-dollar bills; it was steered by a grinning teenage boy, one hand on the mast, the other on the tiller. "Hey," he said as if he hadn't a care in the world. "Am I late for the party?"

The "partygoers" stared at the *X-tra Large* as if it was an apparition rather than a flesh and blood, or rather teak and brass, miracle out of Nantucket's finest shipyard. Then Jessamyn broke the spell. "Here!" she called from the balcony. "Here!"

Timothy Murphy, guiding the ship along the channel between the ever-harder-to-discern banks, heard her voice, but he couldn't tell where it came from. Also, for a second, he was distracted by the dramatic painting of a storm that had passed by more than a century earlier.

Another roll of thunder echoed through the cavern, and another before the first receded, signifying the storm above.

"Let's go," Pym-Gordon ordered his men, and they leapt on

board the barge. One of them set the motor roaring, and immediately they caught the current.

A few cremblers splashed after them. You hauled himself to a sitting position to avoid the rising water, like a toddler by the seashore, and sobbed, "Help . . . Help . . ."

Only Malomi remained calm. One boat that shouldn't be leaving her citadel was speeding toward the exit while another that shouldn't have dared to enter did so as grandly as Columbus cruising into Lisbon Harbor with news of the New World. This *was* a day to remember. Unfortunately, it was also time for the fun and games to cease. It was time to show who owned Undertown.

You was useless, as was Ivan, slumped over the few bills that remained on the table. "Lobo," she calmly directed her lieutenant. "Lower the gates."

The captain of the *X-tra Large* recalled the machinery that sealed off the cavern from the rest of the system. That could pose a problem in a few minutes, but first things first. Where in this mayhem was Jessamyn's voice coming from?

"Tim. Here. Tim!" she called, not from Malomi's side, not from the midst of the milling cremblers, not from the wire cage where the rats were scrabbling frantically to avoid its flooding bottom, not from the already distant motor barge.

More thunder and a horizontal rain obscured his sense of direction.

"Tim . . . Tim," she called, and then, as loud as she could, she screamed, *"Jake!"*

He looked up at the balcony overlooking the lunacy and replied, "Well, why didn't you say so, Kat?"

A lightning flash of anger came over Malomi's usually expressionless face. With the gates about to be lowered, there was no way either the *X-tra Large* or Pym-Gordon's barge could escape, but the teenagers' tender reunion was simply intolerable to her. "Go get the girl," she ordered a crembler wearing the remnants of a tuxedo, probably taken from a fancy men's shoppe on Madison Avenue. He started up the stairs.

Not to be outmaneuvered, however, Timothy—make that Jake—calmly steered the *X-tra Large* to starboard with one hand as if he had the Long Island Sound to play in. But because of the underwater ledge, the closest the boat could get to its passenger-in-waiting was eight feet below and three or four feet away from the balcony. Then, at the last moment, he slackened one half of the sail and tightened the other, and the ship yawed dramatically, practically curtsying to Jessamyn, or Kat, like Juliet on her balcony.

She reached over the railing and grasped the metal knuckle she'd installed near the top of the mast and allowed herself to be swung outward when Timothy straightened sail. She just about flew off the edge, inches beyond the fingers of the tuxedoed crembler.

In a second, she'd shimmied down the mast and joined the captain. "Long time no see."

"Not a second longer than necessary."

"Not a second less, either. But hey," she said, grinning, "I guess it takes a weasel to get into certain places."

He said, "Yeah, but giraffe arms can come in handy, too."

"Nice move," she complimented him.

"Eh." He shrugged modestly. "When you've got a good boat, it will take you anywhere."

"How about out of here?"

"Sounds like an idea."

# CHAPTER

# 30

**H**AD THE CLOCK STOPPED AT THAT MOMENT, ALMOST everyone—with the possible exception of the wounded You—would have made it through the afternoon into the rest of their lives: Dr. Pym-Gordon with his painting and the money, a big winner; Jessamyn and Timothy with the *X-tra Large* en route to rescue and comfort in Montclair; even Malomi, pride shaken but secure in her domain; and the cremblers in their established ways.

Malomi, however, was determined to keep hold of the players in her dramatic troupe. Also, another actor yet unknown to the audience was about to step onstage.

Captain Walter Mullane trotted along the tunnel. It was dark except for lightning flashes from catch basins and the waterproof headlamp he dared not use lest he give himself away. He stepped off the ledge, but instead of sinking under the weight of his metal wet suit, he was buoyed, and half-waded, half-bounced forward against the current. Still, he remembered to give a tug on the rope to signal to Wainwright that he was OK. And then, he heard a motor.

Strange in the sewer. All of the police boats that had been searching for the lost kids were called back hours earlier. If those two bozos who'd wanted to stick around this area had disobeyed a direct order, Mullane vowed to have their heads—after he enlisted their help.

"Which way?" someone called.

"I don't know," another voice shouted back. "Which way did we come in?"

A long, low boat with an enormous box on it, the kind of thing that might be used to pack a wall-size flat-screen TV, puttered into a dim shaft of light under a catch basin. The front of the box was missing, and Mullane glimpsed a painting, dark and startling and literally atmospheric. What was that about?

The men on the boat weren't police and their vessel certainly wasn't the *X-tra Large*. The captain of the 34th Precinct was used to innumerable sects and secret societies in New York—cockfighting clubs in the basements of pizza parlors; Santeria-worshipping dentists; vintage snuffbox collectors—but this boat in the sewer was a new one. *Damn regatta, armada, Fleet Week, whatever*, he thought.

Too bad the policeman's curiosity couldn't be assuaged; if Mullane didn't have a more important agenda regarding two children and a gunshot, he would have pulled the boat over. *For what: Speeding?*

Smuggling, more likely. When Mullane was still a young pup in blues, he'd once been on a detail that nabbed a man rowing across the Spuyten Duyvil with nearly a pound of uncut heroin. Until the police found the drugs inside a suspiciously bulging life vest, the man insisted that he was training for the Olympics.

After the boat passed out of sight, Mullane started forward again, ducking under an amazing spiderweb rather than breaking the product of so much labor, when he heard other voices from around the next bend of the tunnel.

A man with a Latino accent shouted, "It wouldn't close!"

More oddly, a high-pitched female voice—Jessamyn's?—snapped, "What do you mean?"

Mullane waded forward, the water now up to his belly. Visible at the end of the tunnel was an enormous space with erratically pulsating lights and a commotion of people rushing back and forth. Also, he noted another unusual phenomenon. A stream of hundred-dollar bills floated in his direction.

A man no more than twenty feet ahead of him shouted, "They got out. I don't know. I hit the lockdown switch, but the gate wouldn't close. Maybe we need an electrician. My cousin, Rudolfo, could probably—"

"I don't care if your cousin is Rudolph the Red-Nosed Reindeer, you idiot. I just—"

"Hellllp," came a drawn-out cry that was too aged to belong to Timothy.

"And . . . and . . . and . . ." The crembler who'd failed to close the gate couldn't contain himself. "And . . ."

"Spit it out!"

"There was another painting . . ."

The word made Mullane think back to the low-slung boat that had just passed him.

"On the wall. Next to the gate. A painting of a traffic light."

There was a long pause, as if someone was thinking. Finally, the girlish voice asked, "What color?"

"Green."

"Those vandals. They jammed the doors open—they'll flood the place. I'll feed the pair of them to the babies."

*The pair?* There had been more than two men on the boat.

**265**

The angry girl was not referring to the smugglers. Could she mean Jessamyn and Timothy? What were they painting? Who were the babies?

Then, piercing through the angry dialogue and that awful, continuous moaning and the mutter of who knew how many other people, all men, came one last female voice: "Jake!"

Mullane had never heard Jessamyn's voice before, but it was her. He was sure. Of course, he had no idea who Jake was, nor the first girl. Maybe they were friends of the teenagers from Montclair? Maybe they'd come for the regatta? But all of Walter Mullane's speculations were irrelevant. It was time to close the case. He stepped into the huge expanse and shouted those three grand words that never failed to send a shiver down his spine. "Police! Nobody move!"

At that moment, two unfortunate occurrences came to pass, both of them directly related to events in the infinitely, or twenty-foot, distant world up top. There, the storm that had commenced half an hour earlier attained a crescendo.

Midday was suddenly dark enough for sensors to turn on streetlamps, and then their illumination paled as simultaneous multiple lightning bolts flashed. Belatedly, thunder crashed and crashed again. The air was literally electric.

On the street, the vendors of umbrellas were ironically unable to sell any of their merchandise because umbrellas were yanked out of pedestrians' hands as fast as they could be opened. Some skittered along the sidewalks and some flew into the sky like flocks of ungainly birds.

In a normal downpour, people take refuge under awnings. If they have an appointment, they can circle around puddles at street corners. But if the rain continues, everyone eventually leaves the temporary shelters, resolved to the gradual wetness that seeps upward from sodden dress hems and pant cuffs. No big deal until, a block or two later, there's inevitably a misstep. People know it immediately from the sudden wetness inside their shoes. Finally, once pedestrians are as wet as if they'd jumped, fully clothed, into a swimming pool, the rain no longer makes any difference. A giddy community forms as New Yorkers get wet together.

Police, too, enjoy these massive storms, because young hoodlums stay home to play video games and gangs don't hassle old ladies on their way to the market. Officers on patrol can take a break in coffee shops while mist forms on the plate-glass windows.

Generally, summer downpours don't stay long, but this one lasted more than four minutes. Four excruciating minutes in which it felt like the reservoir control house was about to be ripped from its foundations and flung into the sky. Four minutes that felt like four hours to the system's engineer. Four minutes in which hundreds of millions of gallons of water surged through every opening in the earth and into an elaborate network of tunnels.

Four minutes in which the engineer's former companion could have drowned.

Five minutes.

*Not one too many,* Cass Wainwright thought, *five too many.* He never should have allowed the captain to venture into the tunnel alone. He hit the button on the automatic winch in the little house on the city prairie.

In seconds, the revolving spool spun around several dozen times, taking up every inch of slack on the rope that extended down the stairs and into the tunnel. Then, Wainwright could tell, it met resistance. The engine revved higher, but still the wheel turned.

The policeman who'd entered the great chamber of the cremblers lost his balance and fell backward, as the rope attached to his belt reeled him in.

🦫

Jessamyn had seen weirder things in the last forty-eight hours, so she merely rolled her eyes at Timothy as they followed the policeman toward the exit also taken by Dr. Pym-Gordon's vessel.

Timothy, however, had something else on his mind. "Did the crembler say he saw a green light next to the gate they wanted to shut?"

Jessamyn answered with as little interest as she would've if asked the time of day. "Yeah."

Timothy pondered this, until she realized that the information was significant. "Why?"

"Because it must have been DUO, announcing that he overrode the controls to keep it open."

"Maybe."

"Definitely," chimed a familiar voice as the young artist seemed to glide beside the ship, DUO on his skateboard on the last dry sliver of platform. "Told you I'd be back."

Jessamyn turned to Timothy. "Did I miss something?"

"Catch you up later. Which way?" Timothy asked their guide.

"Straight on till dawn, bro."

Timothy was about to reply when he noticed that Malomi's men, even the nearly unconscious You, were staring at him—no, past him, behind the *X-tra Large*—in absolute horror.

He looked back over his shoulder and saw the same thing they did. A wall of water.

# CHAPTER 31

**U**P TOP, THE STORM PASSED AS RAPIDLY AS IT ARRIVED. Rays of sunlight pierced the remaining clouds, which made exactly zero difference underground. Places like the Edgecombe rapids acted like a clogged trap under a kitchen sink, retaining immense volumes of runoff and seep-through, until the strange vegetation that grew there could no longer withstand the pressure. Roots embedded in the seams between stones tore loose and years of accumulated silt studded with garbage—a hat, a pipe, a tricycle —burst apart, creating flood conditions farther along the line. In some spots, where the circumference of the tunnel narrowed, water pushed up through the catch basins, creating urban ponds.

At 125th Street, the roar of rushing water beneath the street was as loud as thunder from the sky.

And in Central Park, conditions were worse. The area between Mount Sinai Hospital, at Fifth Avenue and 98th Street, and the Metropolitan Museum of Art, at Fifth and 82nd, bore the brunt of converging water from Harlem and from its own green expanses. The reservoir overflowed, and that water, too, found its way back into the system.

"Hold on to the boom!" Timothy shouted to Jessamyn as the mighty swell lifted the *X-tra Large* like a toy on an ocean wave.

DUO grabbed onto the rail with one hand and screamed with joy as his skateboard rode the wave. "Hey, I really am surfing!"

Several of the cremblers dashed for the stairs to the upper level of their premises, hoping to find safety in altitude, but the torrent washed them off the steps as if they were made of paper.

What ought to have been You's last gasp—or last gulp—emerged from the corner of the former counting table, now carried like a limb of driftwood on the deluge. Fingers slipping off the edge, again he cried, "*Hellllp* . . ." And then he uttered one simple word—perhaps the simplest word in the English language—"Help . . . me."

Jessamyn crawled along the deck of the pitching craft. Once, twice, a wave knocked her down and still she moved to the rail. There she grabbed the old man's waving hand. He let go of the table, which crashed into a stone wall and shattered, and she hauled him up on deck as the boat sped on.

DUO winked at her. "Nice move."

Men, money, and possessions were tossed back and forth on the water, and the wave itself filled the *X-tra Large*'s sail and ripped it off the mast like a page from a loose-leaf notebook.

Even without a sail, the boat lost no momentum. The current saw to that. Unfortunately, without the sail, Timothy lost any ability to maneuver the boat. He hunkered down, let the wave wash over him, and came up sputtering as they approached the single exit in the great wall adorned with DUO's bright-green Go signal. Most of the wave flowed into the tunnel, but some hit the wall, along with the floating specks of green money and the former sail of the *X-tra Large*.

The last thing the crew and its sole passenger saw before entering the tunnel was Malomi with her diamond tiara sparkling in the manic lights. Maybe she could master men, but the wave was too great even for her. It carried her tiny body faster and faster, nearly adjacent to the *X-tra Large*. She went under and then surfaced again like a dolphin cavorting beside an oceangoing yacht.

Timothy reached out for her, as far as he could, until he was half-overboard himself and his arm ached in its socket. "Grab ahold," he yelled. "Take my hand."

She could have done it. She was that close. Instead, she smiled at her former captive and would-be rescuer, a smile more chilling than ice water. Then she adjusted her tiara to secure its grip on her temples while spreading her arms and riding the wild tide.

Timothy could see where she was headed, literally, and screamed, "No! Try to swim here. Heeeere!"

But the water carried her directly toward the chicken-wire rat cage. Perhaps it was built strongly enough to repel a girl, but the jewels of the tiara cut through the wire as if it was a spiderweb. Malomi's thin chest bounced off the wire and her palms wrapped around the corners, her head lodged firmly inside the cage. Timothy couldn't help but think of a cartoon in which some cat or dog runs into a wall, its body flat as a flapjack on one side, its head protruding from the other, surrounded by a picture frame.

The rats were all swept to the far end of the cage.

Then, as dramatically as it had arrived, the initial flood of water passed. More entered the chamber every second, and every trace of habitation was inundated, but there was enough air to breathe.

There was still a current. The *X-tra Large* was still moving way too fast. Timothy might have been able to navigate now, if only he had his sail. And one more thing: The rats could swim.

First Oahu, then Minorca and the Azores, then the entire rodent archipelago noticed the face inside their cage.

# CHAPTER

# 32

**T**IMOTHY AND JESSAMYN WERE RELIEVED THE moment the current plunged them into the tunnel. Yet relief was short-lived as it became immediately apparent that escape was not the same thing as safety. Water rising throughout the cremblers' cavern was condensed into a much smaller space now and picked up speed.

The *X-tra-Large* was like an Olympic luge, its curved hull scraping against the sewer's rough stone walls. Fortunately, there was a greater danger of falling off the vessel than of crashing. Sometimes it slid down to the bottom of a temporary trough and sometimes it rode straight up a surging wave—there was no telling. There was just hanging on, except for DUO, who allowed the momentum to carry his skateboard's wheels farther up the walls, until he was riding horizontally.

"Get on deck!" Timothy screamed.

"No way, man. You should try—" A bump in the wall knocked the boy off his skateboard, and he dropped across the shuddering wheel.

"Glad you listened to me," Timothy said.

"Hmmph."

Jessamyn briefly recalled a summer outing taken with her parents several years earlier on the Delaware River. But they'd had a pilot and a crewman and were strapped into cozy pockets in the bright-yellow rubber raft. What had seemed like a fantastic rush was in fact a controlled pretence of adventure that would end with a picnic lunch. Afterward, an SUV picked up the Hazards and drove them back to their starting point.

*Hazard.* Her life was a mockery of her name. She'd never experienced genuine danger. Neither had her mother, and her father only once when he made a left turn into oncoming traffic.

New York City's sewers at high tide were nothing like that. They weren't even like the Edgecombe rapids, which ended in the placid pool under DUO's attic. And they certainly weren't like dramatic scenes in Hollywood movies. The water was so fast that she couldn't tell how fast it was. It was rough. It was incoherent. The only thing that began to convey the elemental chaos was a painting.

Timothy shouted over the roar of the water, "We need to control the boat."

Jessamyn shouted back, "How?"

"I don't know, yet." That last word was, he realized the second he uttered it, optimistic—given the circumstances. It implied a future that he would know. "If we only had a sail."

Then, as impressively calm as her companion was irrationally confident, Jessamyn called back, "Why didn't you say so?"

He looked at her.

"There's one somewhere ahead."

Timothy thought that they'd lost their only canvas in the ruins of Malomi's domain, but Jessamyn's words were specific.

She hadn't said "it." She'd said "one." Not the original. He asked, "Where?"

The answer to this question was a bit trickier. "I don't know. Not exactly. It's on the boat that left a few minutes before us . . . couldn't have gone far." As concisely as possible, she explained the elegant doctor and his thugs in the cargo vessel, motor-powered but surely not as well equipped for the SDJ as the battle-scarred, proven, and superbly designed *X-tra-Large*.

Neither of the teenagers had the leisure to consider the moral questions involved in stealing a canvas from someone who had stolen it from a museum that probably ought not to have owned it in the first place, if art was a universal human heritage. Forget about art. There were times when a canvas was just a canvas.

"Watch out!" You screamed as the top of the mast hit a protrusion in the arched ceiling of the tunnel. Timothy and DUO leapt aside as a chunk of cured wood slammed down on the deck.

The level of the current had risen again. The ceiling was no more than a foot over Jessamyn's head.

At last, they saw it, a block ahead, just as Jessamyn had declared. She was also right in believing that the *X-tra Large*'s essential seaworthiness made it more capable of withstanding the chthonic fury than Dr. Pym-Gordon's purloined vessel.

It had been a good day for the soon to be happily retired curator. The altercation with the bizarre creature he'd hired to obtain the painting for a private buyer hadn't turned out too shabbily. Dr. Pym-Gordon could make his peace with the end of a relationship for a million and a half dollars in cash, tax-free, minus a dozen thousand that floated away. The only problem being that he was no longer guided by cremblers, and no longer had any idea where he was.

"Is that a door?" one of Pym-Gordon's men called.

"What?"

"A doorway."

"Where?"

"Back . . . um . . ."

"Spit it out, man."

Pym-Gordon's hired gun couldn't bring himself to describe what he believed they had just passed. Instead, he pointed. "There."

Indeed, the scene behind the boat defied description. A man in a metal suit with a globe-like mask over his head was apparently doing the backstroke in the New York City sewer system. And then he disappeared into a rectangular opening in the wall.

Pym-Gordon, familiar with boats from summers in the Hamptons, yanked the tiller to make a U-turn, but the front of the boat slammed into the right-hand wall of the tunnel and the rear yawed and wedged into the left, pinning the edge of the box that held the canvas in place. The rush of the flood immediately washed one of the crew overboard. No big deal. As long as the painting wasn't going anywhere, he would be fine.

The doctor could risk temporarily leaving his precious cargo behind while making his way along the ledge to the door revealed by the suited man's comic exit. The duffel bag, however, was another problem. What if he lost his grip? He took a stretch of rope and tied one end to his wrist and the other to the handle. He'd deposit the cash in the stairwell and return for the canvas once the flood abated. Of course, the man in the brass suit might be waiting for him at the door, but that was unlikely. He clearly aimed to get out and as far away from the fearful tunnel as possible.

Besides, Pym-Gordon's own man had a gun. "Let's go."

Timothy took the blockade in stride and, noting the large canvas exposed in the open box, said, "Our sail, I believe."

"As long as you don't bereave."

"Been there. Done that."

"Are you sure?"

"Not in the least." It was impressive that Dr. Pym-Gordon had managed to halt the barge even though it was considerably larger than the *X-tra Large*. Had the captain a sail, he might have tried to double-park his own boat alongside the barge, but they were moving too fast. Timothy explained, "See how that boat is leaning toward us? That's because the water is pushing underneath. We might be able to use the slope of the deck like a ramp."

"And if not?"

"You have a better idea?"

"Nope."

"You?"

"Me?" You groaned.

"No . . . him."

DUO shook his head. "Brought you as far as I could, Cap."

"Then everyone hold on."

There were two figures on the boat: men. Both maintained a precarious balance on the tilting vessel, but one was turned away from the oncoming *X-tra Large* and the other was facing it, holding out a hand, as if to gesture *Stop*.

"Um?" Jessamyn gasped.

"Gun!" You shouted.

"Time to go fishing," Timothy declared.

Coolly, he lifted the rod he'd removed from the hold two days earlier, gave himself a second to gauge the shrinking gap between the vessels, and cast the line like he'd never done in Barnegat Bay. The reel whizzed forward, wrapped around the man's wrist, and embedded its hook in the flesh of his palm. The man dropped the gun. The rod itself was yanked out of Timothy's grip.

276

The second man lifted the fallen gun off the deck and aimed.

Too late. The *X-tra-Large* was like a bull infuriated by the taunt of the matador. One bullet pinged off a brass rail; another whistled by Timothy's ear.

"Yeow!" screamed a voice behind him.

Timothy half-turned around in time to see You, who'd managed to lift himself to one of the benches built into the rear of the boat, fall down again just as the prow of the *X-tra Large* plowed into the barge and rode up its sloping deck with such momentum that it left the water entirely and hovered in midair for a fraction of a second.

Timing her own move perfectly, Jessamyn reached out and grabbed the corner of the soaked canvas flapping on its exposed backing and ripped the painting free. The effort made her spin around and collapse onto the deck, next to You, while the canvas snapped taut in the rush of air behind the *X-tra Large*, like a flag mounted on the stern of a racing boat.

Dr. Pym-Gordon spun in the opposite direction, arm extended for another shot between the eyes of the girl who'd just stolen his stolen painting. But the collision loosened his footing and the weight of the duffel bag attached to his wrist made him lose his balance.

The last thing Timothy saw was the flash of the gun firing into the ceiling of the tunnel while the man and his money sank.

# CHAPTER

# 33

UCH! *OW!* OH!" CAPTAIN MULLANE SPUTTERED TO himself inside his helmet as he was hauled one bumpy stair after another into the reservoir house control room. Only then did Civil Engineer Wainwright cut the power to the winch.

Wainwright looked at the gasping policeman in the brass suit on the floor as if he was a remarkable species of fish and said, "Have a good trip?"

Mullane tore the helmet off his shoulders, and a gallon or so of water, which had entered before he'd had a chance to seal the lifesaving device, poured out. "Why in Saint James did you—"

Wainwright tapped at the watch on his wrist. "Time's up."

"I saw them. In another minute, I could have . . ."

"What?"

Mullane immediately forgot about himself. "Those kids. It's a mess down there."

Wainwright nodded slowly and unfurled the map he carried everywhere. "If they missed these stairs . . ."

"They did. The boat passed right by me, along with another one."

"What other one?"

"Weird. Three men. No sail. They tore out of a kind of cave. Nearly ran me over. Inside the cave were a lot more men and a little . . . queen. Crown and all."

"A cave?"

"Yeah. Some deal was going down, going bad. I nearly had a chance to break it up when the water came."

"Just came?" Wainwright repeated. "Into a cave?"

Mullane didn't understand why the engineer was apparently having such difficulty understanding him. "Yeah?"

"There are no caves in the system. Alcoves where there used to be storerooms, maybe, passageways that connect trunk lines, pools in a few places, but no cave as you describe. And the water should have been flowing continuously. I can't see it just . . . *coming*."

"Are you saying that I made this up?"

"Hallucinations are not uncommon in extreme situations."

"I didn't hallucinate."

Wainwright wiped his glasses on the tail of his shirt and shook his head. "No, I don't think so. Whoever was down there must have blocked off a section of the tunnel where a few streams came together. That might create a cave. Then, if whatever barrier they used to isolate themselves from the rest of the system failed during the storm, water might enter at once."

"It was pretty ferocious."

"Hmm." Wainwright peered intently at the map.

"What are you thinking?"

"I'm trying to figure out where the kids might end up. I can't imagine a boat surviving such a flood."

The engineer had referred only to the vessel, not the passengers. Mullane wanted to ask the obvious question but sat silently, until he noticed something. Or rather, he noticed the absence of something. The room was silent. The rain had stopped. He left the engineer absorbed in his calculations and opened the door of the house in the center of the park. Outside, the sun was shining.

The ground was ink black, the grass a brilliant green. Rivulets of water still flowed along the curbs, but here and there patches of sidewalk had already dried out. The air was steamy with evaporation, so different from the burden of imminent precipitation before the storm. Two little boys raced toward a nearby playground, kicking a ball. Off in the distance, across the 79th Street transverse, a couple seated beside the toy-boat basin shook out an umbrella.

"Hey," Mullane called. "Hey!" He was happy.

"What?" Wainwright replied without getting up from his position on the floor of the reservoir house, still looking at his map.

"The rain's stopped. It's over. That means they should be OK, right?"

Wainwright shook his head.

Down below, the flood still raged. Yes, the sky had cleared. Yes, the flow would abate . . . eventually.

Eventually, however, meant that nothing could mitigate the diluvian quantity of water already in the system until the underground rivers made their way to the sea. The barge was breaking up under the pounding. Planks of wood rode along with the *X-tra Large*, now under the minimal control of its captain with a multi-million-dollar sail he'd barely been able to clamp on to the mast.

"Fifteen to port!" he called, and Jessamyn and DUO pushed the boom off in one direction. Then he yanked the wheel in the opposite direction to the stub of the rudder and called out the reverse. "Fifteen starboard."

Back and forth they swerved, aiming to take the brunt of the flood's power on the side of the vessel to slow down its passage, riding out the storm that they couldn't know had stopped above. The mate followed the captain's directions, occasionally glancing back at You, in a puddle of red on the deck. "Hold on," she whispered to him.

Of course, it was impossible to hear anything in the torrent, but his eyes widened.

She nodded and mouthed emphatically, "Hold on."

Still, the turbulence increased. Another wedge of mast fell over the top of the painting that portrayed a two-hundred-year-old storm. A section of rail in front of the mast disappeared as they bounced off an invisible ledge beneath the rising water. Surely there were already holes in the hull, but leakage couldn't swamp the ship as long as the current propelled it along.

Every once in a while, Timothy noticed the sail that helped them navigate the perilous course. J. M. W. Turner's painting of a storm provided strange comfort, implying the contemplation of extremity after the fact.

Unfortunately, there wasn't much opportunity for art appreciation. He had to concentrate on keeping the boat as close to the center of the channel as possible. How much longer he'd be able to maintain control, he didn't know.

They whipped around a bend south of the 79th Street transverse, plunged low, and rose up because of the park topography. Timothy was more than weary, more than exhausted. He was utterly depleted, and yet he summoned energy from some hidden reservoir within himself to keep the vessel from disaster.

Catch basins flew by, a blink, a shaft of light. All the captain knew was that he had to keep going. He had three passengers, one severely wounded, to protect.

Jessamyn screamed.

Timothy turned.

"The sky!" she declared.

"What?"

"Sky!" she repeated. "There." She pointed.

No more than a block ahead of them, along the right-hand branch of a fork in the tunnel, was the most beautiful thing she had ever seen. Surely it was an hallucination, Jessamyn thought, and yet she could see it, robin's egg blue, with tufts of cottony white clouds. The sky.

Timothy wiped the spray from his face and he, too, saw the glorious vision. "Yes!" he cried, and shifted the boom.

But just as the captain aimed toward the light, the mate understood that it was not a reality—though not a hallucination, either. It was merely a painted sky on the rounded ceiling of a distant section of the tunnel.

"Yes!" Timothy shouted again with delight.

"No," she said, shaking her head. It was a cruel mockery. They couldn't afford unjustified optimism.

"Yes," he insisted.

"It's a painting."

"It's a passage. No time for an explanation. Now, let's turn this baby. Boom ninety to port."

They were pushing against the current, against the wind that blew by faster than the current, and the boat was responding, but too slowly. They were still bearing toward the left-hand fork, away from the glimpse of heaven.

"Harder!" he cried.

"I've got it all the way."

Alas, their painted canvas of a storm was not as effective as the imageless stretch of canvas they'd lost in the real storm. Wind passed through the antique weave; flakes of paint flew off it.

Perhaps the real ship was as doomed as the painted trawler. Still, Timothy desperately tried to tighten the nineteenth-century masterpiece against the mast to make the most of its spread.

The fork was perhaps a hundred feet away and he used all the body language he could summon—like a jockey urging a thorough-bred to leap over a steeplechase fence—to direct the *X-tra Large*. He felt his soul bonding with the sailboat. *C'mon*, he thought. *C'mon, just a bit to the right. You can do it. C'mon.*

Still, it was obvious to him that they weren't going to make the turn.

"Weight!" he called. "All weight starboard."

"The anchor?" Jessamyn called back.

No, the anchor would stop all motion—maybe. Besides, there was no time to retrieve it from below. The only movable objects were people. "C'mon." He let go of the useless sail and grabbed Jessamyn's hand, drawing her to the edge of the boat, where DUO joined them. It tilted, but not enough. "Farther," he said.

"Where?"

"Here." DUO grasped the rail with two hands, stepped over it, and lowered his butt toward the water to pull the boat where he willed.

The angle of the boat shifted another degree, not enough, and then Timothy joined the painter. Jessamyn, unsure why they were so determined, added her hundred and five pounds to the equation.

Waves crashed over their heads and made it impossible to see anything, and the boat angled farther to the right, yet still insufficiently, until two hundred more pounds unexpectedly joined the teenagers. Even in the absolute wet, they could smell their new companion.

"You!" Jessamyn cried.

He'd dragged himself to the edge and rolled under the rail beside them. "May not have legs. But . . . *I* . . . l can hold on. *You* . . . told . . . *me*."

Yes, she had, and together they hung on to the boat until they were in danger of swamping the *X-tra Large*. Luckily—was this the first time in this entire saga that Timothy could think of such a word?—that was exactly what they needed to sweep within inches of the dividing wall that separated the main sewer line from a large, round chamber almost like the home of the cremblers.

The space resembled an open-air arena minus the seating, so perfectly circular was its design underneath the achingly blue dome. Yet no matter how beautiful it was, it was just a ceiling, not the sky. A lovely vision didn't compensate for the blunt fact that it might be the last vision they would ever see.

Sewer water entered the chamber, in which, with no place to exit, it spun in a circular, clockwise motion that carried the *X-tra Large* around and around like a carved wooden horse on the Central Park Carousel. Worse, the water continued to rise, so another section of mast snapped off against the clouds, leaving a dark smear on the firmament. If any of the crew had managed to climb back on deck, none of them would have been able to stand upright. Jessamyn looked at her companions and said, "So here we are."

Timothy smiled. "Right where we want to be."

Had he gone mad from the stress? Maybe they could have hoped to escape if they'd continued in the tunnel, but the current here swirled them around like a marble in a bottle, and with every revolution the beautiful, deadly ceiling loomed an inch closer.

In fact, the situation was even worse because every revolution also drew them slightly closer to the center of the circle, where a whirlpool had formed. There were two options: get sucked down and drown now, or wait until the water rose to the ceiling, and drown in five minutes. Unless of course they were crushed between the deck and pale-blue painted sky. Yet Timothy gazed blissfully up at the painted clouds, as if he felt the painted sun on his face.

Jessamyn couldn't bear that idiotic look. "Timothy," she cried, trying to rouse him. "Tim! . . . Jake!"

The name caught his attention. The pleasure left his eyes and clarity returned. Still, his fantasy persisted. All he said was, "It's OK, Kat."

Well, he may have given up hope, but she hadn't. Someone had to try something. She turned to the derelict holding on to the rail beside her. "Can you think of something?"

You said, "Me?"

"Yes, you."

"You mean me?"

What a time to regain his sense of self! "All right, me."

"My name is . . ." It took him a moment to remember. "John."

"All right, John. Do"—she didn't want to say "you" because the dialogue might have revolved as uselessly as the boat—"um, does John have any ideas?"

"No, but . . ." He looked over her head and met Timothy's—or Jake's—eyes and grinned. "But someone else already did. Right, kid?" he asked, addressing DUO.

The creator of the firmament nodded. "Been here. Done that."

All the males started chuckling, and Jessamyn thought they were crazy.

Then Timothy calmed. "DUO always paints whatever's on the

other side of the surface he's painting. The real sky is on top of that painted sky. If we get past the ceiling, we're home."

"Oh, great. If I'd known I'd have to scratch through concrete, I would have sharpened my nails."

"No need," DUO said. "The man's got a plan. *You do have a plan*, don't you?"

"Yes, indeed," Timothy said. But he needed to act swiftly. The mast hit the ceiling and another chunk of wood broke off, causing J. M. W. Turner's painting of a storm to collapse in a sodden heap beneath the Harlem graffitist's rendering of a clear sky.

Jessamyn felt one of her sneakers sucked off her foot by the whirlpool. "What *is* it?"

"Give me a minute."

It wasn't easy to climb on board, what with the circular motion pulling his body sideward and the whirlpool pulling him down, but Timothy hoisted himself back onto the deck and immediately rolled over and looked straight down the hatch.

The *X-tra Large* was nearly filled with water, but the momentum of the current kept it from sinking. They were maybe fifteen feet from the center of the circle, at which point the whirlpool would win. He took a deep breath and dove into the cabin.

"Tim!" Jessamyn shrieked.

You—or John—took one of his hands off the rail and patted her on the shoulder. "He'll be back."

Timothy Murphy had never excelled at sports. He was agile and quick-witted but too short for basketball, too slim for football, barely strong enough to power a baseball out of the infield with a hurricane at his back. Maybe he wasn't the last one chosen in after-school ball games at Brookdale Park, but that was only because of the droolers and stumblers.

Yet he could run faster than most kids his height, and he could swim, if not in competitions. Now he was in the competition of his life. It was a one-boy relay race against his lung capacity.

The first lap between the parallel berths brought him to the storage unit beneath the stern. He groped until he found the door, which had conveniently floated open. Perhaps the leak that would have sunk the *X-tra Large* in any other circumstance was behind the door. Timothy didn't pause to investigate.

*Yes!* The canister was right where it was supposed to be. Thank heaven he had followed his father's advice: Everything in a boat had a place. His fingers grasped the rounded object. Then he dragged the thing out, noting how oddly weightless it felt in the water.

One more task, now. *Now!* He reversed direction and swam forward, using his free hand for propulsion while he tucked the object into his side as if he was playing underwater football. But he overestimated the distance, took a stroke too many, and bumped into the aft of the cabin and fumbled the ball. He felt it slip from his grip and, rather than sink, float upward, grazing his chin.

*No problem*, he hoped. Maybe prayed. The thing should be sitting on the deck, unless it washed away. Since there was no Plan B, he was tempted to go after it, but he needed another item, without which the first was useless. He reached for the pantry door, found the knob, and tried to open it.

The door was forced shut by the same water that opened the storage unit. A few air bubbles dribbled from the corner of his mouth, to follow the metal football aloft.

He gripped the knob with both hands and set his knees on either side of the door and tugged. The knob popped off and he did a slow-motion backward somersault. A large air bubble rose upward from his lungs.

It took another second to reorient himself in the dark enclosure. Hands left, right, locating the refrigerator, he moved again to the pantry and found a hole in the door where the knob had been. He shoved two fingers from each hand into the hole, replaced his knees, and pulled again, as hard as he could.

Still, he could not compete with thousands of pounds of water pressure. The door remained shut, yet a section splintered off in his hands. He squeezed a hand into the hole, its ragged edge scratching his knuckles, and started groping again, while doing his best to ignore the pressure building in his chest.

Was it on the upper shelf or the middle? Everything was supposed to be in its place, but he couldn't remember what that place was. He pushed a few empty plastic containers aside and grasped a metal object.

No, the shape wasn't quite right. At least he didn't think so. It wasn't easy to examine something by feel alone. With one hand. While drowning. A ridged wheel at the end meant it was a can opener. He dropped it and reached farther into the recess of the cabinet, finding a spatula.

Better, much better, because it was on the cooking shelf, but no cigar, either. Not that a cigar would have been helpful fathoms deep. Well, feet, but you could drown as easily in a puddle as an ocean. Spatulas were for turning omelets. You needed to break eggs to make omelets. Another stream of bubbles slid out of his mouth.

At last, next to the spatula, he found something else. Metal, about six inches long. If it was the tongs used to flip corn on the cob on the grill, he'd made a fatal error, but there was no time left for foraging. He extracted the object through the hole and pushed off the floor of the cabin, shooting up the hatch and out of the darkness into the dim catch-basin light that allowed him to see the image of the sky.

"Did you . . . ?" he gasped out while sucking in lungfuls of the air that remained. In the ninety seconds since he'd dived into the cabin, the water level had risen dramatically. The mast of the *X-tra Large* was a mere stump, and he could barely kneel on the deck.

"Looking for this?" Jessamyn replied. She was squatting on the deck, holding the tank of propane gas that had bobbed upward half a minute ago but that seemed like hours before.

"Yes."

"Why? Are you planning to grill some franks for a last meal?"

"Something like that." He held out the igniter he'd retrieved. Of course it was soaked, and who knew if the wet flint would work, but he had a chance. That was all he asked for. That was all that DUO and You, still hanging on to the edge of the boat, could ask for.

Jessamyn looked at the tool, then looked at the tank of explosive gas she was holding, and said, "No."

Timothy asked quietly, "Do you have any other ideas?"

"We can maneuver the boat. Get back in the tunnel. Find an exit."

"Please hand me the tank."

There was no time to argue, no other possibility. The boat was on the edge of the whirlpool, making swifter and shorter revolutions. Jessamyn glanced up at the fake sky, ran her fingers over the rough, painted concrete, and reluctantly held out the canister of gas that was their only chance to break through.

Timothy tried to set the smooth metal container upright, but the tilt of the boat made that impossible. He propped it against the nubbin of a mast, but the deck was too slippery.

And every moment, the ceiling grew closer. He and Jessamyn were both kneeling, then squatting, then sitting cross-legged.

He figured that he'd have no recourse but to hold it, the way older kids in Montclair sometimes held firecrackers until a second before the fuse hit the powder, when Jessamyn said, "Turn your head."

"Huh?"

"Turn . . . your . . . head," she repeated. "And shut your eyes. Everyone," she declared to DUO and You in the sea beside the boat, and began to remove her Hawaiian shirt.

Timothy turned his head.

The bra that Jessamyn wore wasn't strictly necessary for its ostensible function, but it might serve another purpose. Topless now, for the first time in her life in front of several varieties of the male species, even if they couldn't see anything, she wrapped the modest cups around the metal container and tied the elastic straps to the stub of the mast. Then she risked her life—and Timothy's and DUO's and You's—to pause for a second to pull the sodden T-shirt back over her head. Then she said, "OK, what now?"

Of course, she knew. Timothy told her to get back in the water.

She considered refusing. They'd begun this together and they ought to end it together. But his look brooked no dispute. The boy wasn't going to strike the flint until she was as well protected as possible. She lowered herself back into the water, between the urbane child of the slums and the urban derelict clinging with his last bit of strength to the edge of the deck.

Timothy turned the knob on the canister and immediately smelled the gas. Maybe that was because there was so little air left to displace in the chamber. Still, he waited until the odor was nearly unbearable.

Calmly, Jessamyn inquired, "Are we going to drown or asphyxiate?"

"Neither. Now, when I say so, everybody duck."

The *X-tra Large* made its own last revolution on the perimeter of the whirlpool. Then, in an instant, the vessel was spinning rather than riding as if it had been pierced through the middle and could never escape, like an old-fashioned record on its pole. For a second as the gas accumulated beneath the dome, Timothy gazed at the signed corner of the precious canvas, their former sail, lying crumpled over the front of the deck. Sometime around the turn of the nineteenth century, J. M. W. Turner had been drawn to—and drawn—the most dramatic effects of the natural universe. Mostly he was known for his nautical paintings in which the human element was no more significant than a literal drop in the ocean. Toward the end of his career, however, he'd become fascinated with the newfound powers of man. Ultimately, he conferred upon railroad steam engines and train cars the same magnificence he had previously lavished on storms.

So far, the *X-tra Large* had been dominated by the torrent that cascaded through the tunnels. And yet, the tunnels themselves had been conceived and constructed by people similar to the people who held on to the boat for dear life. Once upon a time, the sandhogs who followed the engineers' plans dynamited the bedrock of Manhattan to excavate the sewer for more than a million residents. If they had done it once, Timothy Murphy could do it again.

He held the flint at arm's length next to the nozzle, from which the hiss of gas was audible despite the roar of the flood rising up over the deck. He bent his head down as if in prayer and yelled, "Duck!" and pressed his thumb along the wheel.

Expecting nothing, Timothy heard nothing, saw nothing, but he felt the vibration in every bone of his body.

# CHAPTER
# 34

**U**P TOP, ON THE SURFACE OF PLANET EARTH, THE couple who had left the bench beside the toy-boat sailing pond to start walking back to their hotel heard the sound, as did the pair of civil servants who were dolefully stowing their useless gear in the police car. And though one more loud noise after an hour of rolling thunder ought to have been a trifle to the tempest, all four turned.

A hole had appeared in the center of the boat pond. Chunks of concrete and a geyser of water burst into the sky. A second later, a rain of dust and spray descended.

Captain Mullane started running in the direction of the blast.

Civil Engineer Wainwright huffed and puffed after him.

Miranda Hazard instinctively clutched Thomas Murphy's elbow, and Murphy instinctively threw his arm over Miranda's shoulders to protect her.

Stranger yet was the boat pond itself. Instead of disappearing into the crater/drain in its center, water surged from the gap, instantly overflowing the low wall that defined the structure, inundating the sidewalk and toy-boat rental kiosk and café area. The boat pond was fast becoming a lake, shaped by the contours of the park's terrain. Within a minute, the police captain's footsteps were splashing, while Tom and Miranda stood in water up to their knees.

Most astonishing of all, a life-size—small but life-size—wooden boat bobbed in the center of the pond. Three figures clung to the rail of the boat. There was a boy and an old man and a girl with bright-red hair, who clambered onto the deck and immediately pulled the other two up after her.

Unbelieving, Miranda murmured, "It's . . ."

Tom Murphy saw the same thing. "The *X-tra Large*. But where's . . ."

"Timothy." Jessamyn bent over the boy whom none of the onlookers could see lying flat on the deck. "Timothy," she repeated more loudly as she fell to her knees beside him. "Jake," she sobbed. "Get up, Jake," she cried.

He didn't respond.

Thomas Murphy started running now, approaching the scene from the opposite direction as Captain Mullane, who'd gotten literally stuck in the mud.

Timothy's shirt was in shreds. His hands and face and upper arms, every inch of exposed flesh, blackened. His eyes were closed, and a trickle of water slid out of his mouth and formed a clean line on his cheek.

Jessamyn could have told anyone the difference between positive and negative integers and imaginary numbers, the complex and interrelated causes of World War 1, the theme of T. S. Eliot's *The Waste Land*—et cetera, et cetera, et cetera—down to the last footnote in the most obscure junior high school text. At fourteen, she was destined for some college with a Latin motto on its ivy walls, but she'd never learned an ounce of practical knowledge.

She recalled the horrible day when she'd opened her front door to a pair of uniformed policemen who looked down at her with pity and asked if her mother was home. Immediately, she understood that they bore "news" that no one could do anything about, but for years she lamented her inability to save her father. If only . . . What? She could have begged him to play Scrabble that day. She could have flattened the tires on the family car. She could have . . . What? That was the last day she thought of the Victorian gingerbread house on Bellevue Avenue as home.

She'd never felt at home again, until she and Timothy Murphy set sail on the *X-tra Large*, and there was no way she was going to let their voyage end in a stupid, incoherent tragedy. Desperately, she tried to recall a series of "What to do in an emergency" instructions she'd once heard in a health class—the only class she'd never taken seriously. She inhaled as much breath as she could, maybe as much as Timothy had when he dove into the cabin of the boat, and pressed her mouth to his and exhaled.

Did his eyelids flicker? The area around his lips was smudged where her lips wiped the explosion's charry residue off the skin. The skin appeared undamaged but also lifeless.

Voices called to her from what sounded like hundreds of miles away, or underwater. Two men were standing on the rim of the former boat pond, unable to get any closer because waves carrying floes of concrete pulsed outward from below the *X-tra Large*. She took another breath and again pressed her lips to Timothy's mouth. It wasn't a kiss, but it felt warm.

He coughed and sputtered, and when she turned his head to the side—how she knew to do this, she had no idea—he gagged up more water than one boy ought to contain.

The voices from the edge of the pool were clear now. They were calling her name. Still, she couldn't remove her eyes from Timothy's face, red with coughing, eyes blinking.

You—er, John—said, "Keep going."

"How about yourself, fella?" DUO asked the blood-soaked beggar.

"Flesh wounds . . . *I've* seen worse. And . . . *you?*"

"My momma's gonna be so angry with me."

Eyes opening.

Tom Murphy was the first to see his son's head rise from the broken ship's deck. He jumped onto the concrete lip and slipped into the water and climbed back up, soaking wet, joyous. Miranda Hazard waded in to join him in welcoming the crew of the *X-tra Large*. Captain Mullane and Civil Engineer Wainwright simply shook their heads in amazement.

Jessamyn turned toward her companion in adventure, catastrophe, and triumph. "Not bad, Jake," she said.

Timothy turned to her and said, "We did it together, Kat." Then he stood and picked up the first item that came to hand, an extra-large rectangle of colored canvas, and waved it, shouting, "Land ho!"

# ABOUT THE AUTHOR

**MELVIN JULES BUKIET,** the author of seven previous books of fiction, teaches at Sarah Lawrence College. His stories and essays have been published in the *Paris Review*, the *New York Times*, the *Washington Post*, the *Los Angeles Times*, and more. *Undertown* is his first book for young readers. He lives in New York City and has three children.

This book was designed by Meagan Bennett and art directed by Chad W. Beckerman. The text is set in 10.75-point Rotis Serif, a typeface designed in 1989 by Otl Aicher for Agfa. The display types are Motor Oil 1937 M54 and Headliner No. 45.

The cover illustration is by Jon Foster.

This book was printed and bound by R. R. Donnelley in Crawfordsville, Indiana. Its production was overseen by Kathy Lovisolo.